PROTECTING KELLI

SEAL OF PROTECTION: ALLIANCE
BOOK 6

SUSAN STOKER

This book is a work of fiction. Names, characters, places, and incidents are products of the author's imagination or used fictitiously. Any resemblance to actual events or locales or persons living or dead is entirely coincidental.

Copyright © 2025 by Susan Stoker

No part of this work may be used, stored, reproduced or transmitted without written permission from the publisher except for brief quotations for review purposes as permitted by law.

Without in any way limiting the author's {and publisher's} exclusive rights under copyright, any use of this publication to "train" generative artificial intelligence (AI) technologies to generate text is expressly prohibited. The author reserves all rights to license uses of this work for generative AI training and development of machine learning language models.

This book is licensed for your personal enjoyment only. This book may not be re-sold or given away to other people. If you would like to share this book with another person, please purchase an additional copy for each recipient. If you're reading this book and did not purchase it, or it was not purchased for your use only, please purchase your own copy.

Thank you for respecting the hard work of this author.

Edited by Kelli Collins

Cover Design by AURA Design Group

Manufactured in the United States

DEDICATION

For my editor Kelli...one should always be wary when saying you want to be "featured" in one of my books. You'll find yourself kidnapped and going through some pretty scary stuff. But then again you'll also get a happily ever after with a pretty darn good man. So there's that.
Thank you for your tireless work and for always fixing the same typos over and over again...like imaging instead of imagining and the words definitely and nonsense, and when to use lie/lay/lain, and what/that and a hundred other typos that my brain absolutely refuses to learn.

CHAPTER ONE

One day.

That's all it took for Wade "Flash" Gordon to remember why he didn't vacation at the beach.

He hated sand.

Hated the heat.

Hated the salt that stuck to his skin.

Which was ironic, considering he was a Navy SEAL who spent half his life, or so it seemed, in the ocean.

Flash took a sip of the beer he'd been nursing and grimaced. Warm.

Another reason to dislike the beach...his beer didn't stay cold longer than five minutes.

He was well aware he was being an asshole, but he didn't care. The only reason he was here, sitting in a beach chair, grumpily staring at the gentle lapping of the sky-blue waters off the Jamaican coast, was because of his little sister, Nova.

She was ten years younger than him, and Flash would do anything for her. He'd adored her from the moment his parents brought her home from the hospital, when he was ten. He never cared when she cried at night, that her poops stunk up the

1

house. That she'd followed him around when he was a teenager. He'd loved every second of having a younger sibling. They'd both cried when he'd left home after graduating from high school and joined the Navy.

And through the years, Flash had kept in close contact with his sister. Phone calls, texts, even letters sometimes. So when she'd met Charles Hepworth, Flash had flown home specifically to meet the man and put the fear of God into him. Make sure he understood that if he fucked with his sister, he'd regret it.

Flash wasn't too impressed by Chuck. He was older than Nova by six years and far too...smooth. But then again, Flash could admit that he, himself, was constantly surrounded by men who were a little rough around the edges.

Despite his feelings for the man, when Nova called and asked if he'd be a groomsman at their wedding, Flash didn't have to think too hard. Of *course* he'd stand up with his sister. He might not be her fiancé's biggest fan, but he'd support Nova no matter what.

And if things didn't work out, he'd be there to help her pick up the pieces too.

As a groomsman, when this trip to Jamaica was cooked up as a bachelor party kind of thing, Flash had been invited. He'd planned to turn it down—he definitely didn't want to hang out with Chuck's buddies—but Nova had begged him to go. It was one of the rare times he would've said no to his sister, except he read the concern in her voice when she'd told him about the private resort. How she assumed there'd be plenty of beautiful girls there who might want to hook up with Chuck.

It was obvious she was worried her fiancé might think the same thing.

So here was Flash.

In Jamaica, sitting on his ass on a hot beach, babysitting... no...*spying* on his sister's future husband. Making sure his occasional flirting didn't cross any lines.

Flash had no problem whatsoever reporting back to Nova. Even if it might cause her pain in the short-term, he wouldn't keep any indiscretions by her fiancé a secret from her. But so far, Chuck had been on his best behavior. Hanging out with his friends Rowan, Ben, and Sebastian, mostly at the bar, and not hooking up with any ladies.

Though, not so surprising to Flash, the resort wasn't very crowded. The country was beautiful, as were the grounds of the resort, but Jamaica had been going through a tough period of time with crime and violence. Back home, Flash's SEAL team leader had expressed surprise their commander was even allowing him to go to Jamaica on leave *because* of that violence.

Chuck and his buddies weren't happy with the sparsely populated resort. They'd wanted tons of people they could party with. Instead, they'd gotten families with young children, a smattering of couples on their honeymoons, and only a handful of singles their own age.

A loud crack of laughter sounded from the bar area, and Flash glanced over his shoulder. He saw Chuck and his buds sitting around a large table with a group of four women, all of whom were tall, slender, stacked, and blonde. He'd been introduced to them last night at the resort's indoor bar.

The women were here for a bachelorette weekend. Charlotte was the bride-to-be, and the bridesmaids sitting with her at the table were Ava, Alice, and Afton. Flash had mentally rolled his eyes at the fact their names all started with A.

After hanging around the group for three minutes, Flash had quickly deduced nothing about any of the women would interest him. They were younger, mostly concerned with talking about themselves. And the giggling...

He shuddered. The giggling had gotten on his nerves within seconds.

So he'd ditched the group to enjoy a drink by himself, far

enough away to avoid the high-pitched tittering while still keeping an eye on things.

Now here he was again, glaring at the water, playing monitor, wishing he was anywhere else. He'd much prefer to be home in Riverton, California, in his two-bedroom apartment, studying maps, going over intel about bad guys, watching football... anything other than babysitting Chuck and his buddies.

"It can't be *that* bad."

Surprised out of his thoughts by the husky voice to his right, Flash turned his head to see a woman he recognized, smiling at him from several feet away. She was in her own beach chair, had a book in her hand, and a water bottle stuck in the sand beneath her chair.

Flash searched his brain for her name. He'd been introduced to her last night as well...

Kelli. Kelli Colbert. She was with the bridesmaid group, but it seemed that, like him, hanging out at a bar wasn't exactly her cup of tea. She'd ditched the group even faster than Flash, leaving the bar entirely and opting for a night in her room.

He must've been staring at her for a beat too long, because now she gave him a sheepish grin and shrugged. "Sorry. Ignore me."

"No, I apologize. It's been so long since I've been required to do more than nod in agreement and smile that I've apparently forgotten how to talk to people."

She laughed under her breath.

At first glance last night, the woman seemed...plain. He hated to think that. It was rude as hell. But compared to her friends—overly made up in every way...clothes, hair, makeup—it was true.

Today, Kelli's dirty-blonde hair was pulled into a messy bun at the back of her head. Her cheeks were red, from too much sun most likely, and she was wearing a one-piece black swimsuit covered up by what looked to him like miles of material.

Unlike the other women in her group, she wasn't tall or slender. If Flash remembered correctly, she was at least a foot shorter than his six-two. She was also curvy...the complete opposite of her stick-thin friends.

And today...there was something about her that intrigued him. Maybe it was the genuine smile she flashed at him. Maybe it was her laughter. Flash wasn't sure. But for once, he wasn't annoyed that a total stranger was attempting to chat him up. Usually he hated that kind of thing.

"You aren't over there with the others, hanging out at the bar?" she asked with a small tilt of her head.

Flash shook his head. "Not my thing."

"Yeah, mine either."

"If I'm being honest, I hate the beach."

Kelli smiled, and her light brown eyes seemed to sparkle. "Sure, I can see why. The sun on your face, the relaxing sound of the waves on the shore, servers waiting on you hand-and-foot. It's horrible."

It was Flash's turn to grin. "Let's just say I spend a lot of time trying to get sand out of...sensitive places...in my day job."

Kelli turned more fully toward him. "*Hmmmm*, that sounds intriguing. Beach lifeguard?"

Flash shook his head again. "Nope."

"You run one of those machines that shoot sand into rock formations, trying to extract the oil?"

Flash was a little taken aback. If he was trying to think of jobs that might involve sand, fracking would be the last thing he'd come up with. "Second strike," he joked.

"Sandblaster? Installer of backyard sandboxes? Navy SEAL? Landscaper?"

Flash couldn't believe she'd actually guessed right.

"What? Still way off base?" Kelli asked, with another open and welcoming smile. "Fine. Don't tell me. But me? I love the beach. There's something just so soothing about it."

"If you'll forgive me...you don't exactly look soothed."

She sighed. "Yeah." She looked around, as if to make sure no one would overhear, then leaned in his direction and said quietly as she could over the distance, "I didn't want to come on this trip."

Flash's brows flew up. "You too?"

It was her turn to look surprised. "You didn't want to come either?"

Flash shrugged. "You already know my thoughts on sand. I don't know the guys I'm here with. Not really. The groom-to-be is my sister's fiancé."

"Ah...the obligatory brother-in-law duties," Kelli mused.

"Yup. I want to make sure he behaves, so I don't have to kick his ass for hurting my sister. And you?"

"The bride's my cousin. Our moms are sisters. I think she was guilted into making me one of her bridesmaids. I don't exactly fit in with the Three A's."

Flash almost choked on his lukewarm sip of beer.

Kelli grinned. "I know. It's juvenile, but I can't help it. They look like triplets, act exactly alike, flip their blonde hair all the same way. So that's just how I think of them in my head. Anyway, when this trip was planned, I suspect I wasn't supposed to come. I think Charlotte told me about it, guessing I'd say no. But this time, it was *my* mom who laid on the guilt, so...Here I am. But clearly I didn't think it through. I was just thinking about the beach. Not the part about having to hang out with the Three A's and my cousin."

"What do *you* do for a living?" Flash asked. The more the woman talked, the more intrigued he became. She was a mixture of blunt and shy at the same time.

The redness in her face deepened. "This and that," she mumbled, looking back out at the ocean.

"I'm sorry. I didn't mean to pry."

She sighed, then turned back to him. "You weren't. I just...I don't know what I want to do when I grow up. I'm twenty-eight years old and *still* have no idea what my passion is. I've done lots of things...waitressed, worked at an animal shelter, construction—don't get too excited, I was just the one holding the stop sign directing traffic—fast food, coffee shop, house cleaner. You name it, I've done it.

"Currently, I'm a travel agent. In fact, I arranged this entire trip for my cousin. But I already know the job isn't for me. It's very stressful...which I can handle, but the clients change their minds constantly and are never satisfied, and they call me to complain if the slightest thing goes wrong on their trips, even when it's not my fault. But I still haven't found anything else that I can see myself doing for the rest of my life."

She looked back out at the ocean again, her voice quieter, so Flash had to strain to hear. "My dad was killed on the job when I was a teenager, and just before he died, we had a conversation... and he told me to never settle for anything less than what made me truly happy. I think that's why I've always had a hard time deciding what I want to do with my life. I haven't discovered what *truly* makes me happy. I know I'm probably taking his words a little too much to heart, but it was literally one of the last things he said to me. Anyway..." Her voice trailed off a little self-consciously. "That's why I tried to deflect when you asked me what I did for a living."

There was a lot there. Flash wasn't sure where to start. So he began with the most important. "I'm sorry about your dad."

"Thanks. He worked in construction. He was on a scaffold when it collapsed under him. He fell and was crushed."

Flash frowned. Then he stood, scooted his chair right next to Kelli's and sat back down. Now there wasn't ten feet of space between them. "I really am sorry."

"Thanks. And contrary to what you might believe, I don't go around telling perfect strangers my life history," she said with a grimace.

"We aren't strangers. We met yesterday. I'm Wade. But everyone calls me Flash."

"Because your last name is Gordon," Kelli said with a grin.

"Yup."

"Well, Flash, I'm Kelli, but you probably know that."

Flash nodded. "I remember. And...about an occupation. I think it's admirable that you aren't settling for a job you dislike."

She smirked. "You want to tell my mom that? She thinks it's ridiculous that I'm so unsettled."

"I think that's her job. As a mom."

"True."

They sat in silence for a long moment, and Flash realized that for the first time this trip, he felt content. Kelli was a breath of fresh air. She was down-to-earth, funny, honest, and, it had to be said...hot.

Oh, Flash was aware a lot of men wouldn't find her shape and size attractive, but he'd dealt with plenty of women like her cousin and the Three A's. The type who didn't have an ounce of fat on their bodies and liked to push their fake boobs in his face, wanting a night in his bed simply because he was a Navy SEAL.

They'd say whatever they thought he wanted to hear, just so they could bag a SEAL. The frog hogs were exhausting. Gradually, they'd made him question *every* woman's intentions.

But Kelli...she was interesting. And it had been a long damn time since he'd looked twice at a woman.

"Where are you from?" she asked after a while.

"Riverton, California. You?"

She gaped at him in surprise. "You are?"

"Yeah, why?"

"Because I'm from La Jolla."

It was Flash's turn to be shocked. "Really? That's just north of me."

"I know."

"No wonder you like the beach. They have some wonderful ones."

She smiled. "True. Wow. Small world."

It was.

"You going on the thing tomorrow?" Kelli asked him.

"Thing? What thing?"

It was her turn to frown. "The tubing thing."

"I have no idea what you're talking about."

For the first time, she looked uneasy. "Oh, um...sorry. Forget I mentioned it."

"No, what tubing thing?"

Kelli sighed. "I guess Charlotte and the Three A's are bored. There's not much going on at the resort, and they want to do something more exciting. They contacted a private tour place and decided they just *had* to go tubing on the White River. I guess they asked your friends, and they agreed to go too."

Flash frowned. He hadn't heard anything about going off the resort's property. If he had, he would've tried to talk the guys out of it. While all the people they'd met so far had been kind and courteous, he was well aware of the dangers that lurked outside the fancy resort's gates.

"I haven't been hanging around them much. I'm sure they'll tell me as soon as they get a chance," he said.

She nodded. "I really am sorry. I know what it's like to be left out."

Flash couldn't help it, he laughed. Then, at seeing the look of hurt that flashed over her face before she could mask it, he hurried to say, "I'm not laughing at *you*. It's just that I have no real desire to sit my ass on a tube for who the hell knows how long it'll take to get down whatever overcrowded piece of river."

He was relieved to see the smile return to her face. "Right? I'm so short, my legs usually end up sticking straight up, and it's all I can do to hold onto the stupid tube."

"Are you going?"

Kelli shrugged. "Yeah. I really don't want to because I'm not sure it's safe to leave the resort. But I kind of feel obligated."

Flash didn't want to either, because he knew as well as Kelli apparently did that it wasn't safe. But the last thing he was going to do was leave his future-brother-in-law to get hurt or robbed. His sister would have his head on a platter if he did that. And then there was Kelli...

"So...you think you might want to go?" she asked.

It wasn't hard to see the interest in Kelli's eyes. Normally, that in itself would urge him to say no. He didn't do one-night stands any longer, and he definitely wasn't looking for some kind of vacation fling. But he found himself in a whole new headspace at the moment. He *liked* knowing this woman wanted him to come along. He wanted to spend more time with her. Get to know her better.

"Yeah," Flash told her.

"Cool," she said with a shy smile.

"Cool," he agreed.

A sound behind them had them both turning to see who was approaching. It was Charlotte and the Three A's. Flash chuckled to himself; now *he* was calling the bridesmaids by the nickname.

"Hey, Kelli, we're going to hang out with Seb, Ben, Rowan, and Charles in that little grotto on the other side of the property."

"Um...okay?" Kelli said, obviously confused about why her cousin was informing her of their plans.

"I just didn't want you worrying about where we were or coming to look for us. We'll see you tomorrow after breakfast. The minibus will pick us up in front of the resort at ten. Don't be late." And with that, Charlotte turned, and she and the Three A's strutted back to the bar where the guys were waiting for them, exaggerating the swing of their hips.

Kelli was staring back out at the water, refusing to meet Flash's gaze.

"That was weird," he blurted.

Kelli shrugged.

"Hey," he said softly.

She still wouldn't look at him.

"Kelli," he said, putting a little more force into his voice.

Finally, she turned, and seeing the way her eyes sparkled with unshed tears tore at him.

"What?" she asked a little aggressively.

"You want to have dinner with me?" The words were out before he'd even thought about what he was going to say.

She stared at him with those wounded eyes, and Flash ached to do something that would make them sparkle with humor again.

"I mean, since the guys I'm with are obviously going to be hanging with your cousin and the Three A's, it means we're free to do whatever we want. I've heard great things about the restaurant here. I bet we could even get a table on the beach."

"But you hate the sand," she said softly.

"I hate seeing a beautiful woman torn up because her snobby, clueless, obviously stupid cousin was hateful to her even more."

Kelli sighed. "She knows I made dinner reservations for all five of us tonight. And that dig about not coming to look for her? She obviously doesn't want me anywhere near the guys who'll be drooling all over her tonight."

"Fuck her," Flash said, way past caring that he was being derogatory about Kelli's relative.

"Don't you need to watch your sister's fiancé?"

"He already knows that if he does anything other than talk to another woman, I'll tell my sister so fast it'll make his head spin. And he might be more scared of Nova than he is of me."

Kelli giggled, and Flash was so relieved, his muscles relaxed. He hadn't even realized how tense he'd become.

"Have dinner with me, Kelli. Please?"

"Well, when you ask me so nicely, how can I refuse?"

"You can't," he said with satisfaction.

"What time?"

"Six-thirty?"

She nodded. "Okay. I need to go talk to the front desk and tell them to cancel my previous dinner reservation."

"You need to go right now?" he asked, wanting to prolong his time with this intriguing woman.

"Probably not. Why?"

"Because it's a beautiful day. We could sit here for a while and enjoy it."

She stared at him for a beat, before nodding. "Okay."

"Okay," Flash said, before taking another swig of his disgusting warm beer.

"You mind if I read? I was just getting to a good part."

"Not at all."

Sitting next to Kelli while she read and he stared out at the waves was relaxing. For the first time this trip, Flash felt the tension he always carried on his shoulders dissipating. And it took...what? A pretty woman saying yes to his dinner invitation. Hearing the pages of her book shuffle as she turned them. Her quiet chuckles each time she read something funny.

Flash still hated the beach.

Still despised the sand.

But somehow, it was more tolerable with Kelli Colbert sitting next to him.

CHAPTER TWO

Kelli stood in her hotel room and stared into the mirror. She wiped her sweaty palms down her thighs as she tried to decide if what she had on was appropriate for dinner with one of the sexiest men she'd ever met in her life.

When she'd first been introduced to Flash, she'd dismissed him immediately, figuring he was just like the other four men Charlotte had homed in on at the resort. Out for a one-night stand.

Then her hand touched his when they shook, and it felt as if little electrical jolts were shooting down her arm, straight between her legs. She'd never had a reaction like that to a man before—and it scared the crap out of her. She'd immediately left the bar last night, retreating to the safety of her room and a good book.

Still, she hadn't been able to resist peeking over at him when he'd chosen a beach chair not too far from where she'd been sitting that afternoon. And when he sighed and stared out at the ocean with such...discontent, she also hadn't been able to prevent herself from commenting.

She was too blunt. Always had been. But she hated the games

people played in social situations. She'd always preferred others come out and say what they were thinking. It saved a lot of time and heartache.

Kelli supposed that started after her dad died and people began to tiptoe around her. They'd whisper behind her back, and it drove her crazy. And then she'd found out that her friend, a girl she'd gotten close to during that horrible time, was only hanging out with her because of the money Kelli had inherited, she was *done*.

Done with being socially correct.

Done with hiding what she was feeling.

She was who she was, and if someone didn't like that, tough.

But even so, she was surprised to find herself spilling her guts to Flash earlier that afternoon. Telling him about her many jobs, her relationship with her family, and basically making herself vulnerable to the handsome man she'd met only the night before.

But he hadn't seemed annoyed or surprised. He'd seemed... what? Interested?

No, that couldn't be right.

But he *had* asked her to dinner.

Then again, he'd done so after Charlotte had humiliated her. Maybe he'd felt as if he had no choice. A pity date.

Ugh. She hated being the object of people's pity. Yes, it was embarrassing that her cousin had come right out and said she didn't want her around when she and the Three A's were trying to get some from the bachelor party guys, but Kelli had been embarrassed plenty of times before. She could deal. She knew she was only in Jamaica out of a sense of guilt and obligation. Her mom had probably talked to Charlotte's mom, and her aunt had probably bribed Charlotte into putting her in the wedding and inviting her to Jamaica. And Kelli's own mom had guilted her into attending the bachelorette weekend.

Sighing, she turned her attention back to her reflection. Her hair was actually behaving...right now. Later, it would likely frizz out in the humidity, but for now it hung just below her shoulders with a slight curl in the ends. She'd put on some mascara and lipstick. Her face was pink from too much sun, and a little too round from the sweets and carbs she liked to eat, but she couldn't do anything about either of those things.

She was wearing a dress she'd gotten back in La Jolla that she'd loved at the time, but now she wondered if it was too much. It was a tank dress that stopped just above her knees. It was a little clingier than clothes she usually wore. Frowning at the bulge of her belly, and the way her upper arms sagged, Kelli pressed her lips together.

She'd felt pretty when she'd tried the dress on in the store, but that was before she'd had any inclination she'd be wearing it to dinner with one of the hottest men she'd ever seen.

Flash had eyes so green, they matched the palm trees surrounding the resort. His brownish hair was cut short, and she'd never been with anyone who had any kind of facial hair, so she couldn't help but wonder what it would feel like to kiss him. Would it be distracting? Would he get food caught in his short mustache and beard?

Kelli could admit that she wanted to impress Flash, though it was unlikely anything would come out of these few days of acquaintance. Even though they lived not far from each other back in the "real world," she doubted they'd keep in touch.

But for tonight, they'd be sharing a meal. It wasn't a date, not really. Still, she couldn't help but feel the butterflies that usually happened before going out with someone new.

Shaking her head, Kelli deliberately turned away from the mirror. She was being ridiculous. This was only dinner. Tomorrow they'd go tubing, then the next day they'd all head home. She wasn't going to see Flash again, so thinking about how attractive the hair on his chest was, or how his facial hair would feel against her lips, was nothing more than a pipe dream.

Looking at her watch, Kelli realized she was going to be late if she didn't get a move on. She grabbed her sweatshirt, the only clothing she had that was warm, and headed for the door. The sweatshirt didn't match her dress in the least, but if they were going to sit outside, she'd need something, since it got chilly when the sun went down. And if her putting a sweatshirt on over her dress turned Flash off, so be it.

She was who she was. Blunt, honest...and tonight she'd be warm, if nothing else.

Taking a deep breath, she closed her hotel room door behind her and headed down the hall toward the lobby.

Ten minutes later, she and Flash were being led toward a table in the resort's five-star restaurant. It was almost empty, probably because it wasn't exactly cheap, was the only restaurant that wasn't included in the all-inclusive price of staying at the resort, and because tourism was definitely down in the country.

Flash looked amazing. He had on a pair of khaki pants and a sage green polo shirt that seemed to bring out the color of his eyes all the more. When he'd seen her in the lobby, he'd smiled huge and actually leaned down and kissed her cheek in greeting. Kelli had inhaled discreetly when he was close, rewarded with the crisp scent of whatever soap he'd used when he'd showered. It was intoxicating, and there was nothing more she'd wanted to do than lean in and bury her nose in the crook of his neck.

Now, his fingers briefly touched the small of her back as the waiter led them to their table, and Kelli barely controlled the full-body shiver that tried to break free.

"I hope this meets with your approval," the waiter told them, motioning toward a table.

Kelli audibly gasped.

There was one table set in the far corner of the patio. They had an unrestricted view of the ocean and the coming sunset. The table had two roses in a slender vase in the middle, and the place settings were side by side, facing the water, instead of across from each other.

The chairs at the table were also not your average restaurant chairs. They were leather, with wide seats and no arms, and even from a distance, Kelli could see they looked extremely comfortable. In her experience, restaurants made their seats as uncomfortable as possible so people would eat, then leave, allowing more customers to come in, spend money, and leave just as quickly.

Looking at the romantic setup of the table, Kelli had a feeling she could sit there all right. And since the restaurant didn't seem to be busy, she might be able to do just that.

"This looks perfect. Thank you," Flash told the waiter, as he pulled out one of the chairs and gestured for Kelli to sit.

She smiled at him and stepped in front of the chair. As she sat, Flash pushed the chair under her. He'd done it so smoothly, as if he'd had a ton of practice. And of course, that thought had Kelli assuming he probably took women out to fancy dinners all the time. She was out of her element, but he seemed completely at ease.

The waiter said he'd return with waters and the menus, then left them alone.

Kelli was suddenly nervous and feeling totally out of her league. What was she doing? She should've stayed in and ordered room service.

"I always get confused about which utensil to use. Why do we have four forks and three spoons? What the hell do they think we're going to do, take one bite with a fork, then put it down because it's dirty and use another?"

His joke made Kelli relax. Flash wasn't as comfortable as he seemed, which made her feel so much better. "I have no idea. But I'm thinking they aren't going to haul us to fork jail if we use the wrong one, so we're probably okay."

He chuckled, and Kelli couldn't stop looking at his mouth.

Flash relaxed in his chair, putting his arm over the top of hers. If she leaned back, his fingers might brush against her hair.

She mentally shook her head. She was being ridiculous. Acting like she was fifteen again, sitting with a boy she liked in a movie theater or something.

"This doesn't suck," Flash said after a moment.

Kelli smiled. "Even with the sand?" she asked.

"Even with the sand," he agreed with a small nod. Then he looked at her. "Thanks for coming with me tonight. I was all ready to order room service, but I'm thinking this will be so much better. And I brought my phone, so I can take a picture of the sunset and send it to my sister."

"What? Not post it on social media with a hundred hashtags?" Kelli teased.

"Don't have any social media, so, no."

She blinked in surprise. "Seriously?"

"Yup. My job doesn't allow it."

That's right. She never did find out what he did for a living earlier that day. They'd been talking about sand and she'd guessed a few jobs, and then somehow the subject got changed. "Are you a spy?" she whispered, looking around furtively.

He burst out laughing. "No. But you did guess correctly earlier. I'm a SEAL."

For a split second, the round, adorable, probably annoying-to-fishermen animal flashed in her mind.

"The Navy frowns on its special forces soldiers posting shit on the Net that could be a security breach. I'm not sorry though. I can't stand how some people use the platforms to bitch about every aspect of their lives, or only to show the good stuff. Both ends of the spectrum are distortions of reality, and it's annoying."

"You're a Navy SEAL?"

"Yeah."

Kelli was tempted to push back her chair right then and there. She'd felt out of her element earlier, but now? She was definitely not up to this man's speed. But the moment she told her muscles to do their job and get her the hell out of there, the waiter returned.

"Do you drink wine?" Flash asked.

Kelli nodded. She needed about three bottles right now to find the courage to continue with this dinner.

Flash turned to the waiter. "I'm sorry, I know nothing about wine. Can you bring us a bottle of something light but local?"

"Of course. While you look over the menu, I'll bring the bottle and you can see if it meets with your approval."

The second the waiter left, Flash was leaning toward her. "Does it change things? My job? I can tell you're two seconds from bolting."

Kelli took a deep breath. She was being ridiculous. This was just dinner. That's all. "No. I was just surprised. No wonder you don't like the sand. I've seen the shows about Hell Week."

Flash smirked. "Yup. And my team leader takes great pleasure in having us roll around in the sand during PT in the mornings too. He's sadistic."

Kelli laughed, and just like that, the tension between them broke.

Everything about Flash made so much more sense now. Why his sister trusted him to keep an eye on her fiancé—he'd probably crush the man if he so much as made a move on another woman. Flirting with the Three A's was one thing, but there was little chance he'd risk anything else. Not with Flash around.

And now those muscles made sense. Flash looked like he could bench press...well...lots. Kelli had no idea what a good number was for bench pressing, but it had to be high.

He had an air of confidence that was impossible to miss. Being a Navy SEAL was a tough job. Mentally and physically. He probably had to make split-second decisions all the time, so he had to be smart and intuitive.

She couldn't deny she was intrigued. And yes, attracted.

What woman *hadn't* had fantasies of being carried off by a hot man in uniform? And here she was, having dinner with one.

Deciding to enjoy every second of this night, Kelli smiled at Flash.

Then something else occurred to her...she'd felt safe with this man from the second she'd met him last night. It wasn't a feeling she'd experienced often. In fact, when she'd met Rowan, Ben, and Seb, she'd felt decidedly uneasy. Felt their gazes running over her body when they'd met. Judging her.

But she'd immediately felt at ease with Flash—the excitement of his handshake notwithstanding.

She wasn't an idiot. Not all military men were honorable. But something told her that Flash was someone she could trust. And that made her relax all the more.

The waiter returned with a bottle of wine and, after they both tried it and approved, poured them each a large glass.

The night went by way too fast for Kelli. She found herself enjoying Flash's company immensely. He was easy to talk to, and they never ran out of things to discuss. The sunset was everything she could've hoped for and more. She took around a hundred pictures and loved that Flash did too. He immediately texted one to his sister and showed Kelli the response...about a page full of emojis.

He even insisted the waiter take their picture together in front of the sunset, and that was a pic Kelli had a feeling she'd probably print out, in order to remember such an amazing evening.

When she pulled out her sweatshirt once it got chilly, Flash had laughed outright when he saw what was printed on the back.

Anti-social Wives Club.

She wasn't a wife, and she wasn't really anti-social, but she'd found the company not too long ago and the sweatshirts were perfect. Roomy, not too tight at the bottom—she hated when sweatshirts had really tight elastic at the waist, making her look even heavier than she already was—and while none of the sayings fit her, she still loved the sweatshirt itself.

After they'd eaten, when Flash suggested a walk on the beach, Kelli didn't hesitate to say yes. They didn't have too much beach to walk, as there were fences on either end of the property, but it was still a beautiful evening and after the delicious food, Kelli didn't mind the slight bit of exercise.

"So...you're still going tomorrow?" she asked Flash. They were walking side by side, not touching but sharing the same space. "Going tubing, I mean."

"Yeah. I talked to Chuck, and he gave me the deets."

"Chuck?"

Flash grinned. "He hates that nickname, but I don't give a shit. Until he proves he's a good man who'll treat my sister like the princess she is, he'll be Chuck to me."

"So until they've been married for fifty years or so?" Kelli joked.

"Pretty much."

"I wish I had a brother. Or a sister, for that matter. My mom hoped Charlotte and I would be like sisters at one point, but that wasn't meant to be. We're just too different."

"For the record, I think you're perfect."

Kelli looked up at Flash in surprise. He smiled down at her, then looked in the direction they were walking once more.

"Um...thanks."

They continued in silence, and Kelli was enjoying how comfortable she felt with this man. She didn't feel the need to babble, to fill the silence with conversation. They reached the end of the property line then turned around to walk back. To her surprise, Flash's hand brushed against hers...then his fingers closed around her own.

"This okay?" he asked, looking down at her.

"Yeah."

They walked for a bit, then he chuckled and said, "I can't remember the last time I held a woman's hand. It's nice."

Kelli smiled. It was. It was *very* nice. He had large hands that dwarfed hers. Even if she hadn't known what he did for a living, she would've felt safe with Flash. Not that the resort was dangerous, but she had no doubt if a giant sea creature came up from the ocean, he'd beat it back with his bare hands. Or if someone appeared on the sand with a knife, he'd kick it out of their grip like some sort of ninja, then keep walking like he'd done nothing special.

When they got back to the resort, Kelli was almost disappointed. She was also confused. She'd told herself that this was just dinner. That nothing would come of it. Flash was just being polite. They didn't even live in the same town. True, they'd discovered they lived shockingly close to each other, but still.

And now? After talking for four hours over dinner and wine, walking on the beach, and holding hands...something had shifted within Kelli. She wanted more. Wanted to get to know this man better. Wanted more meals, more walks, more hand-holding.

Hell, who was she kidding? She wanted much more than hand-holding. But she wasn't the kind of woman who jumped into bed with men on the first date. Much to her dismay. It would be easy to invite him back to her room, or for her to say yes if invited to his. But it would also be disappointing. He wouldn't be the man she'd built up in her head if he did that.

Without a word, and without letting go of her hand, Flash walked them back to the lobby of the resort. It was late enough that no one was around. The lights in the lobby had been dimmed and there was only one employee behind the front desk.

"I had a good time tonight," he said, turning to face her.

"Me too."

"We're meeting at ten tomorrow, right?"

"Uh-huh." Kelli stared up at Flash. Wanting him to kiss her, but stressing about it at the same time. Butterflies were swarming in her belly and her heart was beating hard in her chest.

"You want to have breakfast with me before we head out tomorrow?"

Kelli smiled. "Yes."

"Great. Meet you here in the lobby at eight-thirty? We can head over to the buffet together."

"Sounds good."

Flash stepped forward, leaning in, and Kelli held her breath.

He kissed her cheek chastely, squeezing her hand. "Thanks for an awesome night, Kelli. I'll see you in the morning." Then he took a step backward. And another. It was as if he didn't want to leave her either.

"See you later," she said.

"Later."

With one last look she couldn't interpret, Flash turned and strode toward one of the hallways that obviously led to his room.

Kelli couldn't keep her gaze from his ass. It was perfect.

After he was out of sight, she headed in the opposite direction, toward her own room.

By the time she'd changed, used the bathroom, and gotten under the covers, Kelli realized she was still smiling. She never wanted to come to Jamaica, but so far it had been a trip to remember. Even if nothing came of her and Flash's acquaintance, she'd remember their time tonight for the rest of her life. He'd made her feel funny. Interesting. Wanted. That alone made him leaps and bounds above the other men she'd dated in recent years.

Turning onto her side, Kelli snuggled into her pillow. Tomorrow wasn't her idea of a good time. But she'd go because she'd promised her mom that she'd do her best to get along with

Charlotte. And with Flash there, Kelli realized she might just enjoy the outing. She was actually looking forward to it now.

She fell asleep with a huge smile on her face, thinking of the man who'd made her night one of the best she'd had in a very long time.

CHAPTER THREE

Flash resisted the urge to pace. It took a while for him to fall asleep the night before. He'd been thinking about Kelli. There was something about the woman that made him feel as if he'd known her forever. She was comfortable. Funny. Sweet. And he liked all of that. A lot.

There was a moment when he could tell she was seconds away from leaving, but he'd managed to put her at ease. He was more than grateful she'd gone outside her comfort zone and stayed for dinner.

He was also pleased she'd been so down-to-earth. He hadn't lied when he'd admitted that he had no idea which fork to use. And he knew next to nothing about wine, about choosing it, just that he enjoyed drinking a glass or two with a meal sometimes. As it turned out, Kelli was the same.

And he absolutely loved her sweatshirt.

Or really, what he actually loved was the fact that she put her comfort above fashion. Because fashion was something else he knew nothing about and had no desire to learn.

She was also smart, and the fact she didn't have a career

didn't concern him in the least. She'd figure out what she wanted to do with the rest of her life, of that he had no doubt.

He'd had a great time with her last night. And the only reason he'd agreed to go on this tubing trip today was because Kelli would be there.

He *did* try to talk Chuck out of going, explaining that it really wasn't safe to go off the resort grounds. He figured if he was successful, he'd have a similar discussion with Kelli during breakfast. But Chuck had blown him off, insisting it would be fine.

A niggling doubt remained in the back of Flash's mind. He thought of talking to Kelli anyway, suggesting the two of them spend another day on the beach. But he knew he wouldn't forgive himself if something happened to his sister's fiancé. In the end, he justified going today by telling himself he was probably the only person in their group who might be able to recognize danger if he saw it. Hell, his job was to ferret out shit going sideways before it actually happened.

So now he was standing in the lobby waiting for Kelli, anxiously looking forward to seeing her again—and suddenly she was there, walking toward him. She had on a loose bathing suit cover-up that swished above her knees. It was black, made out of a thin, lightweight cotton.

For a split second, an image of her peeling the thing over her head as she stood next to his hotel bed—revealing nothing underneath—flew through his mind.

Flash ruthlessly pushed the vision away. Nothing was going to happen between him and Kelli. Yes, she was gorgeous, and he felt more than the usual spark with her, but they were on vacation. And he wasn't the kind of man who took a woman to bed for a one-night stand...especially while on leave far from home.

"Hey," she said nervously, smoothing an errant piece of hair behind her ear. Last night, when he'd first seen her in the lobby, Kelli's hair had been smooth and silky. But as the evening continued it got curlier and curlier. She claimed it was frizzy, but he disagreed.

This morning, she'd pulled it back with a barrette, but it was still curly, seemed to have a mind of its own, and that made Flash smile.

"Hey," he echoed as she approached. "Sleep okay?"

She shrugged. "Sure. You?"

"Yup." Flash turned sideways and held out his arm to her. "Shall we?"

With a smile, Kelli wrapped her hand around his elbow. "Lead on, kind sir."

Flash had already been up for a few hours. He'd worked out in the resort's gym then ran a couple of miles up and down the deserted beach. Kevlar, his team leader back home, wouldn't be happy if he came home from leave out of shape. Not that a few days off would matter very much, but Flash always felt better after a good workout.

They entered the dining room and headed toward the buffet that was laid out in the middle of the room. As they got close, Kelli dropped her hand upon seeing all their traveling companions already gathered around the food.

"Hey, about time you got up, lazy bones," Charlotte told her.

This morning, she wore a white cover-up that had artfully placed holes, allowing everyone to see the bright red bikini she was wearing underneath. Objectively, Flash could admit that the woman had a nice body, but for him, he much preferred Kelli's curves to her cousin's thin frame.

"You're up early," Kelli noted, as she reached for a plate.

Charlotte giggled, and yet again, the sound grated on Flash's nerves. He stepped up behind Kelli and grabbed his own plate.

"Yeah, well, I had an early night, unlike *some* people," Charlotte tittered, as she looked over at one of the other women going through the line ahead of her.

"What happens on vaca stays on vaca," the woman said with a huge smile as she nudged Ben, who was standing next to her.

"Oh yeah," Chuck's friend agreed, staring at the woman's breasts.

Flash wanted to roll his eyes. He immediately searched out Chuck. Since yesterday afternoon, he hadn't done a very good job of keeping his eye on the groom-to-be.

He was already sitting at a table, his phone in hand, scrolling down the screen. Just because he wasn't currently fawning all over one of the women didn't mean he hadn't slept with any of them, but all the same, Flash was relieved to find him sitting alone.

After going through the line, Flash steered Kelli to an empty table. He put the plate down, then said, "I'm going to go grab some water, want anything? Juice?"

"Yes, please. Orange juice sounds great."

There were waiters around, but there were also pitchers on a table not too far away, and it would be just as fast for Flash to grab one than to wait for someone to come to their table. He'd just picked up two pitchers, one with water and the other with orange juice, when Seb and Rowan came up behind him.

"Where were you last night, man? You missed all the fun," Seb said.

"Yeah, those chicks are fucking *hot*. And horny as hell," Rowan added.

"Not my thing, man," Flash replied. He wasn't that much older than these guys, around four or five years, but at the moment, he felt positively ancient compared to them.

"Seriously, the one I was with did some stuff I'd only seen in pornos," Seb went on.

"Mine sucked my dick so hard, it's actually sore today," Rowan said with a smirk.

The two men high-fived each other.

"If you'll excuse me," Flash said, taking a step to the side, intending to walk around the men acting like a couple of frat boys at some college kegger.

"You with the fat cousin?" Seb asked.

The question made Flash's temper flare. "Excuse me?" he repeated in a low, menacing tone that any of his teammates would've known meant he was on the verge of losing his shit. But since these men didn't know him, they didn't heed the caution they should've heard in his tone.

"You know, that chick Charlotte was obligated to invite. She didn't even want her to come. Said she's a stick in the mud."

"I've heard fat girls are fun in the sack though," Rowan added, leering. "They'll let you do whatever you want since they're so hard up for attention. It's cool that you're showing her a good time. Keeps her off Charlotte's back. I know she's the bride-to-be, but I'm gonna see if I can tap that tonight. Ben said he'd gladly take the girl I had last night, see if she'd be interested in a threesome with him and her friend. Or maybe we can talk Charles into having some fun."

It hadn't escaped Flash's notice that the men hadn't used any of the women's names. He wondered if they even knew them. If they could distinguish at all between the women they were talking about so casually, as if they were merely holes to stick their cocks into.

He opened his mouth to tell these assholes off...when he noticed someone behind them.

Kelli was standing just five feet away, frozen, a look of shock and hurt on her face.

That, more than anything these two dipshits said, *really* pissed him off. This woman, who'd been smiling not two minutes earlier, now looked embarrassed, as if she wanted to be anywhere but in this dining room.

But even as he watched, she straightened her shoulders and lifted her chin. She stepped toward them and shoved between the two men roughly, making them stumble to stay on their feet.

"Sorry," she said insincerely. Then she lowered her voice, as if imparting some deep dark secret. "I have it on good authority that my cousin just got back from the doctor before this trip. Heard her talking with her friends about some test results... something about how it takes chlamydia a week or two to go away."

With that, she took the pitcher of juice out of Flash's hand and sauntered back to their table.

Flash couldn't keep the smirk off his face as Rowan and Seb immediately began to whisper furiously to each other. He quickly followed Kelli back to the table. She was frowning when he sat and refused to meet his gaze.

"Kelli?"

"Yeah?" she asked, staring at her plate as if it held all the answers to every question in the universe.

"Please look at me."

She sighed, then reluctantly lifted her chin. "What?"

"They're idiots. Thinking with their dicks. Don't take what they said to heart."

"They didn't say anything I haven't heard before. It's crazy how being fat is a bigger offense than a lot of other things. It brings out the worst in other people. Everyone talks behind your back. Doctors blame all your symptoms on being overweight without even doing tests to find out what's really wrong. And to men, it's like we have the plague."

"People are morons," Flash said heatedly.

"It's fine," she said with a shrug.

But it wasn't fine. Flash was deeply disturbed. Doubly so that Kelli had heard versions of what those two idiots had said from people in the past.

"I didn't come here to pick up chicks like the others obviously did," he began. "I don't date that much at all. My job takes me away from home way too often for me to be a good candidate for a relationship. The first night here, Afton came onto me.

Actually, she cornered me in the hallway, put her hand on my dick, and invited me to her room. I've never pushed a woman away so damn fast."

"Right. Good for you," Kelli mumbled, looking away again.

"The *only* woman I've noticed since I got here sat beside me on the beach and told me that things couldn't be that bad."

Kelli's gaze, which had gone back to her food, whipped up to meet his own.

"In fact, you're the only woman who's managed to catch my attention in years." The admission wasn't hard to make. And now that he had, Flash couldn't stop there. "You're funny, down-to-earth, easy to talk to, and...this is most definitely inappropriate—but I think frick and frack already crossed that line, so I feel the need to make this point very clear—I fell asleep with my cock hard as a rock last night, thinking about how you'd feel under, over, and next to me. And I woke up the same way.

"You have the body of a Greek goddess, Kelli. Curvy in all the right places. There's *nothing* wrong with you. In fact, seeing you sitting across from me in that coverup makes me want to strip it off you slowly to reveal the gift that's underneath...which is much sexier to me than your cousin and the Three A's showing off their goods to the world."

Kelli's mouth was hanging open slightly, as if she was in shock.

Flash had said too much. Had been *way* too crude. But he needed this woman to understand that all the bullshit Rowan had spewed about women with some meat on their bones wasn't the way the majority of men felt.

"Um...thanks?"

Flash let out a huff of laughter. "I think we can both agree that the people we came to Jamaica with aren't the best examples of how adults should act."

"True. But that now includes me. I was lying about Charlotte. I never heard her talking to her friends about an STD."

"I figured. But it should keep those assholes from making a move on her. Maybe save her marriage."

Kelli shrugged. "I'm not sure about that. And I don't really feel bad about what I did. Serves her right for talking about me behind my back. Are you going to talk to Charles?"

"Oh yeah, Chuck and I are gonna talk," Flash said. Based on what Rowan said, it sounded like his future brother-in-law hadn't stepped out of line last night. But better safe than sorry.

To his relief, Kelli chuckled. "Ah, to be a fly on the wall for that conversation."

"In any other situation, I wouldn't give a shit who the man fucks. But he's engaged to my sister. There's no way I'm gonna let him cheat on her before they even get married. Not if I can help it, anyway."

Kelli glanced across the room, and Flash followed her gaze to his sister's fiancé. He was still sitting at a table by himself, still staring at his phone. This time, he had a small smile on his face. The rest of his friends were at a large table with the Three A's and Charlotte.

Kelli looked back at Flash. "It seems to me that he's not all that interested in the same things his friends are."

Flash had to agree. He could be putting on a front because he knew his fiancée's brother was watching him, but it didn't seem like it. He was completely absorbed in whatever was happening on his phone. As he watched the man, he saw him talking, and it dawned on Flash that he was FaceTiming someone. Probably Nova.

Flash turned back to Kelli. "Are we good?" he asked.

She frowned. "Good?"

"Yeah. You aren't...upset by what I said to you?"

To his amazement, she smiled shyly at him. "No. How can I be when I had the same thoughts about *you* last night when I got into my own bed?"

And just like that, Flash's dick hardened under the table. Fuck. He hadn't had a spontaneous woody in years.

"Good." Then, worried that she'd think he was saying good to her statement that she'd thought about him in bed, he quickly clarified, "Good that we're on the same page. I mean...that we're good. Good that we're good."

He sounded like an idiot. Could he say good any more in one sentence?

Kelli giggled. "Yeah, good that we're good," she echoed.

Reaching for the pitcher of OJ—idly marveling over the fact her giggles didn't annoy him, like the other womens' did—Flash filled her glass. "Make sure you eat enough breakfast, I'm guessing the 'snack' we're promised while on this excursion is gonna suck."

"You don't have to tell a fat girl to eat," Kelli joked.

But Flash didn't find that funny in the least. He reached across the table and put his hand over hers. Her gaze flew up to his in surprise. "Don't," he ordered. "You aren't fat. Not even close. You're curvy. Sexy as hell. Greek goddess, remember? And in my eyes, that's a hundred percent sexier than looking as if you're two seconds from being blown away by a stiff breeze. Or hearing your stomach growling because you aren't eating enough to keep a gnat alive. Okay?"

"Okay," she said softly.

"Good. I see you got some of the cheesy bacon potatoes. They're amazing. I don't know what they put in the cheese... crack? But they're so damn delicious, I'm gonna miss this place for these potatoes alone."

His words seemed to ease the tension in the air, and Kelli smiled. "No. It's the bacon. Everyone knows bacon makes everything better."

"That it does," Flash agreed.

The rest of breakfast was uneventful, thank goodness.

Everyone else in their parties headed upstairs to get ready for the excursion, but he and Kelli stayed where they were. Nursing their cups of coffee and juice, and talking about nothing and everything. And laughing. So much laughter. Flash couldn't remember being this entertained by another human being. Usually he was the first to want to leave a meal. He wasn't much for idle chitchat. But with Kelli? He could listen to her talk for hours.

Eventually, it was time to head out for the tubing trip. Flash's anxiety returned as they headed to the lobby. He wasn't bringing much with him, just his wallet in the pocket of his swimming trunks, holding his ID and a credit card. Kelli had also packed light, with a small bag over her shoulder. The tour company was providing towels and, of course, the tubes they'd be riding down the White River.

To his surprise, when everyone began to board the vehicles, the guys were getting into one minibus and the women in the other. Flash would've thought the horndogs he was with would take every opportunity to stick close to the women. When he neared the minibus already loaded with his brother-in-law-to-be and his friends, he heard Seb and Rowan talking about who might be hooking up with who later that night.

He understood then; they were using the time it took to travel to the river to plot. It just disgusted him further.

Flash met Chuck's gaze—and blinked when the other man rolled his eyes.

It seemed as if maybe, just maybe, he'd underestimated his sister's fiancé. It made him feel better, but he was still going to withhold his approval until the man had proved beyond a doubt that he was loyal to Nova.

Looking over at the other minibus, Flash could see Kelli sitting in the back seat by herself, looking out the window, doing her best to ignore the other women...just as they were doing to her.

"I'm gonna ride in the other vehicle," Flash told Chuck and

the guys, before slamming the sliding door. He didn't wait to stick around and hear the crude comments his announcement was sure to evoke.

He jogged toward the other minibus and opened the front passenger seat and hopped in. It didn't sit well with him that they would be heading off the safety of the resort's property in two vans, one filled with women and the other with men. That wasn't smart or safe.

The driver nodded at him, and Flash turned around to face the women. "Ready?" he asked.

"Hey, Flash!"

"Ready!"

"Ooooh, we've got a big bad bodyguard!"

"Is it getting hot in here?"

Flash ignored the comments and kept his gaze on Kelli sitting in the very back. She gave him a small smile, and that was all Flash needed to see to know he'd made the right decision.

The driver started the minibus and they made their way from the posh beach resort to the heart of Jamaica. The second they passed the resort's security gates, Flash's anxiety increased tenfold. This was a horrible idea, but it was too late now. All he could do was get through it. They'd be back at the resort that afternoon, and tomorrow he'd go home to Riverton.

But Flash felt naked. Wearing only a pair of swim shorts and a T-shirt, without his usual assortment of knives and guns and other SEAL gear, he was completely out of his element.

Doing his best to put his fears aside, Flash concentrated on memorizing the roads they were taking to get to the place where the rafting company put their customers into the river. Without thought, he entered "SEAL mode," as he and his teammates called it. Hyper-alert, ready for anything. Hopefully it was overkill and he was just being paranoid. But better safe than sorry. It had saved his and his fellow SEALs' lives more than once. He'd be an idiot to let down his guard now.

In the back of his mind, Flash had no doubt he was feeling extra protective because of the woman sitting behind him. Kelli had gotten under his skin in the space of a day, and the thought of anything happening to her on his watch was enough to make him even more tense. She, and the others, would have a fun-filled afternoon if it killed him.

He might be the only one on alert, but that was all right. He'd keep watch over them all. It was what he did.

CHAPTER FOUR

Flash looked tense.

Kelli couldn't help but notice, and because he was on edge, it made *her* feel uncomfortable as well.

The other guys had looked a little sheepish when they'd arrived at the put-in spot for their trip, asked Flash why he'd ditched them, riding in the minibus with the girls...and he'd explained that leaving a vehicle full of women unprotected wasn't the best idea, considering the issues in the country.

Kelli could admit to also being confused when he'd hopped into the front seat of their bus back at the resort. Once she heard why he'd done it, a warm feeling settled in her bones. Flash was a good person. And smart. She'd done her research on the country when she'd made all the arrangements for the trip. She knew how dangerous it could be. But she also hadn't been terribly worried, assuming they'd be fine at the private resort.

Now, she could admit to feeling a little nervous ever since Charlotte decided she wanted to head off the secure property. Having Flash along made her feel a tiny bit better. Safer.

Once the tubes were handed out, everyone quickly paired up, leaving Kelli with Flash...which wasn't exactly a hardship. She enjoyed his company, was extremely attracted to him, and the thought of floating down the river with the Three A's and Charlotte for hours wasn't something that sounded fun in the least.

However, Flash hadn't said much since they'd arrived. He was constantly looking around, sizing up the area, the employees and other visitors, and looking worriedly at the river itself. His unease transferred to Kelli. She looked around as well, and didn't see or hear anything concerning. But Flash was the expert; he was a freaking Navy SEAL, after all. He was probably used to bad guys jumping out of the weeds and ambushing him.

But that wasn't going to happen here...right? They were perfectly safe. They were surrounded by tourists, and it wasn't as if the White River was some out-of-the-way place in Jamaica. It was one of the main attractions for people arriving via cruise ships and for people staying at private resorts, like them. Flash was just being paranoid...Kelli hoped.

They were getting a bit of a late start on the river because another tour group arrived just before them, and since the large bunch was from one of the huge cruise ships with a timetable to adhere to, those people were allowed to get their tubes and set out on the river before their smaller group of ten.

But finally, it was time to get in the water.

The Three A's and Charlotte had no problem whatsoever stripping off their already almost see-through cover-ups and displaying their model-thin bodies. Their bikinis were sexy as well as stylish, and Kelli could practically see every guy in the vicinity drooling.

"You guys go ahead. Kelli and I will bring up the rear," Flash told them, taking hold of Kelli's arm gently. "I forgot something at the tube shack. We'll be right back."

Kelli was confused as she watched the rest of their group screech as they stepped into the apparently chilly water and get themselves situated on their tubes to float down the river.

"What'd you forget?" she asked, as Flash led them back toward the shack.

"Nothing."

Kelli frowned. "Nothing?" she echoed. "Then what are we—"

"It looked like you were uncomfortable around them. So I'm giving them some time to get ahead of us a bit, so you don't have an audience while we're getting into our tubes."

Kelli stopped, giving Flash no choice but to stop as well.

He glanced at her. "I'm sorry, did I—"

She didn't give him time to finish his sentence before she practically threw herself at him. He went back on one foot but quickly regained his balance. His arms went around her, and Kelli closed her eyes tightly, trying not to burst into tears.

She couldn't help but remember the *last* time she'd been at a crowded beach and had taken off her cover-up. She could feel everyone staring at her, judging. She looked nothing like the Three A's or her cousin. And she'd always felt self-conscious around them. She was just...herself.

After a gentle squeeze, Flash put his hands on her shoulders and eased her back a little. Kelli forced herself to look up at him.

"For the record? There's nothing wrong with your body. I told you before, you're lush, and those idiots are probably jealous of your curves. So anything they might have said, or will say in the future, is bullshit. Okay?"

Kelli nodded, not really believing it. It was going to take more than one sexy man saying that he liked her shape to break down years of mental conditioning that said tall and slender was much sexier than short and chunky.

His gaze went back to the river. They could just see their group about to round a bend. "You ready?"

Kelli nodded.

Flash turned them back toward the water, where they'd left their tubes. The area that had been crawling with people ten minutes earlier was suddenly eerily quiet and empty, except for the employees of the tubing company.

Back at the riverbank, Kelli took a deep breath and peeled off her cover-up. She put it in a box that had been placed near the water by the tubing company, specifically for their group's belongings. Refusing to look at Flash, she quickly walked over and picked up her tube and stepped into the river.

Despite the sunny day, it was still early, not even eleven in the morning...and the water *was* cold. She inhaled sharply and heard Flash chuckle.

"I'm not sure what you were worried about, it's us guys who should be embarrassed. You do know about shrinkage, right?"

Kelli couldn't help but giggle. "You sound like that episode of *Seinfeld*."

"You like that show?" Flash asked, as he pushed his tube farther out into the current of the river.

"Love it," Kelli told him with a smile. "And that episode...it just makes me giggle... It shrinks? Like a frightened turtle!"

By the time she'd gotten control over her laughter, they were gently floating down the river. Peeking over at Flash, Kelli saw he was staring at her and smiling in a way that made her wonder exactly what he was thinking.

It was taking all her self-control not to stare back.

Flash was...he was beautiful. There was no other word for him. His biceps bulged with muscles, his abs were at least a six-pack, and his thighs were thick. The man was a mixture of muscular while still being long and lean. She could easily picture him in her mind wearing a skintight wetsuit while sneaking through the water doing Navy SEAL shit.

She had no idea what it was he did while on missions, but he obviously looked damn good while doing it.

Kelli felt frumpy and fat all over again. Looking at her toes sticking straight up as she tried to adjust herself in her tube, she could only imagine what he was seeing. Her black one-piece suit covered as much as possible. She'd refused to get one of those suits that had a skirt though; that just screamed fuddy-duddy, as far as she was concerned.

Her suit was actually cut high on her hips, which she thought helped disguise some of the weight she had in her thighs and stomach. It had a U-shaped back that dipped low, which she now regretted, as the rubber of the tube was already rubbing against her uncomfortably. Looking down, she could see her boobs threatening to pop out of the top of the suit, and her belly showed her love of cheese and those Little Debbie snack cakes —Christmas Tree Cakes were her downfall every holiday season.

"How the hell are the girls comfortable in those bikinis on these things?" Kelli blurted, as she shifted once more, trying to find a comfortable position on the tube.

"I'm thinking comfort isn't exactly their first thought at the moment," Flash said dryly.

"True."

"Relax, Kelli. This is supposed to be fun. And soothing."

"I have a confession," she said, looking over at Flash once more.

"Yeah?"

"I'm not the best swimmer."

He looked alarmed.

Kelli went on quickly. "I *can* swim. It's just, as much as I love the sun, spending time in the water at the pool or beach was never exactly my favorite thing to do."

"Well, you're in luck. Because I'm an excellent swimmer."

Kelli figured that was probably the understatement of the century. She rolled her eyes at him and was rewarded with the huge grin returning to Flash's face.

"I know you can't tell me anything specific, but can you tell me a little about what you do? Like, when you're on a mission?"

The next hour or so went by extremely pleasantly. She could hear the laughter and girly shrieks from the others ahead of them, and every now and then they caught up enough to see the group. Flash told her tales about his job, and she learned about the men he worked with. She chuckled at their nicknames—Kevlar, Safe, Blink, Preacher, MacGyver, and Smiley. Individually, they sounded like they were hilarious, and together? She had a feeling they were probably a handful.

But it was the way Flash talked about his friends' girlfriends that had her feeling a little jealous. The women sounded...nice. Which was a totally inadequate word, but it had been a long time since she'd felt as if she were part of a tight-knit group like Flash described when talking about his friends.

And she couldn't help but feel intimidated when he'd told her some of the things that had happened to the women, and how well they'd coped.

"Remi and Kevlar were actually left in the middle of the ocean to die?" she asked.

"Uh-huh. The worst part about that was, it was one of our own, one of our SEAL brothers who did it. Because the asshole was jealous. *Jealous*. It's ridiculous. If he wanted to be team leader, all he had to do was talk to the commander and he could've made it happen eventually. Instead, when stranding them in the ocean didn't work, he kidnapped Remi and tried to bury her alive, in some misguided belief that Kevlar would be so emotionally distraught he wouldn't be able to function, leaving this guy to take over the team."

The absolute fury behind what his teammate had done was easy to hear in Flash's tone.

"Thank God for Blink being in the right place at the right time," he finished.

"He's the one who was a POW in Iran, right?" Kelli asked. She was fascinated by the backgrounds of Flash's friends.

"Yup. He met Josie there. I wish all SEALs were like Blink and the rest of my friends. Unfortunately, they're not. Maggie's ex was also in the Navy, and that asshole had her locked in a box, then he actually arranged for our team to drop that box from a helicopter in Ukraine."

Kelli gaped at him. "That sounds horrible!"

"It was. But MacGyver met Artem, Borysko, and Yana as a result of that mission, and now they're thriving, living in the States with him and Addison."

Once again, Kelli was officially intimidated. The men and women in Flash's inner circle sounded like superheroes. They had their shit together, and when the worst happened, they were level-headed and brave. Afterward, they were somehow able to get past their traumas and have normal lives.

She screamed when she saw spiders in her apartment. She freaked out when she saw someone run a red light because of what *could* have happened if another car had gone through the intersection at the same time. And she couldn't muster up the courage to take off her freaking cover-up in front of the Three A's and the near-strangers they were shacking up with.

"What are you thinking?" Flash asked.

"I'm thinking I don't ever want to meet your friends."

Complete silence met her impulsive words, and when Kelli looked over at Flash, she saw his lips were pressed together and his brow was furrowed.

"I didn't mean that the way it sounded," she hurriedly said.

"How did you mean it then?" Flash asked, his green eyes seeming to bore into her.

"Just that...I'm twenty-eight years old, can't control my urge to eat the Christmas Tree Cakes I've got stashed in my freezer, I have no career, no idea of what I *might* want to do, and if I was left in the ocean, or thrown in a cell in a far-off country, or sold into sex slavery, I'd fall on the ground in a heap and not be able to get up again."

"Christmas Tree Cakes are the bomb, and who cares that you haven't found your passion yet? I have no doubt you will. And trust me, if you asked Wren, or Josie, or Remi how they were feeling when they were in the middle of the shit that happened to them, they'd tell you that they were completely freaked out."

Kelli doubted that. "Uh-huh." She stared at her feet, which she could barely feel; the blood flow had been cut off from her legs because of the way she was sitting with her ass deep in the hole of the tube.

"Look at me," Flash ordered.

Without hesitation, Kelli did as he asked.

"I have no doubt that if the shit hit the fan, you'd handle yourself with grace, bravery, and courage. You're resilient, just like them. We haven't known each other long, but I have a feeling your practicality would be your biggest asset in situations like they were in. You wouldn't panic. You'd stay calm and think through all your options."

It was sweet that he thought that, but Kelli wasn't so sure.

"Right. Tell me this—if your cousin was faced with a hundred-foot waterfall appearing in front of her tube right this second, what would she do?"

Kelli couldn't help but laugh. "Scream her head off."

"Right. And what would you do?"

"Bail out of this tube and swim like hell for the riverbank."

"Exactly."

Kelli blinked. He had a point. She *was* practical, levelheaded. At least compared to her cousin and the Three A's. She was patient and had a tendency to think through all her options before making a decision. It drove her mom crazy sometimes that she couldn't make decisions quickly at all.

"You might have a point," she conceded.

"Of course I do," Flash said with that sexy grin of his.

"Anyone tell you that you're a little bit cocky?" she teased.

"All the time," he agreed.

Kelli rolled her eyes at him, but she felt a little better. Besides, it wasn't as if she would ever actually meet his friends. They were like two ships passing in the night. They were having a good time together right now, simply because they were both so different from the people they were traveling with. When they went home tomorrow, that would be that. They'd go back to their lives and not have a reason to talk to each other again.

They heard some squeals from the girls ahead of them once more, and looking forward, Kelli saw the water they were about to enter was no longer flat and tranquil, but choppy.

"Looks like we're getting to the more exciting part of the trip the employees told us about," Flash commented.

Kelli nodded, but since her anxiety was suddenly spiking, and all she could think about was falling off this stupid tube and drowning, she couldn't speak.

One moment they were lazily floating down the river, and the next they were bouncing along in the whitecaps. It was no wonder the girls had been squealing. Kelli felt a girly squeal rising in her throat too.

"This is awesome!" Flash exclaimed.

He was slightly behind her now, but Kelli couldn't look at him. She was concentrating too hard on holding onto her tube and not dying.

She had no idea how long they were in the rapids, but when Flash suddenly swore in a tone she hadn't heard from him before, she whipped her head to the right, looking over her shoulder to see what was the matter.

She saw Flash's tube heading straight for a huge rock in the middle of the rapids and before she could blink, heard a huge popping noise.

Right in front of her face, Flash disappeared beneath the rolling waters of the river.

"Flash!" she cried.

But he was already underwater. And there was nothing she could do, not with how fast she was floating down the river.

Still, Kelli frantically searched the waters around her for Flash. She didn't see him anywhere. Panic threatened to overwhelm her, but she did her best to stay calm. Her first instinct was to bail out of her own tube, but that would be dumb. She hadn't lied, she could swim, but in water like this she'd be completely out of her element.

"Flash!" she yelled again, hoping against hope he'd somehow be able to answer.

Long minutes went by, minutes during which Kelli didn't know if Flash was dead or alive. He could be still under the waves, trapped against a rock by the current, with no way to break free from the water's grasp.

Just as the rapids began to peter out, she saw something ahead of her.

Squinting, Kelli strained her eyes, trying to spot whatever—

There! She saw it again.

Flash! He was now ahead of her.

The relief that whipped through her body made her weak. Without his tube, he'd obviously moved much faster through the water. She saw him moving toward the bank of the river, and Kelli frantically used her arms to try to steer herself closer to his location.

Her muscles were screaming within seconds, but she somehow managed to get her tube to the left side of the river. She thought she'd float right by Flash, until he saw her. He'd crawled out of the water and was coughing hard, but he immediately waded back in and grabbed her tube right before she would've gone sailing past.

With her frantic movements, Kelli felt like a fish flopping around on the ground, but she managed to get herself out of the tube as soon as the water was shallow enough for her to stand.

"Oh my God, Flash, are you all right? What happened?" she asked, holding onto his arm as he walked them, and her tube, back to shore. It hadn't escaped her notice that for a man who'd been hacking up a lung a minute earlier, and who'd had what would've been a life-or-death experience for her, he was walking just fine and no longer coughing. He was even smiling now.

"Damn tube popped," he said.

"I know *that*," she said a little impatiently. "But after? What happened?"

"The rapids turned me upside down for a bit, but I got my feet in front of me and rode the current downstream. And here I am."

Kelli's gaze moved up and down his body. He had some scrapes on his torso, a kind of nasty-looking gouge in his bicep, his hair was hanging in his eyes...but he was still smiling.

"Let me guess, you thought that was fun," Kelli said.

Flash shrugged. "Kinda."

"I thought you were stuck underwater," she admitted in a small, shaky voice.

"Aw, I'm okay," Flash said. Then he surprised the hell out of her by pulling her into his arms. Kelli gripped him hard, so relieved he was all right, she felt weak in the knees.

After several moments, she took a deep breath and pulled back, but she didn't drop her arms from around Flash's waist. For the first time in her life, she didn't feel self-conscious about being around someone in her bathing suit. Not only being around him, but being in his embrace. Flash felt far too comfortable.

"What now?" she asked with a small frown.

"What do you mean?"

"Well, we only have one tube. And we're who knows how far from the pick-up point."

Flash shrugged. "No biggie. I can swim."

"No, you can't!" Kelli exclaimed.

"Yeah, Kelli, I can. It's not a big deal."

"No," she repeated, shaking her head. "There are who knows what animals in that river. Snakes, crocodiles, leaches, piranha, parasites...yucky things!"

Flash chuckled. "I don't think there are any piranha in there."

"Whatever," Kelli said with a shake of her head. "You can't swim to the pick-up point!"

"We could share the tube," Flash suggested. "Those were the only rapids, at least according to the briefing we got before we put in. We should be fine to float the rest of the way."

"We aren't going to fit on that tube together," she told him with a frown.

"Why not?"

"Um, Flash...look at me," Kelli said, taking a step backward, out of his arms.

The way he licked his lips as his gaze ran up and down her body made Kelli shiver. In a good way. She didn't think she'd ever seen a man look at her the way Flash was in that moment. As if he were starving and she was a hamburger he couldn't wait to sink his teeth into.

"I'm looking at you," he said quietly.

"I just...Flash! Concentrate," Kelli said, a little breathlessly.

His gaze finally came back to her own. "I know you think you're too big or some such bullshit, but I'm telling you right now, Kelli Colbert, you are nothing of the kind. You're tiny."

She couldn't help it. She snorted.

"You are," Flash insisted. "And don't think I missed how uncomfortable you were, sitting in that tube. You're just too short to be able to fit in that huge thing correctly. And that's not a dig, just a fact. I can get in, and you can sit across my lap."

Kelli was shaking her head before he'd even finished speaking.

"Why not?"

"Flash...I...you..." Kelli stumbled over her words, not able to get the image of her sitting in Flash's lap out of her mind. Her butt would be right over his...

Involuntarily, her gaze went to his crotch. Even in the swim shorts, she could tell he was well endowed. Shrinkage didn't seem to be an issue for this man.

When Flash chuckled, her gaze whipped back up to his face. She knew she was blushing, could feel the heat in her cheeks.

"Our other choice is to walk, and I'm thinking since neither of us are wearing shoes, that's out. Or I could hold onto the tube behind you, and float with you that way."

But Kelli shook her head again. She couldn't stand the thought of him being immersed in the water. It was stupid. He was used to the water and was obviously a great swimmer. But she couldn't stop thinking about snakes or seeing the scrapes on his body from where he was already hurt by rocks under the water.

"Fine," she said, before she chickened out and changed her mind.

Flash stepped back into her personal space and wrapped one arm around her waist, putting his other hand under her chin, lifting it so she had no choice but to look at him.

"This is going to be fine. Stop thinking so much. If you think it's any kind of hardship for me to hold you in my lap as we float down the river, you're absolutely, one hundred percent wrong."

"I might squish you," she whispered.

Flash snorted. "As if. You don't weight any more than my pack does when I'm on a mission."

Kelli rolled her eyes. "I seriously doubt your pack weighs as much as I do."

"Come on, let's do this. We don't want to piss the others off by making them wait for us. We'll never hear the end of it if we do."

That was very true. Kelli could just imagine the haranguing she'd get from Charlotte if she and the Three A's had to stand around and wait for them.

Flash hadn't moved. He stayed right where he was, with his

arm around her and his hand under her chin, waiting for her to be ready.

Taking a deep breath, Kelli said, "Okay. Let's do this. I'm about done with this *fun* float down the river anyway."

"That'a girl," Flash said quietly. Then he shocked the shit out of Kelli by leaning forward and kissing her forehead, before letting go and turning to the tube he'd hauled out of the water.

As he leaned over, Kelli couldn't stop herself from staring at his ass. It was almost as nice as his abs. Almost.

Turning, Flash caught her looking at his butt, but he simply smiled and turned back to what he was doing.

Kelli thought she should be embarrassed, but she wasn't. Fuck it. This situation had gotten completely out of control. She had no doubt she'd look ridiculous sitting on top of Flash as they floated down the river. Charlotte would make fun of her when they were alone for sure.

But whatever. Being made fun of wasn't anything new for Kelli, and she'd much rather deal with Charlotte's snide comments for the rest of her life than allow Flash to get hurt or get some tropical disease from being in the water for too long. It didn't matter if the possibility of that actually happening was extremely low, she wasn't going to chance it. Especially since he now had open wounds.

Mentally shrugging, Kelli followed Flash into the water.

CHAPTER FIVE

Flash was in hell.
A hell of his own making, but hell all the same.
And the kicker was, he was enjoying every second of it.
It was a little difficult to get settled when he and Kelli first got into the tube, but now that they were floating down the river once more, and she'd relaxed against him, he'd never felt anything better than this woman in his arms.

She might think she was too heavy, but to Flash, she was absolutely perfect. The sight of her in that black one-piece would be forever etched on his brain. It was a hundred times sexier than the tiny bikinis the other women were wearing.

The high-cut sides empathized her soft thighs, making him think about what they'd feel like wrapped around his hips. The back was nearly nonexistent, and it was all he could do not to put his hand on the small of her back and slip it under the material, down to her ass.

And her tits. Lord. They were a man's wet dream...which was crude as hell, but Flash was almost beyond being a gentleman at this point. Her nipples were hard from the cold, and every time she moved, the globes shifted. He wanted to pull the material down and suck on her nipples until she writhed in his lap.

Forcing himself to think about something else, Flash looked around as they floated, but it was no use. The woman sitting across his lap held all his attention. Every molecule of his body was tuned in to her. Every flex of her muscles, every breath, every time she licked her lips. He noticed.

She was sitting on his lap sideways, so they made kind of a cross in the tube. His legs out in front, hers to the side. She had one arm wrapped around his shoulders, and her other hand sat on his leg just above his knee. He thought they fit perfectly in the tube this way and wished he could've had her this close for the entire trip.

That rock in the river had surprised him, and he hadn't been able to steer himself away from it. Before he'd known what was happening, it had pierced the tube and he'd gone under. He hadn't panicked, even when he'd hit a few rocks under the water pretty hard. He'd simply gotten himself turned around so his feet were facing forward and rode the current until he could get himself to the bank.

He hadn't meant to scare Kelli, nor had he meant to swallow so much river water. He'd almost missed grabbing her as she floated by. Thank goodness he hadn't.

The world was silent around them as they rode the now quiet current toward their pull-out point. He couldn't hear anyone from their group ahead of them and realized he and Kelli had probably been standing on the riverbank for longer than he'd thought.

"Are you sure I'm not squishing you?" Kelli asked nervously for what was probably the tenth time.

"I'm sure. Are you uncomfortable?"

"No. You're surprisingly comfy," she said with a shy smile.

Flash's dick twitched under her ass at her words. "Ignore that," he told her.

"Kind of hard to," she said.

"It's hard, all right," Flash murmured.

Kelli giggled, and he felt the movement throughout his body.

Yup. This was hell.

Staring at the woman he couldn't stop thinking about last night, having her laid out in front of him as if she were a buffet and he hadn't eaten in months...Utter torture. But he was obviously a glutton for punishment. Flash hadn't felt this alive in years.

He'd gotten into a rut and hadn't even realized it. He did his job, came home, then went into work the next day. Over and over. It was like the movie *Groundhog Day*. He hadn't wanted to come on this trip, but he was so damn grateful he did. If he hadn't, he wouldn't have met Kelli. Wouldn't be floating down the White River with a gorgeous woman on his lap. Wouldn't be feeling her fingers dig into his leg every time the tube bounced in the water.

Flash had been using both hands to steer the tube, but he couldn't *not* touch her right now if his life depended on it. He put one of his hands on her thigh, and she jerked at the feel of his fingers, cold from being emersed in the water.

"Sorry," he said. "I just wanted to reassure you. We're okay. We're going to get to the pick-up point without any issues."

"Do your cuts hurt?" she asked.

"No." The truth was, Flash had forgotten all about them.

"Good. Flash?"

"Yeah?"

"I'm glad we met. This trip would've sucked without you being here to keep me sane."

He wasn't too surprised they were thinking along the same lines. "Same," he agreed.

If he had his way, Flash would've floated down this river until it joined the ocean, but like all good things, this too had to end.

Ahead, he saw the spot where they would be getting out of the river.

But strangely, it was almost deserted. There was one man sitting on a bench and a minivan in the small covered parking area.

"Where is everyone?" Kelli asked, obviously having seen the deserted area herself.

"Guess they got tired of waiting for us," Flash said.

But inside, every nerve was on alert. Something felt off.

He tried to reason with himself that he and Kelli *had* been a ways behind the rest of their companions, and they were the last tour group to enter the river that morning.

Still...they couldn't have missed their one o'clock pick-up time by *that* much.

"I guess we should be glad someone actually waited for us. It would've sucked to have to hitchhike back to the resort."

Flash shivered at her words. That would've been the worst-case scenario for sure. There was no way he wanted to hitchhike in this country. He was sure most of the people who lived here were perfectly nice humans. But it was the small percentage of people who were desperate enough to do anything for a buck that worried him.

He steered them as close to the edge of the river as he could. "I'll help you out," he said.

After Kelli nodded, he easily lifted her off his lap and held onto her arm as she got her balance in the knee-deep water. Well, it was knee deep for him; on her, the water was lapping at her—

Nope. He wasn't looking there. Wasn't going to stare as the water gently caressed her pussy while she waited for him to get out of the tube.

Fuck. Now he was hard again.

"Go on, I'll bring the tube," Flash said in a raspy tone.

She smiled at him, then nodded before turning and wading out of the water.

For a second, Flash stared at her ass, imagining what it would look like as she knelt in front of him on her hands and knees, waiting for him to take her.

Moving quickly, Flash rolled out of the tube and into the chilly water. It had the effect he wanted, shrinking his cock.

Shrinkage. Thinking about George Costanza and the *Seinfeld* episode once more, he grinned. Standing, he whipped his head from side to side, flinging water in all directions, before running a hand through his hair to get as much moisture out of it as he could. Then he picked up the tube and followed Kelli onto dry land.

She was smirking as he came toward her.

"What?"

"You totally looked like a hair commercial when you did that."

"Did what?"

"Shook your head. Water sparkled in the sunlight, and after, when you ran your hand through your hair? If I had that on camera, I could sell it to some shampoo company and make a million bucks."

He snorted. "As if."

"You two ready?" the employee asked.

Flash turned. The man had an impatient look on his face.

"Your stuff is over there," he said, pointing at a plastic crate sitting off to the side.

Flash wanted to ask what the guy's hurry was but held his tongue. He quickly walked over to the crate and pulled out two towels. Kelli followed him and without a word, they dried themselves off as best they could, then got dressed.

Flash could admit he was sad to see Kelli's curves covered up once more. Out of habit, he double-checked his wallet to make sure everything was still inside. The last thing he wanted to deal with was his credit card being stolen.

He approved of Kelli doing the same thing with her purse, looking inside to make sure all her things were still there. "Ready?"

"Ready," she said with a firm nod. "I'm ready to hit the buffet. Even though I don't think we burned many calories today, I'm still starving."

"Me too," Flash agreed, then held out his hand.

Kelli glanced at it, then at him, and for a second Flash thought she'd blow him off. But to his relief, she wrapped her fingers around his.

They walked toward the minivan hand-in-hand...and any contentment Flash might've felt disappeared as they climbed into the vehicle. He had no idea what it was that had him on such high alert. But something just didn't feel right.

It wasn't until the driver pulled out of the dirt parking area that he realized this wasn't the same minibus they'd taken to the tubing place. It was more run-down. There was trash on the floor and the seats weren't nearly as clean as the ones in the other vehicle.

Flash sat next to Kelli in the seat behind the driver. He remained ramrod straight as he watched out the front of the minivan. Driving on the left side of the road always seemed a bit disconcerting. Seeing cars come at you from the "wrong" side of the road felt as if they were always two seconds away from a head-on collision.

They'd been driving for five minutes when Flash realized they were going in the wrong direction. They were headed away from the resort instead of toward it.

The bad feeling intensified.

"Hey, where are you going?" he asked the driver.

"To the resort," the man answered tersely.

"This isn't the right way."

"Of course it is. You aren't from here. I know a shortcut to get you back faster."

Kelli's grip tightened on his hand, but Flash didn't dare look away from the road in front of him. He did his best to see street signs, to find any landmark he could use later to find their way back. Because he knew without a doubt that they weren't taking a shortcut. His gut churned.

Things got worse when the driver slowed down, then stopped for a man standing on the side of the road. The guy climbed into the front seat of the minivan and as soon as the door shut behind him, they were moving again.

The newcomer turned around and met Flash's gaze. Then he looked at the driver, frowning. "What the fuck? Why're there only two?"

"Everyone else was whining about going back. I couldn't exactly tell them some had to stay behind."

"Damn it!"

"Stop the bus," Flash ordered. But the men ignored him.

"I knew you'd fuck it up."

"This isn't my fault!"

"The hell it's not!"

As the two men argued, Flash once again interrupted to bark, "I said, pull over. Right now!"

The man who'd been picked up turned around, and this time he had a pistol in his hand. He pointed it right at Flash's face and said, "We aren't stopping. Shut the fuck up, unless you want a bullet in your head."

Flash's first instinct was to reach out and grab the gun, but if something happened to him, Kelli would be left alone with these two assholes. The better plan was to sit tight. These guys would fuck up sooner or later. And he'd be ready when they did.

"Give me your wallets," the man ordered, waving the gun at them.

This was a robbery? Flash was confused, but he didn't hesitate to say, "I don't have any money on me."

"Don't care. Wallets. Now!" the man ordered again.

Moving slowly so as not to alarm the man, Flash reached for his back pocket. Kelli loosened her fingers around his right hand, but Flash refused to let go. He felt a crazy need to stay connected to her. Like if he let go of her, he'd lose her.

He felt more than saw her fumble one-handed with her bag as he handed his wallet to the asshole in the front seat. The man didn't even look inside it, just threw it to the floor at his feet. He did the same with Kelli's wallet.

His suspicions that this *wasn't* a robbery were confirmed, Flash tensed even more, if that was possible. He could feel Kelli shaking next to him, but he didn't take his eyes off the man with the gun.

And the passenger didn't take the gun off him for a second either. He was in his mid-forties, had dark skin and black hair, wore an old, tattered navy-blue T-shirt and shorts that went down to his knees...but it was the blank look in his eyes that worried Flash. He didn't seem to have a soul. He'd seen men like this before. Desperate men who would do whatever it took to accomplish their goal...whether that was killing civilians, setting off bombs, or protecting their leader.

It seemed like they drove for an eternity, and Flash's concern grew even greater when they left the city and the roads they took got rockier and more rustic. Soon they were driving through thick trees, the minivan bouncing up and down so hard, Flash hit his head on the roof a few times.

Though, he wasn't exactly disappointed with where they were. He had extensive training on jungle survival and evading tangos. If he and Kelli could get away from the men, he had no doubt he could get them back to the resort. They might miss their flights, and they'd have to deal with replacing their IDs and credit cards, but all that was better than being shot in the head and left for dead in the forest.

When the man behind the wheel finally stopped, silence filled the minivan for a moment.

"Out. And if you try anything, I'll shoot her," the second man said.

Fuck. That was the one thing that could get Flash to cooperate. He could deal with a bullet wound, but the thought of *Kelli* getting hurt because of something he did, or didn't do, made him physically sick.

Moving slowly, Flash scooted toward the door, which opened for him. The driver had gotten out and come around to open it. The man with the gun—clearly the leader of their little duo—now aimed the weapon at Kelli's head as they exited the minivan.

"That way," the gunman said, gesturing behind him with a nod.

Flash followed the driver, his hand clutching Kelli's as they walked into the jungle. He estimated they walked about half a mile before the driver stopped.

"Get in."

Flash frowned in confusion. Get in? Get in what? Where?

"I said, get in!" the leader yelled. Flash turned in time to see his hand swinging but before he could act, the gunman hit Kelli on the back of the head with the butt of the pistol.

She let out a surprised and pained yelp, and Flash immediately yanked her hand, pulling her toward him. Far too late to keep her from getting hurt. She whimpered as she put her free hand up to the back of her head.

Flash could smell the iron in her blood before he even saw her pick up her hand to look at it. Her fingers were covered in red.

Turning, Flash growled at the man who'd hit her.

He simply smiled. "I *said* get in. I meant it. Now...Get the fuck *in*, unless you want me to shoot her this time."

Flash looked where the man was pointing...and saw what seemed to be a manhole cover on the ground. He was even more confused. What the hell was a *manhole cover* doing in the middle of the jungle?

The driver crouched, grunting as he shifted the heavy cast-iron circle to the side, revealing a black hole underneath.

"What the fuck?" Flash muttered.

"It's your new home," the man with the gun said almost gleefully. "You and your friend are going to spend some quality time together down there. It won't be long...assuming we get what we want."

"And what's that?"

"Money," the man said without hesitation. "We're gonna contact your families and tell them if they ever want to see you again, they'll transfer money into an untraceable bank account."

Flash couldn't help it. He laughed.

Which pissed off their kidnapper.

"What's so funny?" he demanded.

"This. My mom is barely scraping by. And I have no siblings." He was lying, of course, but there was no way he was going to have Nova involved in this shit if he could help it.

"Neither do I," Kelli said in a soft voice from next to him. Flash was proud of her for hanging in there, especially with that head injury, but he couldn't risk looking away from the man with the gun. He needed an opening. Just one. And he could get him and Kelli out of this.

"Then I guess you'll die down there," the man said, not seeming concerned in the least. "There'll be *someone* willing to pay to get you back. There always is. The company you work for, friends...someone."

The man wasn't wrong. As a Navy SEAL, he actually made a pretty good kidnapping victim. It infuriated Flash that that's what he was. A victim. He wasn't ashamed, but more pissed off.

Without warning, the man aimed at the ground and squeezed

the trigger on the gun, shooting the ground near their feet, and Kelli's little scream of fright ate at Flash's soul.

"The next bullet goes into her leg. How long will it take for her to bleed out, I wonder? Get down that hole. Right fucking now."

Turning, Flash stared at the hole in the ground. Every muscle in his body was screaming at him to make a move. To fight the asshole holding the gun. As he prepared himself to do just that, movement in front of him made him look up.

The driver was now holding a gun on them too.

Fuck! He might be able to stop the first gunman from shooting Kelli, but the driver would easily be able to get a round off before he could take him out.

Feeling naked without his KA-BAR knife, or any other kind of weapon, Flash did the only thing he could think of to keep them both alive at that moment—he turned to Kelli and said, "Come on, I'll help you down first."

Her eyes were huge in her face, and he was afraid he'd see some sort of blame in their depths. But other than her obvious fear, she seemed calm. And the trust she showed him when she put her now bloody hand in his made Flash mentally promise to do whatever it took to live up to that trust. He'd figure a way out of this. Somehow.

He led Kelli to the hole, and she sat down with her feet dangling over the edge. Looking down, Flash couldn't tell how deep the hole was. Glancing at the gunman, he asked, "How far down is it?"

"Guess you'll find out. Hurry up, we don't have all day."

Turning back to Kelli, his gut clenching, Flash said, "Turn around and brace yourself at the edge. I'll take your hands and lower you down."

"Okay," she said, her voice only quivering a little.

They maneuvered, and Flash felt like throwing up. He had no idea how far Kelli would drop when he released her. The only thing that gave him the ability to let go of her hands when he'd lowered her as far as he could was the fact that there was no way these assholes could dig a hole in the jungle so deep, it would kill her when she fell.

He hoped.

"Ready?" he asked.

Kelli's head was tilted back to stare up at him. "Do it," she whispered.

It felt like a betrayal when he loosened his grip, and he heard her frightened inhalation as she fell.

"Kelli?" he called out, crouched on his hands and knees beside the hole, desperately looking down. He couldn't see a damn thing.

"I'm okay!" she said a moment later. "It's about ten feet or so from the top, I think."

Flash sighed in relief. "Stand back. I'm coming down." He sat on the edge and, before dropping into the hole, turned to the men still pointing their guns. "This isn't the end of this. When I get out of here, I'm going to hunt you down and make you regret fucking with me."

"Whatever, lover boy. If I was you, I'd enjoy the little time you have left with your girlfriend. Fuck her good and hard, because it could be the last time you get the chance if your people don't come through with the money."

"You have no idea who you're messing with."

"Fuck you!"

Flash moved a split second before another gunshot echoed in the woods around them. He hit the surface below hard, rolling as his knees buckled, taking the bulk of the landing off his joints.

As the kidnappers maneuvered the cast-iron cover, he took a quick look, trying to get the lay of the land. As soon as that manhole cover was in place, he knew it would be pitch black in there, and he needed to see what he was working with.

To Flash's shock, he and Kelli were inside what looked like an old bus with all the seats taken out and the windows removed and replaced with planks of wood. Someone had driven the thing out here, somehow placed it into what had to be a massive hole, then covered it with dirt. He had no idea how they'd managed it, but the how didn't matter at the moment.

There was a cardboard box in one corner of the otherwise empty space, and that was it. No seats, no blankets, nothing he could see to use as a weapon or a tool to dig themselves out.

Just before the light from above was cut off, the man they'd picked up from the side of the road looked down at them.

"The plan was to have more of you, so you better hope your people come through with our money and make this worth our while."

"And *you* better hope you've covered your tracks. Because we *will* be getting out of here. And you have no idea who my people are. They'll never give up. They'll find you. And when they do, you'll wish you'd never come up with this asinine plan."

"Fuck you," the man growled again.

Then the manhole cover slid across the hole, cutting off all light. It was so dark, Flash couldn't see his hand in front of his face.

This wasn't good. Not good at all.

CHAPTER SIX

Kelli inhaled sharply when the manhole cover above their heads shut out every scrap of light. She wasn't usually scared of the dark, but this was...all-encompassing. She couldn't see anything. She immediately began to shake. It started with her arms, then her legs, and before she knew it, her entire body was trembling.

She'd never been so scared in her entire life.

And now they were...what? Being held for ransom? It was ridiculous and unbelievable, and yet here they were.

Her head throbbed where the guy had hit her, and she could feel the blood still oozing from the back of her head, down her neck, soaking into the coverup she was wearing.

A small whimper left her mouth involuntarily.

"Kelli?"

She couldn't speak. Couldn't answer Flash. She felt paralyzed with fear and disbelief.

"Where are—ow, fuck! I'm coming, hang on, sweetheart."

The touch on her shoulder startled Kelli so bad, she literally gasped and wrenched away. Before her brain could process that it was Flash who'd touched her, and not the boogie man in the dark, she was in his arms.

Closing her eyes—not that it mattered, she couldn't see anything with them open—Kelli held onto Flash with both arms and squeezed him as hard as she could.

"It's okay. We're all right. We're going to get out of here. I give you my word."

That made her feel better, even if a part of her deep down knew he couldn't promise any such thing. They'd been buried alive, and it was terrifying.

"Come on, I want to look at your head."

She couldn't help it. She snorted. "Look at it?" she mumbled against his chest.

"Yeah, bad choice of words. But we need to stop the bleeding. Head wounds bleed like motherfuckers...Um, sorry. I tend to use more swear words when I'm stressed."

At that, Kelli's head came up. She couldn't let go of the man she was clinging to as if she were a spider monkey, but out of instinct, she tried to look at him. "You're stressed?" she asked.

It was his turn to snort. "Yeah. Stressed. Pissed off. Confused as fuck. Angry. Worried. Furious. All the adjectives you can think of. Come on, let's sit here."

Kelli wanted to ask where, but before she could, Flash was lowering her down onto something metal.

"It's one of the wheel humps," Flash told her, as if he could read the confusion in her body language. "I need you to let go of me for just a second. I'm not going anywhere, I'm right here. I'd never leave you alone. Understand? We're sticking together. Period."

Swallowing hard, Kelli forced herself to drop her arms from around Flash's body. One hand still gripped the edge of his T-shirt. Even though there was no place for him to go, she still needed to keep contact with him. She couldn't even imagine what she'd be thinking or doing if she'd been dumped in here alone.

"Does it hurt? Your head? Sorry, don't answer that—of course it does. Motherfucker clocked you good." She felt his fingers in her hair, gently probing. "Yeah, it's still bleeding. Damn, I wish I had my KA-BAR. I'm not sure I can rip my shirt without a knife or something."

Kelli felt Flash's large hand cup the back of her head. It hurt for a moment, but then she leaned into his touch. Intellectually, she knew he was putting pressure on the gash, but feeling him cradle her head so intimately was incredibly soothing. He pulled her forward until her forehead was resting against her chest, as he did his best to stop the bleeding of her wound.

Her arms went back around him, and she inhaled deeply. He smelled...sweaty. With a slight tang of river water. He definitely wasn't fresh and clean, but neither was she. And it wasn't as if they had any way of getting any cleaner. Their situation was beginning to sink in. They were in big trouble. Buried alive in a swath of jungle in the wilds of Jamaica. No one was going to notice a random manhole cover that was completely out of place in the middle of the woods.

She was going to die here, which sucked.

But all Kelli could think was that at least she wasn't alone.

"We aren't dying here," Flash said, startling Kelli.

"Stop reading my mind," she complained, mumbling against his chest.

"Not hard to know what you're thinking," he told her. "There's no chance in hell my friends won't come to Jamaica to look for me when they get that fucking ransom request. Our kidnappers will find out who I am soon enough, when they open my wallet and find my Navy ID card. They'll think they hit the jackpot, that they might be able to get the government to pay for my return, but that's not going to happen. Everyone knows the US doesn't negotiate with terrorists, and while Heckle and Jeckle might think they've covered their tracks and no one will find us—they're wrong."

He sounded so sure of himself. So positive that someone would find them. But Kelli wasn't nearly so confident.

"We might need to be here a few days, but trust me when I tell you that we'll be out of here as soon as my friends can arrange it."

Kelli nodded. Even if she didn't believe it, she wasn't going to disagree with him. "Heckle and Jeckle?" She asked the first thing that popped into her head.

Flash chuckled, and Kelli could feel the laugh rumble through his body.

"Yeah, they're cartoon magpies who cause problems for others and for themselves by their crazy actions. They're supposed to be funny, but I found the cartoon to be fairly violent. Then again, I guess that's kind of the nature of some of those older cartoons."

He kept talking about his favorite episodes of the cartoon, and to her amazement, Kelli found his chatter about something so inane helped her relax.

"I think the bleeding has slowed down. How do you feel? Are you dizzy? Nauseous? Have a headache?"

It took Kelli a moment to realize that Flash had stopped talking about Heckle and Jeckle and was asking her questions. "I'm okay," she told him. She wasn't, but what was she supposed to say? It wasn't as if he had some painkillers in his pocket or he could get her to a doctor.

"Right."

Then he shocked the hell out of her by putting both hands on either side of her head and tilting it back. She felt his lips against her forehead, then he simply held her for a moment. She imagined he was staring at her, and if they had light, he'd be searching her eyes and facial expression to try to ferret out her true thoughts.

"Thank you."

"For what?" Kelli asked, confused.

"For not making that fucked-up situation worse."

She couldn't help it. She laughed. "I don't think it could've gotten any worse."

"Of course it could've been worse," Flash said calmly. "You could've screamed, freaked out Heckle and Jeckle, and they might've shot one or both of us. They could've beaten the hell out of us, or killed one of us in the jungle, leaving the other in here alone. You did exactly what you should've done. Kept quiet and followed directions."

"I thought it was always better to fight," Kelli said softly. "I've watched a few of those crime shows that are super popular on TV these days, and they always say that if you let someone take you somewhere in a car, that's the worst thing you can do. That you should fight."

She felt Flash shrug. It was almost weird how, without sight, her other senses became so much sharper. "That's not always true. Every situation is different. Fighting an attacker or kidnapper could result in them killing you while trying to subdue you. Other times, fighting is your only chance of survival."

"How do you know which is more appropriate?" Kelli asked.

"Intuition."

"Is that why you didn't do anything to take that gun away from the guy? I have a feeling you could've done it without too much issue."

"Yeah, pretty much. The main thing was, while I could've taken that gun away from Jeckle, I didn't know what Heckle would do. I had no idea if he had a weapon as well, and concentrating on Jeckle would have left you vulnerable. And my fears were right. Heckle *did* have a gun. He could've shot us both while I was subduing his partner."

Kelli shivered.

"Besides, I have confidence in my team. They'll find us, Kelli. We just have to stay alive until they can get here."

She wanted to ask how long it would take for his friends to

find them, but it was a stupid question. Flash didn't know that. So she kept her mouth shut.

In the eerie silence of their tomb, her stomach suddenly growled loud enough to almost echo off the sides of the metal vehicle they were in. She could feel her cheeks getting hot and was briefly thankful that it was so dark.

"Sorry," she whispered.

"Don't be. I'm hungry too," Flash told her. "Maybe they left something for us to eat."

The possibility perked Kelli up, but she quickly sagged again. "I didn't exactly see crates of supplies before they shut us in."

"No, but there *is* a box in the corner. I saw it...before."

"A box?" Kelli didn't remember a box, but then again, she'd been freaking out and looking up at the hole, and then Flash as he'd dropped down next to her.

"Yeah. From what I can tell, we're in a stripped-down bus. At least that's what it looked like in the short glimpse I got before they turned out the lights. No seats, just the humps of the wheel wells. Even the steering wheel is gone. They took out the emergency exit in the roof and somehow replaced it with the manhole cover. I think we can probably reach it if I put you on my shoulders, but I want to make sure Heckle and Jeckle are far away from here before we try to mess with it. Just in case they're up there watching."

"This bus is much taller than usual, isn't it?" she asked. "I mean, I don't remember the bus from middle school being this tall."

"Yeah, I noticed that too. But if they retrofit the emergency exit with a circular manhole, I guess they could've somehow raised the roof too. Making it harder to reach the ceiling, and thus harder to escape."

His words made Kelli shiver. "Do you think we can just push the lid up? I mean, I know manhole covers are heavy, but it's not like, welded shut, is it?"

"We would've heard them doing that if it was, I think. I want to inspect that box before we do anything else though. Wait here."

Before she could protest, Flash was gone. Like before, when the cover was put in place and she'd had a small panic attack, the loss of his presence was disconcerting and terrifying.

"Flash?" she called out, unable to stop herself.

In a few seconds, she heard footsteps approach right before she felt Flash's hand on her knee. "I'm here. I'm not going anywhere. You're okay."

And just like that, Kelli felt stupid. Of *course* he wasn't going anywhere. Neither of them were. They were stuck down here. "Sorry," she murmured.

"Don't be. This isn't a situation you've ever been in before. For what it's worth, I think you're coping amazingly well. You're doing great."

"I'm not," she protested. Then asked, "Wait, have *you* been in a situation like this before? In the dark? Buried underground with no way out?"

"Not exactly. But there was this one time when I was diving. My job was to place an explosive against the hull of a ship that... well, that doesn't matter. But I was underwater and visibility was shit. Like, I couldn't see a damn thing, kind of like now. I was fumbling around, trying to feel my way to where I was supposed to attach the explosive. After a while, I decided that I needed to just do it and get the hell out of there. But after I set the timer, I got turned around. I didn't know which was up and which was down. I couldn't see the bubbles from my equipment to follow them to the surface. I panicked. It was as if I was in a coffin."

"What did you do?" Kelli asked with bated breath.

"I got lucky," Flash told her. "One of my teammates appeared as if out of thin air. He realized I was panicking and got me out of there. We didn't get the second set of explosives set, so technically the mission was a failure, but I'll never forget the feeling of being disoriented and not knowing which way was up or down."

Kelli couldn't imagine. "I'm glad your friend found you and got you out of there."

"Me too. And he'll find us again this time, and get us out of here too."

For the first time, Kelli understood Flash's confidence. The things he did, the places he went, he had no choice but to rely on his fellow SEALs to have his back. It was literally a matter of life or death. And if he said they'd be looking for him, and could find him, who was she to disagree or not believe?

"I'm okay now," she told him as firmly as she could.

"How about we both go and check out that box?" Flash asked.

Kelli liked that idea. A lot. "Yeah."

Flash took her hand in his and she could feel him stand in front of her. She got to her feet, swayed a little, then got her balance.

"The bus is empty, but stay behind me anyway," Flash told her. "Against the sides are where the wheel humps are, so if you're using the walls to guide you in the future, be aware of that."

Kelli nodded even though he couldn't see her. It was time to stop being a baby. Sitting around crying wasn't going to help their situation. Yeah, she was hungry, thirsty, and scared. But she was alive.

Flash was right. Heckle and Jeckle—she smiled at the nicknames he'd given their kidnappers—could've shot one or both of them. She was grateful they hadn't. And she had to trust that Flash's SEAL teammates would come for him.

* * *

Flash felt as if he was going to go out of his skin. He wasn't a fan of the dark, especially now. He could still feel Kelli's blood on his hand, and he didn't like that he couldn't see how bad that cut was. If she needed stitches.

A little light would also help figure out how to get the fuck out of this damn bus. How the hell had Heckle and Jeckle gotten equipment into the jungle to bury the stupid thing? It would've taken some backhoes and some serious digging to accomplish it. He wondered how long the bus had been here, how many other hapless tourists had been held captive.

His anger simmered just below the surface of his skin. He hadn't lied to Kelli earlier. He was scared and stressed. But he was more furious. He knew better than to go off the resort's property. And yet he'd let himself be talked into it. So stupid.

Actions had consequences, and here he was. Here he *and* Kelli were. That was probably the worst part of this. That she was terrified and hurt and there wasn't much he could do about it. If they'd been left in the jungle, he could find her something to eat, get her some water, and make a shelter. But here? Inside this fucking underground bus, he was helpless to do much of anything except reassure her that Kevlar and the rest of his team would be coming.

Pressing his lips together, he just prayed they'd be able to find him. He wasn't sure how they would. Unless they found the kidnappers, there wasn't a definitive way to determine where he and Kelli had gone after leaving the river tour. And of course, he wasn't wearing his tracker. Tex wouldn't be able to just pull it up on his computer and lead his team straight to him. He was on vacation. Why would he have brought his tracker?

One more thing he kicked himself for. Again, he should've known better. The travel advisory for Jamaica should've been enough to make him extra cautious.

Sighing, Flash held out his hand so he wouldn't bump into

the front of the bus as he walked. The last thing they needed was a second head injury.

It wasn't long before his hand made contact with the front of the vehicle. He considered seeing if he could break through the plywood that had replaced the windows, but decided that wouldn't help their situation. Would only make it worse if the dirt all around them filled the bus.

"I wish MacGyver was here," Flash muttered.

"The guy from that TV show?" Kelli asked.

He'd almost forgotten she was there.

No, that was a lie. He couldn't forget. Her grip on his hand was tight, almost desperate. But he'd been lost in his head for a minute, and Kelli was staying quiet, her steps equally silent. He hadn't lied when he'd said she was doing amazingly well for someone so outside her comfort zone. The last thing he needed was to deal with a hysterical companion, not that he'd blame her if she was. But other than a little trembling and the way she was reluctant to lose contact with him, so far, she was doing great.

"Yeah, but that's also one of my teammates."

"Oh, right. He's the one who's trying to adopt the three kids from Ukraine?"

"That's him. He got the name MacGyver because he's a magician when it comes to making something out of nothing. He's gotten us out of more jams because of his ability to make a fucking time machine out of a brick, some dirt, and a rubber band."

"If I could go back in time, I'd tell Charlotte that I didn't want to go tubing, and I'd stay on the beach sipping frozen drinks and reading a book."

"Same," Flash agreed. He felt around with his foot until he found what he was looking for. The box he'd seen before they'd been sealed inside this bus. "Did I tell you about Little Mac?"

"No, who's that?" Kelli asked.

"She's MacGyver's stepdaughter, Ellory. She's twelve going on about twenty-seven. She has Crohn's disease, do you know what that is?"

"I think so. Something to do with the intestines not working correctly."

"Pretty much. Anyway, she's struggled a lot. Bullies in school, delayed puberty because she simply doesn't want to eat because it hurts too much, things like that. When her mom married MacGyver, the two got close. My teammate and Ellory, that is. They tinkered in his garage all the time, and he showed her lots of tips and stuff. Then she and her little sister were kidnapped and put into a Conex container, and they escaped because Ellory used the tricks MacGyver taught her…so we started calling her Little Mac."

"Wow! Well, if a twelve-year-old can figure out how to save herself, maybe we can too," Kelli said.

Flash closed his eyes for a moment, more grateful than he could articulate that this woman was as strong as she was. She could be flipping out, probably *should* be. Could be complaining about how hungry she was—her belly was still growling; they were both doing their best to ignore it—and yet she was trying to stay positive.

She was exactly the kind of woman Flash had been looking for. The kind of woman he wanted to spend the rest of his life with. Someone who wouldn't dwell on the bad, but would find the good in every situation. Because Lord knew dating him would mean she'd find herself in plenty of situations where things weren't great. His long absences, the dangerous aspect of what he did. But there would hopefully be good things too. Lots of them. Family, friends, reunions.

"Did you find it? The box?" Kelli asked.

Her question snapped Flash out of the rabbit hole his mind had fallen into—again. "Sorry, yeah. Although now that I'm here, I'm thinking you should probably go to the other end of the bus. Just in case."

"In case of what?"

This was one time he kind of wished she was a little less naïve. "I don't know what's in here. And since I can't see, the only way I'll be able to figure that out is by picking things up and feeling them. If Heckle and Jeckle are sadistic enough, which I think they could be, they may have put something explosive in here."

At that, she didn't step away from him—her hand around his tightened. "If you're going to get blown up, so am I. I'd rather go that way than have to sit in here with your body parts strewn all over the place."

Flash couldn't hold back the bark of shocked laughter that left his lips.

"Sorry, was that too gross?" she asked. "It's true though. I'd rather die with you than have to be here by myself. So we'll investigate this box and whatever's in it together."

Flash couldn't stop himself. He turned and unerringly found her cheek with his free hand. "We aren't dying," he said, the thought completely unfathomable, now that he'd gotten to know Kelli a little better.

"Well, I hope not," she said with a shrug he felt.

"Right. Okay. Let's sit. Might as well be comfortable while we check it out, yeah?" he said, tugging on her hand, pulling her to the metal floor with him.

She situated herself right next to him, her thigh touching his. "For the record, even though I said I'd rather be blown up with you than sitting on the other side of this bus, that doesn't mean I'm brave enough to touch whatever's in that box. There could be mice or something. So I'll leave that up to you...if that's okay."

It was more than okay. Flash didn't mind that she was relying on him.

Moving slowly, he reached forward, finding the edge of the

box. From what he remembered, it was about the size of a medium shipping box. Maybe a foot square.

Taking a deep breath, he reached in.

The first thing he touched was small and soft. He turned it over in his hands, not sure what he was holding but guessing it was some sort of cloth. He brought it up to his nose and sniffed. A little musty, but no alarm bells went off in his head. This could be useful.

"Hold out your hand," he told Kelli.

"This isn't one of those times you put something gross or scary in my hand and laugh at my reaction, is it?" she asked.

Flash laughed. He couldn't believe he was finding anything funny about this situation, but he was. "No, promise. This feels like some sort of towel or cloth. I want you to hold it to your head."

"I think the bleeding has stopped."

"Even so. You can probably use it to clean your neck, if nothing else."

He felt her fingers brush against his as she took the cloth from him.

"It's tiny. Like, smaller than a washcloth. What *is* this, and why would it be in the box?"

"Not sure. But I think it's a torn piece of T-shirt. Probably their way to mess with us by not giving us an entire shirt. Hang on, let me see what else is in here," Flash said, as he reached back into the box. He picked up something that felt somewhat heavy. Running his hands over it, Flash's heart rate sped up. "Holy shit!"

"What? What is it?" Kelli asked, sounding a little alarmed.

"Sorry, nothing bad. I think it's a radio."

"A radio?"

"Yeah." Flash turned a knob but nothing happened. No static, nothing. "Damn. It doesn't work. But...hang on..." Turning it over, he found the compartment on the bottom that should've held the batteries. Opening it, he smiled. "It has batteries."

"But it doesn't work," Kelli said, sounding confused.

"Yeah, but depending on what else is in here, we might be able to get some juice out of them anyway. Maybe even make a light."

"A light?" The hope in Kelli's voice had Flash realizing he'd fucked up. He shouldn't have said anything until he was sure. But the thought of having some sort of light was too tantalizing to keep quiet about.

"Maybe. I'm no MacGyver, but I've seen him use wires with batteries enough that I think I can do it."

"I have no doubt. What else is in there?"

The more stuff he found, the more Flash was sure that Heckle and Jeckle were fucking with them. They'd put things into this box that they probably thought were completely useless. That would demoralize them more than help.

There was water, which he recognized by the shape of the bottle—and was relieved the safety seal was still intact—but only one. That sucked, but it would've sucked more if there'd been no water at all...or additional captives in this bus, as it sounded like they'd planned.

A ballpoint pen, what felt like a conch shell, a couple of coins, a thick candle—but no matches or lighter—two cans but no can opener, a key—which was especially ridiculous, considering they were underground and Flash was certain there was no engine in this piece-of-shit bus—a Band-Aid, a bullet, a condom, a handful of what felt like uncooked pasta noodles, and a spoon.

Again, their kidnappers probably thought giving them all this stuff was a joke...but it was a treasure trove to Flash.

"I was hoping there might be something we could use," Kelli said, sounding dejected.

Flash realized that while he'd kept up a running commentary

of what he'd discovered, he hadn't shared the usefulness of the items.

"We *can* use most of this."

"How?"

"Well, first things first, the cans. We have no idea what's in them, it could be dog food, which would suck, but hopefully it's human food of some sort."

"But we can't open them."

"Yes, we can. They gave us a spoon. Again, probably to torment us mentally, but in lieu of an opener, that's exactly the tool we need to get in. All I have to do is rub the edge of the spoon back and forth in the same spot on the top, and it'll break through."

"Really?"

"Yeah. The tops of cans aren't as thick as the sides. So we can definitely get into them, and again, hopefully it'll be something we can eat."

"What else?" Kelli asked, scooting closer to him and sounding much more interested now.

"The one bottle of water isn't super convenient, but listen..."

They were both silent for about a minute.

"I hear dripping," Kelli whispered.

"Right. We're in the jungle. It's wet. It's not surprising that this bus isn't waterproof. We can drink this water, then use the bottle to catch more from wherever it's dripping. It'll probably have dirt in it, but *any* water is better than none. And they gave us a freaking container. If they were trying to demoralize us, they definitely failed there."

"What about the shell? What can you do with that?"

"It could be another container, but I'm thinking if I break it, the edges will be sharp. It could be a useful weapon."

"Cool! And?"

"Well, not everything is useful, although I bet MacGyver could come up with a use for literally all this shit. I'm not sure about what we can do with the Band-Aid or the coins. And the bullet is pretty useless."

"Did they think we were going to have sex while we're in here? I mean, really? A condom?"

"Actually, that could be the most useful item of all," Flash told her, glad she couldn't see his grin. "A condom can hold water. We could use it as a kind of glove if we had to, or an improvised pressure bandage for wounds. It can be used to make a splint for a broken finger; it's rubber, so it could also be a rubber band, except we don't have anything to cut it up...but maybe the shell would work if it had to. It can be a slingshot, an emergency sealant, like on a pipe or something. And I've even seen MacGyver start a fire with one."

"Now I *know* you're lying."

"I'm not. I swear. He filled one with water and used it as a magnifying glass. It took a good bit of time, and there were a lot of bad words, but damned if he didn't get smoke, then flame. I was as surprised as you."

"Okay. So the condom can be used for more than...you know, the obvious."

"Yup. We can take the ink out of the pen and use the casing as a straw, and while the uncooked pasta will be hard on our teeth, it does have some caloric value. And lastly, the candle is pure gold. Assholes thought they were taunting us, but I think I can strip the insulation off some of the wires in the broken radio, hook them up to the battery, and maybe get a spark that will light the wick."

"Holy crap. That would be awesome!"

It would. If he could get it to work. Flash usually left this kind of thing to MacGyver, but it was his turn to step up. If he could give Kelli the comfort of some light, he would.

To his surprise, she chuckled.

"What's funny?"

"Just that Heckle and Jeckle thought they'd break us by

leaving a box of worthless crap. Except they didn't know they'd kidnapped a freaking Navy SEAL. Idiots."

Kelli had a lot of faith in him. Flash hoped it wasn't misplaced.

Determination swelled inside him. He'd do whatever he could to make this experience as painless as possible for the woman at his side. They'd be uncomfortable, and until they climbed out of this damn bus, he wouldn't let his guard down, but maybe, just maybe, they'd come out of this dented instead of broken. He hoped.

* * *

Brant Williams looked at the US Naval ID in his hand and smiled. His plan had been to contact the families of the American tourists they'd kidnapped and demand ransoms, but knowing he had a member of the military in his grasp was even better.

The Navy would want to rescue this guy. They'd definitely pay.

"I'm not sure the Navy is gonna pay a ransom," Errol said, the uncertainty clear in his voice.

"Of course they are," Brant retorted. "There's no way they'll ignore me. They'll have to pay, or I'll go to the media and tell them the US government is letting one of their own die."

"But the US doesn't negotiate with terrorists," Errol told him.

"We aren't terrorists," he argued.

When Errol continued to frown, Brant felt irritation rising. "You were the one who fucked things up. If you'd done what I told you, brought at least four or five people with you, we would've been able to get more money. But instead, you only brought two."

"I told you! I couldn't just *force* some of the others to wait while those two were still on the water."

"Why not?"

"Because! They were bitching about leaving and the other driver offered to cram them all into his bus!" Errol yelled. "You know what? Fuck this! I'm out."

"What? You aren't out!" Brant yelled back.

"I am. You aren't listening to me. You think I'm stupid. *I'm* the one who found where Wade Gordon is stationed in Riverton, California. *I'm* the one who found Kelli Colbert's Facebook and discovered she works for a tiny travel office. She doesn't make shit for salary. Without me, you wouldn't even know who to contact to ask for money in the first place. And you *still* aren't listening! The Navy isn't going to hand over fifty thousand dollars for this Wade guy. He's enlisted. Not an officer. That makes a huge difference."

"No, it doesn't!" Brant argued.

Errol rolled his eyes, which pissed Brant off all the more. "Whose idea was this? Mine! Who paid for that bus to be buried? Me! This whole plan wouldn't have happened without me. I invited *you* to join *me*, not the other way around. I'm in charge. And I'm telling you that this is going to work just fine. Now chill!"

"Nope. I'm done. Good luck. Don't contact me again. Ever," Errol told him.

"Fine. Good. All the more money for me."

"There won't be any money," Errol muttered, as he turned and left Brant's small rundown house.

Brant dismissed the asshole before he'd even slammed the door. He didn't need him. He already had everything he needed. He had the addresses of his captives, and Errol had given him the contact information for Wade Gordon's commander. He also had an untraceable cellphone that he'd use and get rid of right after the call was made.

Then he just had to sit back and wait for the money to be deposited into the account Errol had already set up.

The man was good with computers, and it was a shame to lose someone with that skill, but Brant would find another partner.

Starting with someone to remove the bodies from the bus after his captives died.

But he'd worry about that later. First things first, call this Navy commander and let him know Wade Gordon was in imminent danger—and the only way to save him was to send fifty thousand dollars.

Brant was done living in squalor. He wanted more. What he deserved, which wasn't to be living here. And this job would be the first of many. Once he had a million dollars, Brant would move to Los Angeles, buy a huge house, and live like the king he was meant to be.

And it all started with Wade Gordon.

Brant glanced at the drivers licenses on the table, then back to the Navy ID in his hand. The Navy would be desperate to have their soldier, sailor...*whatever* back. He was sure of it.

CHAPTER SEVEN

"What the fuck?" Kevlar bit out, after he and his team were abruptly pulled out of an important meeting about a possible upcoming mission...to talk to the commander about something entirely different.

They'd all thought they were summoned about an emergency mission. And they were—but nothing at all like what they'd expected.

"I told that asshole Jamaica was a bad idea," Kevlar bitched under his breath.

"Are the guys he went with okay?" Safe asked the commander.

"Yes. They don't even know he's missing yet. And apparently there's a woman missing too."

"This just keeps getting better and better," MacGyver said dryly.

"There was a group of women there on vacation, and they all went tubing together. Flash and a woman named Kelli Colbert didn't return. I've got a call into the hotel to talk to the men Flash was with now."

Kevlar's gaze went to the phone in the middle of the table.

He noticed the light flashing for the first time, indicating the connection was on hold. "That him?" he asked, nodding at the phone.

"Yes."

The team wasn't yet up to speed on what the hell was happening, but obviously it was imperative they talk to the people who were with Flash before he disappeared. He leaned forward and reached for the button that would reconnect the call, looking at the commander for permission.

The other man nodded.

As soon as Kevlar pressed the button, the commander said, "Hello?"

"Um...hello?" The man who responded sounded confused and worried. Probably wondering why he'd been summoned to whatever office he was currently sitting in by resort security.

"Is this Charles Hepworth?"

"Yes. Who is this?"

"This is Wade Gordon's naval commander back in the States. I need to know what the hell happened today."

Kevlar leaned forward, as if that could make the man on the other end of the phone give them the information they were after faster. He noticed his teammates all did the same thing.

"Um...I'm not sure what you mean?"

"When did you last see Mr. Gordon and Ms. Colbert?"

"Uh...when we were tubing. We got separated on the water, and we waited around for a while but they weren't appearing. Flash is a Navy SEAL, so I wasn't worried about him, but Kelli... she's not built for the water, if you know what I mean."

"No, I don't know what you mean," the commander said in a low tone. "Explain it to me."

"Just that she's not the best swimmer, apparently. Doesn't have the body for it. That's what her cousin says. I don't remember who suggested it, but we all piled into one of the two vans to go back to the resort, leaving the other one for Flash and

Kelli whenever they finally appeared. Wait—why are you asking about them? They're okay, right?"

Kevlar wanted to roll his eyes. This Charles person wasn't very quick on the uptake.

"No. They've been kidnapped."

To everyone's surprise, Charles laughed.

"That's funny?" the commander barked.

"This is a joke, right? Flash is pissed at me for hanging out with the girls last night, so he's getting back at me. He set up this elaborate prank and convinced Kelli to go along with it."

"This is not a joke," Kevlar said, not able to keep his mouth shut anymore. "My teammate is missing, along with Kelli Colbert, and you're fucking *laughing*."

There was silence on the other end of the line before Charles said a little uncertainly, "You're not kidding?"

"No, we aren't kidding. We need to know *everything* that was said when you and the rest of the group decided to leave the river to go back to the resort," the commander ordered.

"Holy shit. Okay, I'll tell you everything I can remember. Jesus...Nova's gonna be so upset about her brother."

As Kevlar and the rest of the team listened to Charles tell them how Flash and Kelli came to be left behind—because everyone was eager to get back to the resort to resume their drinking and flirting, apparently—it became clear that the entire group had been very lucky. It was quite possible *everyone* had been targeted...but because they were inconsiderate and horny, they'd actually lucked out. For some reason, their driver brought them back to the resort, instead of to wherever Kelli and Flash were being held.

It was also obvious Charles was now extremely upset about the fact his brother-in-law-to-be was missing. He wasn't faking his agitation over the situation and was now almost tripping over his words, eager to tell the commander and Flash's team anything and everything they wanted to know about the tubing trip. Including descriptions of the men who'd driven them there, and then the ones who'd been waiting to take them back to the resort.

"Are they going to be okay?" Charles asked.

"If we have anything to say about it, yes," the commander said.

"What do we do now?"

"You keep your asses at the resort. Do not leave the grounds again. The police are being called as we speak. Talk to them. Tell them everything you told me. Then get a flight back to the States as soon as the officers there say you're cleared to leave."

"Are we in danger too?" Charles asked, sounding as if he was in shock.

"We don't know. But it's better to get you back to the US as soon as possible."

"Yeah. I need to get to Nova," Charles said quietly, as if talking to himself.

The commander ended the call after briefly speaking with the security chief at the resort to make sure the police had been called, and that the groups Flash and Kelli had been with would be safe until they could get out of the country.

"I can't believe Flash got kidnapped," Smiley said, clearly pissed.

"Wait—if Hepworth didn't even know, how did you find out about Flash?" MacGyver asked the commander.

"Because the kidnapper called my office to demand a ransom."

Kevlar stared at his commander in disbelief. "He called *you*? How did he know who you were?"

"No clue. But if Flash had his Navy ID on him—which we all know he probably did, because he's a stickler for that kind of thing—it was probably taken. The kidnapper obviously has some knowhow with computers, because he knew Flash was stationed here, and he called my office line. Not the general base number."

"Has anyone called Tex? Can't he just track him and we can go and pick him up?" Safe asked.

"He doesn't have his tracker on him," the commander said grimly.

"Fuck!"

"Damn it!"

"Didn't he learn *anything* from the rest of us?"

Kevlar's mind was spinning. He itched to get on a plane to Jamaica. To find his friend. It was one thing to be sent on a rescue mission for a stranger, or several strangers, but this was one of their own. Their brother. "Is he alive?"

The question seemed to hang heavy in the air.

The commander pressed his lips together. "I don't know. I asked for proof of life, but the kidnapper said the only proof of life I'd get was when he got his money and Flash was released."

"How much did he ask for?" Blink asked.

"Fifty thousand."

Kevlar blinked in surprise. "That's it?"

"Yes. But as you know, many Jamaicans live in extreme poverty. Fifty thousand dollars is more money than a lot of them can imagine making in a lifetime," the commander said.

"And it's an amount he probably thought he could get," MacGyver added. "If he asked for ten million, he had to know he'd never get it."

"So? What now? Are we paying it? Are we going to Jamaica? What?" Kevlar asked impatiently.

"We're not paying it, but we're going to string this guy along. Give you six time to get to Jamaica. But if any of *you* get kidnapped, I'm going to be pissed," their commander said. "Their government has been made aware of the situation and we've all agreed to keep this hush-hush. The last thing they want is word getting out that tourists are still being kidnapped. The tourism industry has already taken a hit over there with the increase in violence."

"When do we leave?" Blink asked.

The commander looked at his watch. "Wheels up in three hours. Go home, kiss your women and kids, and meet back here at eighteen hundred."

"I'll stay here and call Tex," Smiley volunteered. "Since I'm the only single one. I'll also research the area where Flash disappeared. Get the lay of the land. He and this Kelli woman are being held *somewhere*, I'll see if I can come up with possibilities. And if they aren't alive..." His voice trailed off.

"He's alive," Kevlar said, his voice thick with emotion. "I don't know what happened, but if a woman was taken with him, my guess is that he would've done everything they asked of him, just to keep her safe. To bide his time. I'm guessing they've been stashed somewhere, and it'll be up to us to find them. No Tex. No trackers. Just some good old-fashioned detective work. Which is fine—we're more than hired muscle. We're smart. We can do this. We get our brother back."

"Hooyah!" all six of the other men yelled...their commander included.

* * *

"That's it. Right there, don't move," Flash told Kelli.

They were kneeling on the metal floor of the bus and he was attempting to light the candle. Kelli was still terrified, but now that they had some sort of goal, something to *do*, she felt a little better.

Flash had taken apart the nonfunctioning radio and, while she couldn't see him, she could hear him grunting, muttering under his breath, and swearing when something didn't go the way he'd hoped. He also gave her a running commentary of what he was doing while he was doing it, which she liked...since she couldn't see him.

Currently he had the wires of the radio exposed, the

batteries out, and was going to attempt to make some sparks that maybe, just maybe, they could use to light the candle. They were using the padding from the Band-Aid to hopefully catch the sparks, which would in turn light the padding on fire, and they could use that to then light the wick. It was her job to hold the Band-Aid close enough to the battery for the sparks to take hold, which was made more difficult by the complete darkness.

She could only hold the Band-Aid still where Flash directed and hope his plan for light worked.

Her hands shook, with both fear and nervousness, but she was very glad that Flash was letting her help. If he'd had her sit off to the side and do nothing, it would've hurt her feelings. Which was stupid, because she was definitely out of her element here and this was what Flash did for a living. Well, not really, but he had more experience at being held captive than she did.

The fact that he saw her as an asset and not a liability meant a lot. No, it meant *everything*. He didn't treat her as if she was stupid or "less than." They were a team. Partners. And that made her feel so much better about the situation.

"All right, here we go. Ready?"

"Ready," Kelli confirmed, trying to control the shaking of her hands.

The spark that was created when Flash touched the wire to the battery almost hurt her eyes. Going from pitch blackness to that quick flash of light was startling.

"Holy shit, it worked!" Flash said a moment later, giddiness in his tone. "Scoot closer, Kelli, hold that bandage as close as you can."

Doing as he asked, keeping her gaze where she thought she'd seen the spark, Kelli pressed her lips together in determination. This had to work. It *had* to.

"Here we go," he warned.

Kelli was a split-second too late trying to catch the spark on the tiny piece of gauze. They did it again and again, and Kelli missed the spark every time.

After what seemed like the hundredth time, she let out a defeated breath and sat back. "It's no use. I can't do it."

She wanted to cry. She'd been so hopeful that they'd be able to have some sort of light, but it was just too hard to try to catch that tiny spark, get it to land exactly where she needed it, on the miniscule piece of gauze from the Band-Aid.

Tears sprang to her eyes, but it didn't make her vision go watery because she couldn't see a damn thing.

"I can't do it," she repeated. "I'm sorry. How much air is down here, anyway?" she asked out of the blue. "We're going to die, aren't we?"

She heard Flash shuffle, and then his hands were on her. He'd been facing her moments ago, both of them huddled around the radio and the candle, but now he was sitting next to her. Before she knew what he was doing, he'd lifted her, and she was sitting on his lap.

In any other situation, she'd be pissed that a man touched her without her permission. That he'd touched her so intimately. But this was Flash. And this wasn't any kind of normal situation.

Without a second thought, Kelli turned into him. She was sitting sideways across his lap, much like she'd been while in that tube on the river, which seemed like such a long time ago now. She leaned into him, put her arms around his shoulders and buried her face against his neck.

"I'm sorry."

That had Kelli frowning. "For what?" she mumbled into his skin, grateful for his warmth. Surprisingly, even though they were in the rainforest and she'd been hot earlier, being buried in the ground, without the sun shining on them, had chilled her to her bones.

"For forgetting that you aren't used to this. That you aren't one of my teammates. That you have to be terrified. I think I forgot because you've been doing so well. You haven't lost your cool even once."

"Inside, I'm a mess," Kelli admitted.

"And that's why you impress me so much," Flash reassured her. He began rocking back and forth a little, and Kelli almost moaned with how good it felt to be held. The tears she'd desperately held back rolled down her face and dripped onto his shoulder.

"Let it out, Kelli. I've got you."

That was all it took for the dam to break.

Kelli cried because she was scared. Because she was sick of the dark. Because she was hungry. Because, despite Flash's reassurances, she had no idea how anyone would be able to find them. Their kidnappers had obviously planned this meticulously. They'd stripped a bus and buried it in the *jungle*, for goodness sake. Then to further torture them, they'd purposely left a box full of ridiculous crap. This sucked!

As she cried, Flash kept rocking. He stayed silent and let her express everything she was feeling through her tears.

When she was all cried out, her head hurt, and she felt dehydrated and kind of sick. Flash shifted under her. Thinking he was getting uncomfortable, Kelli sat up and prepared to get off his lap, until she felt something on her face.

Freezing, she realized Flash was using part of his shirt to dry her face.

"Blow," he ordered, putting the material over her nose.

In response, Kelli gently pushed his arm away from her. "I'm not blowing my nose into your shirt," she told him with as much force as she could muster.

He chuckled, and she could feel the rumble all along her body. "I'd give you the cloth we found earlier, but it's got blood on it now. I wish I had a real tissue for you."

"Yeah," Kelli responded, because she wished that too. If he did, they probably wouldn't be where they were right now.

Leaning away from him slightly, she brought the hem of her coverup to her face and blew her nose. In any other situation, she'd be disgusted. But she felt better afterward, and it wasn't as if she was as clean and fresh as a daisy anymore. What was a little snot to add to this already fucked-up situation?

"Better?" Flash asked as she leaned back against him.

"Not really," she said honestly.

"I know this situation seems hopeless, but it's not," he said.

Kelli rolled her eyes. "Uh-huh," she told him without much conviction.

"It's not. Let's go over the positives. I'll go first, then you. We have water."

Kelli wanted to counter that with a snarky comment about how, yay, having water would only prolong their deaths, but she took a deep breath and tried not to be a negative Nelly. "We aren't alone."

"Good one. This would really suck if you weren't here," Flash agreed.

"It's not as if I'm doing anything," she felt obligated to say.

"The hell you aren't. You being here is forcing me to keep my shit together. I probably would've gotten shot if you weren't. I would've attacked Jeckle and gotten shot by Heckle."

To her amazement, Kelli found herself giggling. "Heckle and Jeckle. Those names are so stupid, and they sound so funny coming from you."

"You got better names?"

"No." She sobered. "They were careful not to say their real names in front of us."

"I noticed that too. Doesn't matter. My team'll figure out who they are."

"How?"

"No clue. My forte is not computers and ferreting out information. I'm more of a muscle man. A man of action. Of getting physical shit done."

"I think I'd rather be in this bus right now with someone like you than a computer geek," Kelli said.

"You haven't met Tex. From what the ladies say, even with one leg and a couple decades on us, he's hot."

Kelli laughed again. Hearing Flash say another man was hot was funny. "One leg?" she asked, when she had herself under control.

"Yup. Okay, what else? Your head isn't bleeding anymore."

Oh, they were back to listing positive things about their situation. "Um...we have cans of food? Maybe?" She wasn't so sure that was a positive, because even though Flash said he could open the cans with the spoon their kidnappers had left, they had no idea what was inside.

"Yup. How about this, we have plenty of space to walk around. We aren't confined to a tiny room or space."

Kelli hadn't thought about that. "Have you ever been confined in a small space?" She felt him shudder under her, and she tightened her arms around him. "Sorry, forget I asked."

"No, it's okay. And yes. Trust me, this is much better."

Kelli didn't ask him for details. The last thing she wanted to do was bring up bad memories at a time like this. "Um...you can make a weapon out of that shell they left us?"

"I can," Flash agreed. "See? We have plenty of things to be positive about. After we get some rest, drink some water, and maybe see what's in those cans they left for us, we'll check out that manhole cover. See if we can open it."

Kelli wasn't sure how they were going to do that, but she nodded anyway.

"Think we can try again to light the candle? Do you still have the Band-Aid?"

To her amazement, Kelli realized she was still clutching the stupid bandage in her hand. "Yeah."

"Good. And I'm not just saying this to make you feel better —although I hope it *does* make you feel better. I once saw

MacGyver do exactly what we're trying to do, use a battery and wires to make sparks to light a fire, and it took him five hundred and twelve attempts making sparks to get a flame. And he was using a piece of his shirt that had been soaked in a flammable liquid...something he'd found in the room we were locked in. No clue what it was, I didn't ask. But my point is that it took *him* forever, and he's MacGyver. We can do this, Kelli. Besides, what else do we have to do right now?"

She wasn't so sure, but he had a good point. Although, she could probably sit on his lap all night and feel content. It wasn't a hardship to be surrounded by his heat and larger-than-life presence.

"Okay, let's do this."

"That'a girl."

Before she could scoot off his lap, Flash gently grasped her shoulders.

To Kelli's surprise, his lips brushed hers.

He froze under her, and his muscles tensed. "Fuck. Sorry. Didn't mean...I was...*shit*. Sorry."

"You're sorry for kissing me?" Kelli asked.

"No. But I was aiming for your forehead. Which is stupid, because I can't see a damn thing. I just didn't mean to overstep."

"Flash, I think we're past having to apologize for touching each other," Kelli told him. "Besides...it was nice."

"Nice." Humor was back in his tone. "I guess I need to do better next time. Can't have you thinking my kisses are *nice*."

Kelli chortled.

"Love your laugh. It's much better than your tears. Come on, let's get this damn candle lit so we can see what kind of food Heckle and Jeckle left, then explore this damn bus and see if we can find anything else to help us."

He sounded so positive. Truthfully, Kelli was glad for it. The last thing she'd want was to be stuck in this situation with someone who moaned and groaned and bitched nonstop.

They moved back into position, kneeling with their heads nearly touching. Kelli touched Flash's hands to figure out where exactly to hold the gauze to hopefully catch a spark.

"Here we go," Flash said.

Kelli had no idea how many times he'd touched the wires to the battery, how many times sparks flew from the current, but she was seeing spots and her arms shook with the effort it took to keep them still and try to catch the falling sparks. It might've taken his friend MacGyver five hundred and twelve times to make fire, but it felt as if they'd tried at least double that.

Just when Kelli was about to give up again, tell Flash that it was impossible...one of the sparks fell directly on the gauze.

Automatically, she leaned forward and blew very gently on the Band-Aid.

"That's it!" Flash crowed. "Move back a little, let me get the wick in there. Easy...one more little blow... We did it!"

The wick of the candle flared to life—and the sense of relief hit Kelli *hard*.

She sat back on her butt and stared at the little flame. The candle was fairly large, both thick and tall, and while she had no idea how long it would stay lit, having any light, even for a little while, felt like the most amazing accomplishment ever.

"We did it!" Flash said again, his features lit by the candle he was holding. He had a huge grin on his face, and Kelli couldn't help but smile back at him.

Then he leaned forward and kissed her again. Not on the forehead either. But purposely on the lips.

"We did it," he whispered a third time, against her lips.

Kelli wanted to throw her arms around him again. Wanted to feel him under her, around her. But he was already moving back, getting to his feet and looking around.

Moving more slowly, Kelli stood as well.

As naturally as if they'd done it a million times, Flash held his arm up and Kelli slid in next to him, wrapping an arm around his waist as his came down around her shoulders. They fit together perfectly.

"It's not exactly the Taj Mahal, but we can work with this," Flash said.

Kelli let out a snort of laughter. "Yeah, right."

Flash shrugged. "I just...now that we have light, everything seems brighter...literally and figuratively."

The crazy thing was, Kelli realized he was right. Being able to see had changed *her* entire perspective as well.

Now all they needed was for his friends to come and get them the hell out of there.

CHAPTER EIGHT

Impatiently, Kevlar looked at his watch. It was eight in the morning, and none of the team had gotten much sleep. They'd arrived in Jamaica just before three a.m.—roughly thirteen hours after Flash had gone missing—and they'd been going nonstop ever since.

Even though it was the middle of the night, they'd gone straight to the resort where Flash and both wedding parties had been staying and interviewed as many employees as they could. The resort had driven the two groups to the tubing place, but they hadn't been responsible for bringing them back to the hotel. That was the responsibility of the tubing company.

They were let into Flash's room, which hadn't given them any leads. While Blink and Safe packed up his belongings, Kevlar and Preacher went to the missing woman's room. MacGyver and Smiley had continued casing the resort, talking to anyone who was up and about for any information they could get.

Kelli Colbert's room, like Flash's, had been neat and tidy. There was a book on the nightstand, along with a half-empty water bottle...a set of clothes neatly placed in a drawer. She'd even folded her dirty clothes and placed them back in her suitcase. She was mostly packed, obviously ready to leave the day after the tubing trip. Kevlar had been relieved to find her passport tucked under the clothes in her suitcase.

They'd packed up her few belongings as well, and left her and Flash's bags in the security chief's office for the time being.

Now they had to wait for the tour company to open before they could talk to them, and none of the team was happy about the delay. Flash was out there, as was Kelli, and they wanted to find them as soon as possible. In the meantime, they contacted Tex, the former SEAL who'd dedicated his life to finding missing people…civilians, former military, other SEALs, Delta Force… anyone who went off the grid without a good reason. He supplied special forces teams with trackers that he could use to pinpoint the wearers' locations. But as they'd already discovered, Flash hadn't brought his tracker to Jamaica. So they were flying blind.

Tex was doing his best to use his computer skills to track Flash, but Jamaica wasn't like the US or a lot of other countries. There weren't surveillance cameras literally everywhere, and so far, there weren't any suspicious transactions on either Flash or Kelli's credit cards. It was as if the two had disappeared into thin air.

But Kevlar and the rest of the SEALs weren't going to lose hope. Flash was out there somewhere. They'd find him.

After getting all the information they could from the resort —which wasn't much—the team headed for the White River tubing company in time to be there when they opened. They were led into a back room in the small building, where they met with the manager of the operations, who was flustered when confronted with six intense, large, pissed-off men.

He told them what they already knew, that the party of ten had checked in the morning before, and they had to wait about twenty minutes to go into the river, until after a group from a cruise ship had gone first due to their rigid timetable. No, he didn't see them put in, as he was in his office doing paperwork, and he didn't see them leave because the river tour ended at a location downriver.

Yes, he'd find the employees who helped them enter the river.

Interviewing the men who'd helped the group choose tubes and get into the water didn't give Kevlar or the others any useful information. Just insistence that everyone looked happy. No one seemed concerned as they set off into the river's current.

"What about the men who picked them up to drive them back to the resort? Can we talk to them?" Flash asked the harried-looking manager.

So far, he'd answered all their questions without reservation. Hadn't seemed to be hiding any information, though he *was* getting a bit testy. But they had to keep pressing. They needed some sort of lead to know where to start looking. And at the moment, they had bupkis.

Impatiently, the team waited while the manager left to find the drivers who'd been scheduled to take the group back to the resort. After twenty minutes, he returned with a nervous-looking young man who couldn't have been much older than eighteen.

"This is Mark. He drove the first group," the manager said.

"Give us a minute," Smiley told the manager, standing by the door and gesturing to it with his head.

"Um...okay."

Mark's eyes widened as his manager left him with the group of six angry-looking Americans without a second glance.

Safe turned a chair around and motioned to it. "Sit," he told Mark.

Nervously, the young man did as ordered.

"Tell us everything about the group of men and women you drove back to their resort yesterday. Don't leave anything out," Kevlar said.

"Um, I was waiting for the group at the pick-up point. They were all laughing. Seemed to be in good moods."

"How many?" Safe asked.

"Eight."

"But you knew there were ten in the group, right?" Preacher asked.

They were all standing around Mark, intimidating the hell out of him, but Kevlar didn't care. Neither did the others. They were purposely attempting to put the teenager at a disadvantage.

"Of course. I asked one of the men where the other two were, and he didn't know."

"So you left?" Safe asked in disbelief.

"I suggested we wait, but no one wanted to. They were hungry and thirsty, and one of the women said they had some sort of going-away party that evening, and they wanted to get back to the resort so they could change and meet at the bar."

Kevlar was disgusted but not really surprised. From everything he'd heard about the men and the women, except for maybe the bride- and groom-to-be, they'd had only one thing on their minds...sex.

Okay, two things...sex and alcohol.

"It wasn't a huge deal! Errol was there, and he stayed to take the other two back to the resort when they got off the river," Mark said hurriedly, as if realizing the men around him were one second away from losing their shit.

"Errol?" Kevlar asked, standing up straighter. "Where is he?"

Mark shook his head quickly. "I don't know. He was supposed to work today but hasn't shown up yet."

"How long has he worked here?" Blink asked.

Mark looked terrified. "He's new. A few weeks maybe?"

"Do you know him?"

"How old is he?"

"What's his last name?"

The questions were coming fast and furious, and it was obvious that Mark was shutting down in fear.

Kevlar held up a hand, stopping his friends' questions.

"Thank you, Mark. You've been very helpful. My friends and I are going to get your information from your boss—you know... address, family, things like that—so if we have further questions we can find you. Is there anything else you want to tell us? Anything you haven't already said? Anything that will help us find our missing friend?"

"No," Mark said, shaking his head almost violently.

It was obvious he got the message Kevlar wasn't too subtle in sending. That they could find him at any time, and if he'd lied about anything, it wouldn't go well for him.

"You can go. But in the future, I'd advise you to make sure that all members of a tubing party are accounted for, and *never* leave anyone behind again."

"Yes, I will do that. Of course. Good idea. Thank you! Yes. All right." He was tripping over his words, trying to appease his interrogators.

"Leave," Smiley said, opening the door.

Mark was out of his seat and out the door before anyone could blink.

The manager was obviously waiting nearby, and Smiley gestured him into the office.

"Errol. Who is he? Where can we find him?" Kevlar asked, the second the man stepped back into the room.

"His last name is Brown. He was hired about a month ago, and he just got out of his probation period. I can give you his home address. He didn't show up for work today, which is why I didn't bring him in with Mark. I'll get you the info you want right away."

Kevlar watched as the manager shuffled through some papers in a filing cabinet against the wall. It struck him this was the reason Tex couldn't find much information on the employees of the company, because they still kept paper files.

But they were on the right track. He suddenly felt it in his gut. They just had to locate this Errol Brown and find out what happened after Mark had left for the resort with the others. They were getting answers, but every minute that went by was one more minute that his friend and teammate was in danger.

It was possible both Flash and Kelli were already dead...but Kevlar didn't think so. Whoever had called in that ransom request was a coward. He suspected they'd stashed them somewhere, hoping they'd just die. That they could get their money, then disappear.

His fists clenched as the manager gave Safe the information they needed on Errol Brown. They'd find Flash. The alternative was unacceptable.

* * *

Flash had meant to open one of the cans as soon as they'd gotten the candle lit, hopefully get some food into Kelli...but somehow they'd fallen asleep instead. He had no idea what time it was. The darkness skewed his sense of time and, of course, neither of them were wearing a watch. To his huge relief, the candle was still flickering when he woke up.

And he wasn't just relieved because they still had light; that flame still flickering also meant there was sufficient oxygen in the bus. He'd been a little worried about that when Kelli brought it up earlier but didn't want to admit it.

There was air getting in somehow, which was one more thing he could cross off his "oh shit we're screwed" list. He was trying to stay as positive as he could, for his sake and Kelli's, but it was difficult.

Looking down at the woman in his arms made Flash feel crazy protective. She'd done an amazing job of staying calm.

PROTECTING KELLI

Other than her one moment of weakness when she'd cried in his arms, she'd held up remarkably well.

He could still picture the way her face flushed when she admitted that she had to pee before they'd fallen asleep. They'd decided the opposite corner of the bus would be the best place to relieve themselves, because the whole thing was just slightly tilted down in that direction, and their waste wouldn't flow toward where they sat now. It wasn't ideal, but Flash hoped they'd be out of here before the smell became an issue.

They'd settled into the slight indentation where the bus driver's seat once sat. Flash was getting used to holding Kelli in his lap. She felt right there, fit against him as if she was made for him.

Once she let down her guard, she'd immediately fallen into a deep sleep. The metal of the bus wasn't comfortable in the least, but Flash wasn't about to move. He'd act as Kelli's pillow, because keeping her comfortable and upbeat was vitally important.

It struck him that this must be how his friends felt about their girlfriends and wives. He'd always been protective, but with this woman, those feelings were in overdrive.

Kelli shifted in his arms, and Flash waited for her eyes to open. Her hair was tangled and matted in the back where her head wound had bled. She had dark circles under her eyes, and her face was filthy from whatever crud was down here in this damn bus, but honestly, he'd never seen anything as beautiful as her big brown eyes when they opened and immediately locked onto him.

"I thought it was a dream. A bad one," she said softly.

"What? Waking up in my arms?" Flash quipped.

That earned him a smile. Each and every time he could get her to laugh or smile felt like a victory.

"No. That's the best thing about this. Being with you. The candle's still lit," she said, changing subjects abruptly.

"Yup. And one more thing to add to the positive pile. It's burning evenly and slowly. Heckle and Jeckle left us the perfect long-lasting candle. Idiots."

The giggle that left her lips made Flash mentally put another tick mark in the "I made her smile" list he was compiling.

"You need to use the facilities?"

She frowned and shook her head.

Flash didn't like that. Not peeing meant she was dehydrated.

"Right. I don't know about you, but my stomach is eating itself. How about we check out those cans?"

"With our luck it really *will* be dog food," Kelli murmured, but she shifted off his lap.

Flash held her hand until she had her balance, then they both walked the few steps to where they'd left the box. He reached for the bottle of water and handed it to her. "Small sips," he warned. They'd already cracked the seal the day before—at least, by now, he *assumed* it was the day before—and they'd each taken one large swallow. It wasn't enough, but even with water dripping into the bus, he didn't want to take the chance of them running out. Besides, at least he knew the water in the bottle was clean; the last thing he wanted was either of them getting diarrhea after drinking from an unknown water source.

He was also a little suspicious that there was water dripping inside the bus in the first place. Upon inspection, he guessed their kidnappers might have set it up somehow, to make sure they didn't die before they'd gotten their money. The water just looked too clean to be leakage of rain or some other naturally occurring source through the soil.

If they were in the bus long enough, they'd have to drink the dripping water...but he wanted to put it off for as long as possible.

The possibility that the water was tainted...some other way for their kidnappers to torture them...wasn't something he was going to bring up at the moment. He needed to be nothing but positive for Kelli. There was no use scaring her with scenarios that might not even happen.

She nodded and closed her eyes as she took a single swig of the water.

He accepted the bottle and took his own drink, before replacing the cap and putting the water aside. He urged Kelli to sit and made himself comfortable next to her. He said a little prayer that whatever was in the unknown cans was edible. He definitely hoped what they had wasn't dog food either, but he could eat it if it was. It would totally suck, but nutrients were nutrients.

Both cans in the box had their labels stripped off, and he balanced them in his hands, trying to decide which to open first.

"Eeny meeny miny moe?" Kelli asked with a smile.

"How about you just pick a hand?" Flash countered.

"Right."

He waited. When she didn't say anything, he asked, "Are you gonna pick?"

She chuckled—Flash ticked off another line on his mental chart—and said, "I just did."

"Oh! I thought you were agreeing with me," Flash said, returning her smile. "Right it is."

He put the cans down and reached for the spoon. "I think I told you yesterday that the lid's thinner than the actual can itself. So if you use the tip of the spoon to rub over and over in the same spot, making a groove, eventually you can break through the thinner tin." He demonstrated by gripping the spoon firmly, holding the can still, then carefully putting force on the spoon as he rubbed the tip over and over at the edge of the lid.

Before too long, the spoon punctured the surface.

"Voilà!" he exclaimed happily.

"It worked! You did that fast!" she said.

"I'll let you do the next one."

"Oh, that's okay."

"Nope, you need to learn how to do it too. Doesn't matter if you aren't as fast as I am. I've had more practice. Besides...what else do we have to do?"

"True," she said. "What is it? What do we have?"

"After you make the hole, use the spoon to cut all the way around the top. You can fold the top back when you get far enough around. But the lid is super sharp with the jagged edges, so you have to be careful not to touch it."

"Yeah, yeah, yeah...what's in it?" Kelli asked, leaning forward eagerly.

Flash carefully peeled the lid back, then picked up the candle and held it closer.

"Is that...spinach?" Kelli asked.

"If I had to guess, I'd say it's probably canned callaloo."

Kelli looked at him with both brows furrowed. "What's that?"

"A Jamaican vegetable that's rich in iron, calcium, and B2. It's in the spinach family."

"So...it's spinach," Kelli said, licking her lips. "Can we eat it raw?"

"Yes." Spinach wasn't Flash's favorite food, but right now, his mouth was watering and he couldn't think of anything more delicious than the leafy vegetable in the can.

He dipped the spoon in and held it up to Kelli.

Her gaze came up to his, then she leaned forward. Without taking her gaze away, she opened her mouth and let Flash feed her...then moaned as the vegetables hit her taste buds.

The sound went straight to Flash's cock.

He was embarrassed by his reaction. This was the absolute last time he should be thinking about anything other than survival. But this woman did something to him. Turned him inside out. In a good way.

"Go on," she urged. "Try it."

Flash did, and it was all he could do not to moan himself when he chewed.

"We need to make this last," Kelli said, her gaze fixed on the can now. It was obvious how hungry she was, how badly she wanted to shovel the food into her mouth. But she knew they needed to prolong their meal. "How about we tell each other something about ourselves between each bite. Wait? Are we eating it all right now? Or should we save it?"

Flash's first inclination was to hoard the food. He had no idea how long it would take Heckle and Jeckle to get a hold of someone back home with the ransom demand. And then how long it would take for whoever was contacted to believe the threat was real and not some joke. Then his team would have to be notified, probably Tex, and then they'd have to get approval to come to Jamaica—

He cut off his thoughts. They were most likely still days away from being rescued.

"I'm thinking we should finish this. The last thing we want is to let it go bad," he told her. "Besides, it would be stupid to be rescued with uneaten food. There's a show I found on TV called *Alone*. It's a reality show, but not like most. Men and women are dropped into remote locations, and they have to be the last one of the group to call it quits...or to be taken out of the game for medical reasons. They have no contact with anyone else and they have to film themselves, so there's no fake drama or alcohol used to make things more, quote, 'interesting.'" He held up his hand, making quotation marks as he said that last word.

"Anyway, this one guy, he caught a ton of fish. I think it was fish. Anyway, he had a ton of food that he smoked and was hoarding in his shelter. He lost a gazillion pounds but was more worried about having food for the future than eating it in the moment. He ended up being medically evacuated because he'd gotten too skinny. He had all that food, but still lost because he just didn't eat it."

Kelli nodded. "I'll have to look up the show when we get home."

"We'll watch it together," Flash said impulsively.

"I'd like that," she told him with a shy smile.

And just like that, Flash realized they'd decided to see each other again when they got back to California. He liked that too. A hell of a lot. "So...I think we should eat this entire can now."

"I'm not going to disagree with you," Kelli said. "But we should still make it last."

"Agreed. Okay...let's see...my favorite color is...black."

"Why am I not surprised?" Kelli said with a grin. "Mine is pink."

"Why am *I* not surprised?" Flash repeated.

"I've always wanted to play the piano. It seems like such an elegant instrument. But I learned in elementary school that the recorder is about the extent of my musical abilities," Kelli told him.

"I played the clarinet all throughout high school."

"You did?" Kelli asked, sounding shocked.

"Yup."

"You don't seem like the band type."

"Oh, I was a nerd through and through, and happy to be one. I was also in theater."

"Me too!" Kelli exclaimed happily.

They spoke about the plays they were in and some of the shows they wanted to see on Broadway.

"Time for another bite," Flash told her, scooping out another spoonful of callaloo.

"Seriously, this stuff is amazing," Kelli said, as Flash chewed his own bite. "I bet it's even better steamed, or cooked with some of the fish dishes the Jamaicans are known for."

"Didn't we have some of this on the buffet at the resort?" Flash asked.

At his question, Kelli's gaze dropped and her shoulders sagged.

Mentally kicking himself for ruining the good mood, Flash reached out and put his hand on Kelli's shoulder. He didn't say anything; what *could* he say? He knew she was thinking how, just yesterday—*was* it yesterday?—they'd been stuffing their faces at the resort with no cares in the world.

He felt her take a deep breath, then look back up at him. "Dogs or cats?"

"Both," he said without hesitation. "I like all animals. Never been able to have one with my work schedule, but if I could, I'd like to go to the shelter and ask for the oldest animal they have. One that has very little chance of being adopted. Then spoil him or her rotten until the end of their life."

"That's...that's awesome," Kelli said.

Flash shrugged. "Beach or mountains?"

"Beach. I think I know what you'd say to that question."

Flash grinned. "You know how I feel about the beach."

"Ebook or paperback?"

"Audio," Flash said.

They continued like that, asking questions back and forth, getting to know each other better as they took turns eating the callaloo. When there were no more leafy vegetables in the can, they slurped up the juices left over.

"It's crazy how full I feel," Kelli said when they'd finished every drop they could get.

Flash wanted to tell her it wouldn't last long. That when her body was finished sucking all the nutrients out of the food she'd just consumed, she'd likely feel even hungrier, even more desperate for more. But of course he didn't. He'd just distract her if and when that happened.

"Oh, you know what? We should've put the uncooked pasta in the juice of the spinach stuff. It might've softened it up."

She was right. They absolutely should've done that. "We'll do it with the next can." He just prayed whatever was in it would be edible and have some juice.

"I have a confession to make," Kelli said out of the blue.

"Yeah?"

"Uh-huh...something I should've told you earlier."

Flash frowned. He had no idea what deep dark secret she thought she should've shared...but suddenly she sounded almost nervous.

"I told you that I've had a lot of jobs, basically because of what my dad told me right before he died. Well, the reason I'm *able* to jump from job to job is because there was a large settlement from his death—and I got the bulk of it, since I was a minor.

"I've got money, Flash. Lots of it. I think that could've been why we were kidnapped. The men who took us must've somehow found out about it and decided to kidnap me. And you just got swept up in the whole thing. I'm so sorry."

Flash was shocked. Not about the money. Surprised she was rich, yes...but shocked because she thought their kidnapping was because of her. "I don't think that's why we were taken."

"You don't?"

"No."

It was Kelli's turn to frown. "Well, I mean...I guess it doesn't matter at this point. But I have no problem using my money to get us out of here. I'd pay anything if it meant saving us both. I'm not sure how that would work. Maybe if they come back to check on us, I can tell them that I'm rich and I'll pay the ransom?"

"No one's gonna have to pay anyone any money if my team has their way."

"I'm just saying—" she started.

"And I heard you. But you'll get to keep your money, so you can continue to search for a career that you love." He was glad she had money. That she could be independent. But she wouldn't be giving a damn dime to the kidnappers. Not if he could help it. "Now...you want to check out that manhole?"

Flash decided it would be a good idea to see if they could move it while they had some energy from the food. Later, they might be too weak.

"Sure. Although it's pretty high off the ground. Not sure how we'll reach it."

"You can stand on my shoulders," Flash told her.

"That's probably not the best idea," she said, biting her lip. "I'm not exactly light."

Flash gave her a look. "I thought we already talked about this. You're perfect, Kelli. I mean it."

"I know, but—"

"No buts."

"Okay, *however*, I don't think I'm strong enough to lift that manhole cover."

Flash grinned at how she'd avoided using the word but. "Don't underestimate yourself. Even if you can't, I'll be under you, all you have to do is put your hands on it and lock your elbows. I'll push upward, and hopefully that will be enough to move it. All I need is just enough of a lip to get my hands out, and I can get it moved."

"Then what?" Kelli asked. "We drove pretty far into the jungle. We have no idea where we are, or who are the good guys and who are the bad guys."

"I've had extensive jungle survival training," Flash reassured her. "I can find us food, water, make a shelter, we can hang out in the rainforest until my team finds us. Being out there in the jungle is way better than being in here."

"Yeah. You're right. Okay, let's do this," Kelli said, sounding more confident.

Flash couldn't keep himself away from her if his life depended on it. After they stood, he stepped into her personal space and pulled her against him. Her hands landed on his chest, and she blinked in surprise.

"Flash?"

"I'm going to kiss you," he warned. "More than a brushing of our lips. Is that okay?"

"Um...I'm not sure my breath is all that great," she admitted.

He grinned. "Mine isn't either. But since we both smell like callaloo, I think we're okay."

She stared up at him.

Flash licked his lips as he stared back. "If you don't want this, it's alright. I just—"

She didn't let him finish his sentence. One of her hands moved up to tangle in his hair, and she pulled him down at the same time she went up on her tiptoes.

Flash took over from there. As soon as he knew he had her consent, there was no way he could hold back.

His lips covered hers, and he groaned as her tongue immediately found his. She wasn't shy about taking what she wanted, and the feel of her against him was like...coming home.

Flash bent Kelli backward until he was holding her up as he devoured her. Their kiss went from a tentative exploration to a deep, carnal exchange of what was to come in the future.

He would have this woman. In all ways. Not just physically. He wanted to know everything about her. Her hopes, fears, dreams. He'd make those hopes and dreams come true and slay all her demons.

He lifted his head, but didn't bring her back up.

"Flash?" she whispered, licking her lips.

"When we get back to California, I want to see you again. I want to take you out. Bring you to my crappy apartment and make dinner for us both. We can watch all ten seasons of *Alone* and be all judgmental about the decisions they make. I want to be your boyfriend, Kelli. *Exclusive* boyfriend. I want to introduce you to my friends, pick you up from a girls' night out, help you find your dream career, and watch you shine from the inside out. Please say yes. Give me a chance. I swear I won't let you down."

Kelli put her hand on his cheek and said, "I know you won't."

Flash's arm was beginning to tire, so he stood them up straight, but he didn't let go of her. He realized how hard he was pushing. He'd come on *way* too strong.

He had a gut feeling that was going to be an ongoing problem when it came to this woman.

"And if we get out of here, yes, I'd like to see where things might go between us."

That wasn't the firmest yes, but Flash would take it.

"*When* we get out of here. It's a date then. Come on, let's check out that manhole cover."

He took her hand in his and walked over to where they'd been dumped inside this tomb of a bus. He jumped, and could just barely touch the ceiling.

Turning to Kelli, he said, "I think you'll be able to just sit on my shoulders." He squatted down and held out his hands.

She looked skeptical, but bravely went behind him and took hold of his hands. She awkwardly climbed onto his shoulders, and Flash held her thighs tightly as he stood.

Kelli was at the perfect height. She was practically nose to nose with the cover.

She did her best to push the lid, with no luck. Then Flash crouched, Kelli straightened her arms, locked her elbows, and he used his leg strength to try to push the cover up and off, but again, it didn't even budge.

Frustrated, he put Kelli back on her feet and began to pace. He'd been counting on being able to break out. But Heckle and Jeckle must have put something on top of the manhole cover to hold it down.

"We're never getting out of here, are we?" Kelli asked, sounding despondent.

That wouldn't do. Not at all.

"We are. Think about it, if those assholes parked a car or something on top of us, that's like a huge beacon for my team. I mean, a car in the middle of the jungle? That'll stand out like a sore thumb. And anything else they might've done to make the cover heavy enough not to be moved will also stand out. We might not be able to break out, but my team will break in. I give you my word."

Kelli took a deep breath, then nodded.

Flash was overwhelmed with his feelings for this woman. She had every right to be freaking out, and yet she was putting her trust in him. In his team. It was humbling.

"How about we check out that conch shell. See if we can break it? Make us some shanks in case Heckle and Jeckle come back." He needed to keep her busy.

"Okay."

"Great. Come on, let's have some more water before we start." It was Flash's responsibility to take care of her physical needs. He knew what could happen to the human body in survival situations. He'd make sure she conserved her strength and got what she needed to keep going.

It wouldn't be long before Kevlar or one of the others stuck their head down that hole and asked what the hell he was doing down there. He hoped.

CHAPTER NINE

The second the door opened, Smiley pushed his way inside and grabbed the man on the other side around the throat, pushing him backward into the hut.

"Easy, Smiley," Kevlar warned. He'd been concerned about his friend for a while now. The whole thing with the missing Bree Haynes, and Smiley not being able to find her, was pushing the man to the edge. It was frustrating for all of them, knowing the woman was close yet not being able to locate her. But Smiley was taking it personally.

They'd found Errol Brown, however. It wasn't hard. They simply went to the address the tubing company manager had provided and knocked on the door. The man lived in a very poor neighborhood. People were cooking over open fires outside their front doors. The neighbors had watched without much expression as the minivan the SEAL team was using pulled up. Kevlar couldn't decide if they were used to strangers approaching Errol's house, or if they just didn't care.

Kevlar shut the door behind them and watched as Smiley pushed the man into a chair.

"Errol Brown?" Kevlar asked.

"Yes? Who are you? What do you want?"

"We want our friend back," MacGyver said in a low, pissed-off voice.

At his words, Errol tensed. The man knew something. He was the key to finding Flash. Kevlar had no doubt.

He grabbed the only other chair in the room. It was made out of wood, and when he turned it around and plopped it down in front of Errol, Kevlar wondered if it would even hold his weight. Mentally holding his breath, he straddled it and crossed his arms on the back, staring at their "host."

Several tense moments went by, and Kevlar purposely didn't speak. He and his team had discussed strategy on the way here, and they'd all agreed to let Kevlar take the lead.

Safe, Blink, Preacher, MacGyver, and Smiley all stood around Kevlar with their arms crossed and scowls on their faces. They were an intimidating bunch, which was their intention.

"So...Errol. Here's the thing," Kevlar said. "There we were, minding our own business back home, when we find out someone had kidnapped our friend while he was on vacation here in Jamaica. They had the balls to call our commanding officer and demand fifty thousand bucks to get him back. That wasn't cool. Not at all. So you know what we did?"

Errol glanced away from Kevlar, up at the other men standing around him, and then the door, then he met Kevlar's gaze once more. He visibly swallowed and shook his head.

"We got on the first plane to the island and our investigation immediately led us here. To you. What do you think of that?"

"I don't know nothin'," Errol said.

"You see, I just don't think that's true. Your buddies at the place where you work—the same place where you didn't show up today—said you were the last person to see Flash and his friend. That you picked them up from the river and were supposed to take them back to their resort. But surprisingly, they never arrived. You want to explain that?"

Errol pressed his lips together.

Kevlar sighed. He was tired of this already. Didn't have the patience to drag this out. He needed answers, and he felt in his gut that this man had them.

He stood up suddenly and kicked the chair he'd been sitting in. It went flying sideways, breaking into several pieces from his vicious kick alone.

He stepped up to Errol and pulled out the KA-BAR knife that never left his side. Visions of Remi being tortured by his former teammate swam in his mind. Her scared eyes as she floated next to him in the ocean in Hawaii...

How Josie had looked when they'd broken her and Blink out of that Iranian prison cell...

Wren, Maggie, and even MacGyver's kids, Ellory and Yana...

He was sick and tired of men praying on women and children who they believed were somehow lesser than them. Of course, he had no way of knowing what Errol's motivation was for kidnapping this Kelli person along with Flash, but he was done.

D. O. N. E. *Done*.

The tip of his knife pressed against Errol's throat as the man wrenched his head backward, trying to get away from the deadly weapon.

Preacher and Blink had already stepped behind him, and they grabbed his arms, holding him still in the chair.

Kevlar was in complete control. He wasn't going to kill this asshole. He just wanted information. Now. And he'd do whatever was necessary in order to get it.

"Talk to me, Errol. It's obvious you aren't living the high life here. I don't see a woman around, no luxuries...few belongings at all. That tells me you're probably sick of scraping by every day. Is your belly growling with hunger? It sucks, I know. Maybe you were offered money you couldn't turn down. Is that it? Or maybe you're the one who came up with the plan to kidnap and ransom who you thought were a couple of rich Americans. At this point, I don't care *what* your role was. I just want to find my friend."

Every muscle in Errol's body was tense as he stared up at Kevlar. The urge to plunge the knife through his throat was strong. But Kevlar wasn't that kind of man. The kind who killed out of frustration.

"I don't think you understand," Blink murmured, leaning into Errol as he held him. He was almost whispering into his ear as if they were lovers. But his words were anything but loving.

"You have no idea who you kidnapped. If you did, you would've chosen one of the other pansies who were on the river that day. See...our friend, Flash? He's a Navy SEAL. Just like us. You kidnapped one of the most highly trained men the United States government has to offer—and you pissed off his teammates."

Blink's tone became almost conversational. "Do you know we've been taught ten ways to kill a man and make him bleed out in seconds? The jugular is such a cliché vein to sever. Too easy. Myself? I like the femoral artery."

The snick of his own KA-BAR knife being flicked open was loud in the suddenly quiet room. Blink held it against Errol's inner thigh.

"Personally, I like to distract my target by cutting off their dick, and while they're screaming and crying about that, they don't even notice the pain from me slicing their thigh open and severing their artery. It makes a bloody mess, but it's *very* effective."

"Please, man! Don't! I'll tell you what I know. We didn't know he was in the Navy! It wasn't until we took their wallets and found his military ID that Brant came up with the idea to find his commander and call him for the ransom."

Blink straightened, and the knife he'd been holding disappeared back into a pocket.

Kevlar smirked with satisfaction. They were finally getting what they came for. "Brant who?"

"Williams. He's the one who came up with the plan! Said we could get easy money from the tourists. I thought he meant *robbing* them. I didn't know nothin' about any kidnappings until the day before. I swear!"

"Where are they? Flash and the woman?" Safe asked.

Kevlar hadn't moved. He still had the tip of his knife against Errol's throat.

"He'll kill me, man!" Errol whined.

Kevlar didn't feel the least bit sorry for him. "You should be worried about *me* killing you," he bit out, pressing his knife a bit harder against the man's skin. A bead of blood welled up and dripped down his neck.

"Stop!" Errol cried.

Kevlar held onto his patience by a thread. Taking a deep breath, he straightened, taking his knife with him. He made a big show out of putting it back into the hidden sheath at his waist. Then he leaned over, getting right in Errol's face. It was difficult, as the man smelled horrible. Body odor like onions, and his breath could kill. But he didn't let his disgust show.

"Here's what's going to happen. You're going to tell us everything about the plan. About Brant Williams. His family, where he lives, about this bank account he told our commander to deposit the money into…and we'll *think* about letting you live."

Errol swallowed hard and nodded.

"If you lie to us…I'll let Blink have his fun with you."

Errol's gaze whipped up to his teammate, still holding one of his arms, then back to Kevlar's. He nodded again.

"Good. We're on the same page. Let him go," Kevlar said, nodding at Blink and Preacher.

They did, stepping back but staying close to Errol. The terrified man rubbed his upper arms where he'd been held down, then brought a hand up to his neck. He wiped away the blood, stared at his hand for a moment, released a shuddering sigh... then began to talk.

Twenty minutes later, Kevlar and the rest of the team knew everything about the plan to kidnap clueless Americans through the tubing company. Flash and Kelli had been their first attempt, and even though Errol was an asshole, he wasn't dumb. When his accomplice began talking about getting the Navy to pay the ransom, Errol had allegedly tried to convince him the plan wouldn't work.

Errol admitted that he'd been the one to figure out where Flash was stationed, and he'd found Kelli Colbert's Facebook account and deduced that she wouldn't make a good target. With her job at a small travel agency—and a somewhat recent hire, at that—he figured Flash was the one who made more money, the one they should concentrate on.

He also swore that he'd walked away from the entire fucked-up plan. That he'd left Brant on his own.

When he'd reluctantly admitted that this Brant character had buried a stripped-out bus in the middle of the jungle, one that he'd had altered by fitting a cast-iron manhole cover into the roof—and that they'd left Kelli and Flash inside—Kevlar saw red.

His Remi had been buried alive, and she still sometimes had nightmares about it. And she'd only been in that box for minutes. Flash and Kelli had been there for nearly a full day now. Yes, a bus was way more roomy than the box Remi had been forced into, but still...buried was buried.

He took a step toward Errol, and surprisingly, it was Smiley who took hold of his arm and held him back. Safe stepped in front of his team leader and took over the interrogation as smoothly as if they'd done it many times in the past.

It took Kevlar several moments to regain control. He heard

Errol trying to give the others directions as to where he and Brant had buried the bus. All he could think of was getting there as soon as possible. There was a possibility that Flash had found a way out of that bus, but given how Errol was describing the area, and what they'd done to try to make sure no one could escape from the buried vehicle, Kevlar wasn't so sure.

When Errol was done talking, he asked, "What now? What are you going to do with me?"

"You're coming with us. You're going to tell the police everything you just told us. Without leaving anything out," Safe said.

Errol winced.

It was a crapshoot if the local authorities would do anything to the man. Unlikely that he'd be prosecuted. But since the team's goal in coming to Jamaica was to find Flash, Errol's future wasn't their concern.

Now, Brant? *That* man had to be found and needed to pay for what he'd done. What he'd planned on doing to as many tourists as he could. According to Errol, he had plans to use the buried bus many times over. Apparently, once he'd received money from a family, or a group of families, his plan was to wait until his captives had passed away, remove their bodies, then play his sick game all over again.

Errol Brown was a patsy. A small-time punk who'd gotten mixed up with the wrong person.

Kevlar was itching to head to the jungle. It was obvious they'd put the bus in a place known to locals but difficult to access. The easiest option would be to take Errol with them, make him show them exactly where they'd stashed Flash and Kelli. But they had enough info to find the bus without him, of that Kevlar was certain.

No. He'd prefer Errol be taken into custody right away by the Jamaican authorities, and he didn't want to have to worry about the man trying to get away when they *did* find this damn buried bus, and their attention was focused on their missing teammate.

Everyone would give Flash a ton of shit for getting kidnapped. Personally, Kevlar couldn't wait to tell him "I told you so." He was the one who'd warned against coming to Jamaica in the first place.

Once they made sure Flash was all right, of course. Wasn't hurt, or was getting any medical attention he needed.

Then they'd make fun of him for getting hurt in the first place. It was just how the team was. It was a coping mechanism. A way to release tension.

Suddenly needing some air, Kevlar turned and headed for the door. The second he stepped outside, all conversation from the neighbors stopped. Their visit was obviously being gossiped about. Kevlar had a feeling everyone on the island would know about it in the next day or so. Which meant they needed to move fast.

If Brant Williams got word that they'd been here, and Errol had been taken away, he'd get spooked. But Kevlar wasn't willing to split up his team. Flash was the most important thing right now. If Brant disappeared, they'd find him. Eventually. There was nowhere the man could hide.

* * *

It took longer than Kevlar wanted to bring Errol to the police station and force him to give a full confession to the authorities. He wasn't feeling confident that the police would do much to him, other than make him pay a fine and send him on his way with a slap on the wrist.

Eventually, they had no choice but to leave Errol in the custody of the local authorities. They'd done all they could to see that he was punished for the kidnapping. One of the officers had demanded to come with them when they went into the jungle to try to find Flash and the woman who'd been kidnapped.

It made sense; Errol couldn't be charged without proof. But Kevlar was still annoyed. He didn't want anyone tagging along. He simply wanted to find his friend without having to worry about being politically correct. He could almost hear his commander in his head, telling him to do things by the book, to not ruffle any feathers, to not turn this into an international incident.

But to Kevlar's way of thinking, it *was* an international incident. Keeping a Navy SEAL's kidnapping a secret wasn't a smart plan. It wouldn't be good for Jamaica, since they relied on tourist dollars. He couldn't stop thinking about Remi, and how she'd been kidnapped and buried alive. There were too many similarities to what happened to her and what was going on with Flash for him to remain rational.

The trip to the jungle was long...and more difficult than Kevlar anticipated. They got lost once or twice as they tried to follow Errol's verbal directions to where the bus had been buried. Many of the dirt roads looked the same and, of course, the terrain didn't help. The minivan they'd rented was taking a beating, but Kevlar didn't care.

The officer following them looked bored. Every time Kevlar looked behind them to see if he was still there, the man was on his cellphone. Amazingly, one time, it looked like he was smoking what Kevlar thought was a joint, but he couldn't be sure.

Before long, he was kicking himself for leaving Errol behind. Even though bringing him would've added more stress to the situation, he could've led them straight to the damn bus. They should've waited to turn him in after Flash and Kelli were found...but it was too late to change that now.

His stress levels were sky high, especially since it was creeping toward evening. They'd lose the sunlight soon, and if that happened, if they hadn't found the damn bus, they'd have to wait until morning to start the search again. The thought of his friend having to spend another night underground was unacceptable.

Finally, they got to a point where the road abruptly ended, just as Errol said it would.

Anticipation rose within Kevlar. They'd done it! Found the place Errol had described, where they'd made Flash and Kelli get out and walk into the jungle.

All four doors opened at the same time, and the six SEALs climbed out, eager to find their teammate. The officer got out of his car and leaned against the door.

"I'll wait here," he said.

Disgusted, but not caring anymore *what* the man did, Kevlar followed the tracks on the forest floor that had probably been made by whatever large piece of equipment Brant had used to bury the bus.

Kevlar had no idea how the man had done it. Or when. Yes, they'd obviously used heavy machinery, but the logistics of the entire operation were mind-blowing. Ultimately, though, the how didn't matter right now, only the where.

They walked for around half a mile, and looking around, all Kevlar saw was trees and vines. The forest floor was covered in vegetation. A tropical rainforest. How the hell they were going to find anything buried out here was a real concern.

Until he saw it.

Exactly as Errol had described.

Three large tires stacked on top of each other. Two had the rims still attached, which would make them extremely heavy. Kevlar knew that from experience. He'd had to change a tire on large trucks a time or two. Three of them on top of that cover would prevent anyone under it from being able to escape.

Running toward the tires, he said in a voice much calmer than he felt, "Preacher, grab the other side. Safe and MacGyver, get the second one. Smiley, I'll help you with the last."

No one argued. They got to work doing what needed to be

done. No one spoke out loud about what they might find when they opened that manhole cover. True, it hadn't been all that long since Flash and Kelli had been kidnapped and buried alive, but depending on what condition they were in when they were left, and what supplies, if any, were inside with them, they could be facing the worst-case scenario.

Taking a deep breath, Kevlar reached for the first tire.

CHAPTER TEN

Kelli felt like crap. She was exhausted but couldn't sleep. She was terrified that she'd fall asleep and wake up to pitch darkness again. The candle had been a godsend, but it had finally burned down to almost nothing.

Flash had been the most amazing partner in this...what was this? Adventure? No, that wasn't the right word. Nightmare? Yeah, that was closer. Having Flash with her made everything that had happened not quite as scary. If she'd been by herself, she would've been a basket case. And she couldn't even imagine being stuck in this hellhole with her cousin and the Three A's. They would've been unbearable.

Amazingly, she'd learned stuff from Flash. He'd let her...no, *made her* open the second can of food. She'd wanted to save it, because in the back of her mind she still wasn't so sure that Flash's friends would find them. But she let him talk her into seeing what was inside the can.

He'd made opening the first can seem so easy. She sawed back and forth with the tip of that spoon for what seemed like an hour before she'd finally been able to weaken the tin enough to break it. Inside had been what looked like peas, but they were a speckled brown. Flash thought they were probably gungo peas. Another common Jamaican staple. The liquid they were in smelled really good, but that was probably because she was so hungry.

This time, they'd remembered to put some of the uncooked pasta into the can. Her mouth watered as they waited for the pasta to soften. When they couldn't stand waiting any longer, they both popped a few pieces into their mouths.

Never in her life would Kelli have thought just soaking pasta in liquid, without any kind of heat source, would result in anything edible. But the tiny morsels were a feast. She imagined she could feel her body soaking up the carbs and other nutrients from the pasta as it settled in her belly.

The peas weren't great, but again, since she was so hungry, Kelli didn't think twice about eating them. When the can was empty of peas, and after they'd drunk every drop of the coconut milk the vegetables had been packaged in—the little that wasn't soaked up by the pasta—it was all Kelli could do not to break down in hysterics.

That was it. The end of their food. They'd also finished the water. They'd found the source of the dripping, and had begun collecting water in the empty bottle, but starving to death wasn't her idea of a good way to go.

"Come here," Flash said, from where he was leaning against the side of the bus. He held his arm out to his side. Without hesitation, Kelli crawled over and leaned into him. His arm around her felt like coming home. He was her safety net. Being close to him helped her believe that someone *would* be coming for them. That they'd be found.

"Once upon a time, there was a girl. She had an evil mother and stepfather. They made the poor girl work from the time the sun came up to when it went down. But the girl didn't mind. Staying busy kept her mind off other things. Like her empty belly and the taunting of the other little girls in her village. None of them had to work like she did. They all got to wear pretty dresses and sit outside in the sun and have tea parties."

Kelli smiled as she snuggled into Flash's side. She'd told him hours ago about her love of fairy tales. How the happy endings soothed her soul. They'd taken turns telling little made-up stories. It was his turn, and she was content to listen to him talk as she watched the last of the light from the flickering candle.

"One day, a possum waddled into her yard. Her stepfather wanted to kill it. Said it was vermin and would dig holes and destroy their crops. But of course, he wouldn't do the deed himself, he ordered the girl to do it. So she dutifully set a trap, putting some of her own dinner inside. Before long, the possum took the bait and was inside the trap.

"But the girl couldn't kill the beast. It was ugly and scarred, and it hissed at her, but she didn't care. It was just scared. Trapped. Like her. All it wanted was to live its life. So in the middle of the night, when everyone was asleep, she went out to the trap and set the possum free, warning it not to come around in the daylight when her stepfather could see it. She also promised to leave food out, if he came back.

"For the next year, that's what she did. Even though she was always hungry, she saved some of her dinner every night to bring outside for her possum friend. Then one night, her stepfather got angry with her and began to beat her. The girl was crouched down, trying to cover her head, enduring the pain from the much larger man's fists, when she heard a noise outside. Scratching at the door.

"It got louder and louder, until finally her stepfather couldn't ignore it any longer. Angrily, he stalked to the door and wrenched it open. Looking down, he saw a possum.

"As he stared at it, the animal began to grow. It grew and grew—until standing at the door was a giant! A huge, ugly, scarred giant. It hissed at the stepfather, then grabbed him by the throat, pulled him out of the house, and stomped on his head. Squishing it.

"The girl stared at the giant, wondering if she was hallucinating. Then the giant ducked his head and came inside the small kitchen. He picked up the girl ever so gently and carried her outside. He stepped over the wall around their yard and stopped. They were surrounded by almost a dozen possums. As she watched, they all began to grow, just like the one at her door. Now she was surrounded by giants, male and female.

"'This is my family. My brothers and sisters and my parents,' the giant said. 'Because of you, not killing me a year ago, we've thrived. To thank you, we're going to bring you to our world. You'll marry me and live happily ever after.'

"The girl was confused. 'But you're a possum,' she said.

"'I am and I'm not. That's our secret form. I'm really a prince. But maybe you think I'm ugly and don't want to be with me.'

"He sounded so sad, and the girl felt for him. 'I don't think you're ugly. My stepfather was ugly. Deep in his soul. You aren't. I'll come with you. Be your princess.'

"That night, there was a huge party. The giants celebrated a new princess—who was healed by their prince's touch, so no more bruises marred her fair skin. And they lived happily ever after."

Kelli smiled against Flash. His stories...they weren't exactly the best. They made no sense. But she loved them anyway. Because they all had happy endings, just like she'd told him she loved. "That was perfect," she told him.

He chuckled, and Kelli felt it reverberate against her side. "It sucked. But I'll get better."

It was strange that she was smiling. She was filthy, smelled horrible, was thirsty and hungry, and yet, she was content.

Just then the candle flickered and abruptly went out. Kelli

could smell the smoke from the smoldering wick in the air. She inhaled sharply.

"Easy, Kelli. We're okay."

Swallowing hard, Kelli nodded against him. The dark seemed darker now. Which was silly, but she couldn't help thinking it was true.

"Your turn. Tell me a story," Flash ordered.

She knew he was trying to distract her. From their situation, from her growling belly, from the dark.

What Kelli *really* wanted to do was scream. Have a tantrum. This wasn't fair. What did she do to deserve this? She was a good person. Didn't cut in front of people on the interstate, said please and thank you even to people who were mean. She put her cart in the thingy in the parking lot at the grocery store instead of leaving it in the middle of another parking space. She paid her taxes on time and ignored all of Charlotte's nasty quips against her. And for what? To end up buried alive in a bus in the middle of some stupid jungle.

Flash's arm tightened around her, then she felt his lips on her forehead.

But...she wasn't alone. She had Flash. And the more time she spent with him, the more she liked him. There was probably some psychological reason for that. She was dependent on him. Shared trauma, something. But Kelli couldn't imagine him *not* being in her life now. She liked talking to him. He was smart, had good instincts, and was incredibly calming. Besides that, he made her feel alive. He didn't see her flaws, and there were many.

Instead, he saw *her*.

"Come on, your turn," Flash said, nudging her gently.

Taking a deep breath, Kelli began telling a story about a grasshopper named Fred who left home to see the world, only to discover that what he'd been searching for was back home the entire time.

She'd just finished, and was basking in Flash's gentle chuckles, when a loud sound echoed throughout the metal bus.

Like his namesake, Flash moved so quickly, Kelli couldn't even begin to process what he was doing or what was happening. Before she knew it, he'd pulled her to her feet and put her back against the far corner of the bus. Away from the manhole they'd been dropped through when this whole nightmare started.

"Stay here," Flash ordered in a tone of voice Kelli hadn't heard him use before. It was hard and cold and completely businesslike. This was the SEAL behind the man she'd gotten to know. It should've scared her, but instead it made her feel protected.

"I've got the conch shell knife we made. If it's Heckle and Jeckle, I'll make sure they don't get a chance to hurt you."

His first thought wasn't even about getting out of there—it was for her safety. "Be careful," she whispered.

She felt his hand on her upper arm a split second before his lips unerringly found hers. The kiss was hard and fast.

"I will. Unlike Fred the grasshopper, I know exactly what I've got, and I'm not going to do anything to fuck it up now."

Then he was gone.

Kelli couldn't see anything, but she could just hear Flash moving quietly through the bus. She held her breath and strained to see something, any speck of light. But it was no use. Their tomb was just as dark as it had ever been.

The odd scraping sounds continued at the top of the bus, making the hairs on the back of Kelli's neck stand up.

Whatever Heckle and Jeckle had put on top of that manhole cover sounded heavy, just as Flash had thought. She wasn't sure why they hadn't heard them piling whatever it was on it when they were first put in here, but she supposed it was because of the shock of the moment.

Then...the cover began to slide to the side.

The light that poured into the bus wasn't overly bright, it

wasn't direct sunlight, but it was still more than enough to make Kelli wince as her eyes struggled to adjust.

She'd just made out Flash, pressed against the side of the bus beneath the hole—half the conch shell in his hand and ready to strike—when a voice called out from above.

"Flash? You in there?"

Kelli blinked in surprise. Did Heckle and Jeckle know Flash's nickname? It wouldn't have been on his IDs, and she couldn't remember if she'd said it when they were in the van at the start of this nightmare.

"Flash?" a different voice called out.

Then a man's head appeared in the hole, looking down. His gaze met Kelli's, and they stared at each other.

"Smiley?!" Flash asked, sounding both elated and shocked at the same time.

The man's head turned, and he smiled when he saw Flash standing under him.

"In the flesh," the man named Smiley said.

Kelli knew that was one of Flash's teammates. He'd told her all about his friends and their women. She felt as if she knew them now, just from Flash's stories.

"Holy shit, am I glad to see you! Took you long enough."

"Fuck off," another man said, pushing Smiley out of the way and sticking his own head into the hole. "It's been less than a day and a half."

"That's it?" Kelli said without thinking.

"Damn, it feels as if it's been at least a week," Flash said at the same time. "Who's here?"

"We all are. Come on, let's get you two out of there, then we can chat," he said, before climbing to his knees. Before Kelli could blink, the man's legs were dangling from the opening and he jumped inside the bus.

Flash dropped his makeshift weapon and gave the guy a huge hug. "Man, it's good to see you, Kevlar!"

"You too. Although, dude, you need a shower."

Kelli frowned at that, thinking it was a pretty inconsiderate thing to say, considering the circumstances. But since both men laughed, she assumed Flash wasn't offended, given he hugged his friend once more.

Then he turned toward her. "Come here, Kelli."

Suddenly self-conscious for the first time since they'd been kidnapped, Kelli hesitated. She was filthy, still had blood in her hair and down the back of her cover-up. Was wearing a *bathing suit*, for goodness sake.

Flash didn't wait for her to come to him. He quickly strode over to where she was standing. He blocked her from Kevlar's view and put his hands on both sides of her head, tilting her face up.

"It's okay. We're safe now."

"Aren't you going to say 'I told you so?'" she teased.

"No. But I *am* going to ask you to trust me. These men, my friends and teammates? They're good men. They understand what we've been through. There's no judgement here. Okay?"

This man could read her way too easily. It was uncomfortable and kind of scary.

Then he leaned in and kissed her forehead. Right there in front of his friend. Kelli couldn't believe it.

"Come on. Let's get out of here. We've got food, water, and a shower waiting for us back at the resort."

Now *those* were three things she couldn't resist. Flash took her hand and turned. Kelli looked down as she started to follow. Then she stopped.

"What? What's wrong?" Flash asked, concern heavy in his voice.

Kelli knelt and picked up the spoon that had been in the box. The one they'd used to get into the cans. It was just a stupid spoon. A cheap one at that, as it was now bent from the pressure she'd used to try to open the can of peas. But for some reason, she didn't want to leave it behind. It was a reminder of what she'd survived.

Some people might think it morbid that she wanted a reminder of this horrible experience at all, but it hadn't been *entirely* bad.

The kiss she'd shared with Flash popped into her head. That had been…not horrible in the least.

Flash squeezed her hand and led her over to where Kevlar was standing.

"Hi. I'm Kevlar," he said with a smile as she got close.

"I'm Kelli."

"It's very good to meet you, Kelli. How about we get you out of here?"

"Yes, please," she said.

Kevlar grinned at Flash. "She's a polite little thing."

"Yup. How we doing this?"

Kevlar glanced up at the hole above their heads, then back to Flash. "How about you have her stand on your shoulders. The guys can take it from there."

Flash nodded and turned to Kelli. "We'll do this just like we did before, except this time you'll be standing. Don't worry about falling. My team won't let that happen, and neither will I."

Kelli was still nervous about her weight and standing on top of Flash, but she wanted out of this damn bus more than she wanted to brainstorm other ways to climb out of that hole above their heads.

Before she knew what was happening, Flash had turned and was crouching in front of her. Kevlar moved behind her, to help her climb onto his shoulders.

"Damn! You didn't say she was hurt!" Kevlar exclaimed. "Preacher! She's bleeding! Run back and see if the officer has a first-aid kit."

"Don't," Flash called out. "She's okay! It's from when we were taken. Jeckle hit her with the butt of his pistol. It's old blood."

"Ma'am, are you sure you're okay?" Kevlar asked.

The concern from these men was overwhelming. "Flash is right. It's old. I mean, I do have a headache, but I think it's from the bright light after so long in the dark."

"We'll get that cleaned up and checked out as soon as we get you topside," Kevlar reassured her.

"Step up, Kelli. Let's get you out of here."

It didn't take long at all. Kelli stepped onto his shoulders, and once she was secure—with Kevlar's help—Flash stood. Then her head was actually above the level of the ground. It didn't take more than a second for two of the men waiting outside to grab her biceps and pull her up and out of the hole.

One of Flash's friends kept hold of her and gently backed her away from the hole, and before she could blink, Flash was out and striding toward her. She watched as two of the men lay on the ground and reached into the hole, obviously to help Kevlar out, before her line of sight was blocked by Flash.

He took her into his arms almost roughly, and just held her as they both breathed in the fresh air.

After taking a moment to appreciate that she was free, Kelli looked around. All she saw was trees. It was hard to believe these men had actually found them. It seemed like a miracle.

"Come on, we need to get you two back to the resort and cleaned up. I'm sure the police will have questions."

Kelli blocked out the rest of what Kevlar was saying as Flash turned her, keeping an arm around her shoulders and walking her away from the tomb she'd thought she was going to die in. The fact that she was still here was a direct result of the man at her side. And she had no idea how she was going to function when they parted ways.

But that time was coming. She knew it down to her toes. He had a life, friends, a job. And she had...what? A crappy job she did just to stay busy? Yeah, her mom loved her, but she was occupied with her own life. Somehow over the years, Kelli had become isolated by her own making, with no friends to speak of, while saying yes too many times to her mom and cousin and not putting her foot down when she didn't want to do something. Doing whatever they asked just to avoid conflict.

Well, she was done with that. She wasn't going to be in her cousin's wedding. But she *was* going to sit down and talk to an advisor at one of the local colleges, to see if she could figure out what she wanted to do with her life.

And she was going to take self-defense and survival training. She never wanted to feel as helpless as she had when she was inside that bus, ever again.

And Flash? She wanted him too. But she had no idea if what she felt was one-sided or not. Yes, he'd said he wanted to date her, and he'd certainly kissed her as if he wanted more than just friendship...but now that they were free, things could change. His feelings about her might be different in the light of day, literally.

She'd have to see how things played out.

First things first. Shower, food, water. Then she'd worry about everything else.

But even as she walked toward the vehicle to get the hell out of this jungle, she couldn't help but love the feel of Flash's arm around her. Couldn't help but feel safe and protected. Getting used to that would be a bad idea, but for now, she allowed herself the moment of weakness. She'd find her backbone...later.

CHAPTER ELEVEN

Flash was tense the entire ride back to the resort. He couldn't help but remember what happened the last time he'd been in a vehicle in this country. It helped that his team surrounded him, keeping his mind occupied with questions about the abduction. He couldn't concentrate quite so much on how bright everything was after being in that damn bus for so long, or how every time he looked out the front window of the van, it seemed as if they were going to crash head-first into another car.

Instead, he did his best to pay attention to what was being asked of him, and the soothing feeling of Kelli's thumb brushing back and forth over his hand.

He hadn't let go of her since he'd joined her outside of the bus, in the jungle surrounding that damn hole in the ground. He'd held her hand as Kevlar inspected the wound on the back of her head, confirming that he didn't think she needed stitches, but suggesting it should be looked at again once the wound was clean, just to be sure.

Even as they'd crawled into the van, Flash couldn't let her go. He was feeling off-kilter. So many emotions swam through his veins. Anger, frustration, worry, and of course relief that his team had come through so quickly and found them.

He recounted everything that happened, from the time the inner tube had popped in the rapids, forcing him and Kelli to share a tube and making them late to reach the pick-up point. He described Heckle and Jeckle as best he could—even though his team told him the names of the two men who'd kidnapped them, he preferred the stupid nicknames he'd come up with—and how they were forced into the buried bus.

"How come you didn't disarm him?" Smiley asked. "And don't say you couldn't have. We all know it would've been easy for you."

Flash pressed his lips together. He'd already had a similar conversation with Kelli and didn't really want to rehash it. He still felt a little guilty because if he'd done what he'd been trained to do, it was likely they wouldn't have had to spend any time in that buried bus.

"I didn't know if Heckle...er...Brown had a weapon. I didn't want to risk him shooting Kelli while I was dealing with Jeckle," Flash said as succinctly as he could.

To his relief, his teammates all nodded. They understood. Yes, he could've taken out Brant Williams. Disarmed him in seconds. But if the consequence of that meant Kelli getting hurt, he wouldn't risk it.

"Besides, I knew you guys would figure out what happened and where we were," Flash said.

"He could've shot you after you were in the bus," Safe said. "Like fish in a barrel. Easy pickin's."

Flash felt Kelli tense next to him. "But he didn't," he said firmly. "Did Jeckle really call the commander and ask for only fifty thousand dollars?" He wanted to change the subject. Talking about Kelli getting shot made his stomach clench painfully.

The rest of the trip was uneventful, and Flash and Kelli were brought up to date on what had happened since the guys arrived on the island. How they'd talked to the tubing company, found Errol Brown. And in the morning, they'd see if they could round up Brant Williams.

Flash didn't volunteer to go with them. He didn't want to leave Kelli alone at the resort. No, that was incorrect. He didn't want to leave her alone *anywhere*. The two of them had been through some bad shit together, and while he wanted to make sure she was all right emotionally, he also wasn't anywhere near ready to let her out of his sight.

When they arrived at the resort, everyone was wearing clean and pressed uniforms. Flash felt uncomfortable...grubby and out of place. The lights annoyed him. All the people annoyed him. This happened sometimes after missions in remote places. It was hard to acclimate back to normal life.

"Come on, I talked to the manager. We packed up yours and Kelli's things, and the resort put you guys in connecting rooms. Tex is getting us flights out of here tomorrow afternoon, so you have plenty of time to eat, sleep, and get clean," Kevlar told them. "If you need anything, all you have to do is ask. Everything has been comped."

Flash looked at Kelli. She was staring at the floor, not meeting anyone's gaze. Her shoulders were hunched and she looked completely uncomfortable. He needed to get her out of there.

"Sounds good. We still have our passports, right?"

"Yeah, you're good," Preacher said.

"I'll order you guys some food so you don't have to come out of your rooms until we're ready to go tomorrow. Protein, bread, and some dishes without too many spices. Again, if you need or want anything else, just pick up the phone and order it," MacGyver told him.

"Thank you," Flash told his friend. He was grateful that was one less thing they needed to worry about. "Let me know how tomorrow goes. Looking for Jeckle."

"We will," Blink said. "Take care of her." He gave a small nod toward Kelli, who was glued to his side.

Flash nodded, then turned toward the lobby doors. They stopped at the front desk to get their new keys, and the entire time, he could practically feel the stress radiating off of Kelli. He needed to find out what was wrong, but that would wait until they were alone.

Their rooms were on the other side of the resort from where he'd stayed before—was it only a day ago?—and by the time they arrived at their doors, Kelli still hadn't said a word.

Flash was even more worried. This wasn't the woman he'd gotten to know. It was as if she'd closed in on herself. Shut herself off. He wouldn't allow her to pull away from him though. He knew exactly how she was feeling. He'd been there in the past, after especially gnarly missions. But he'd been trained. Knew what to expect. The adrenaline drop from being a captive one minute, then rescued and on the move the next...It was a lot.

He slid one of the plastic keys into the slot in the first door and stepped inside with Kelli's hand still firmly in his. He didn't even offer to open the other door, since they were connected anyway. He simply pulled her inside with him.

The room he'd been given was big. Much larger than the one he'd had before. This one was a suite. It had a full kitchen, complete with a sink, stove, and refrigerator. There was even a dining table and chairs in a sitting area. A couch was against one wall, with a huge TV on the opposite wall. Sliding glass doors opened onto a huge grassy area of about twenty yards across, before meeting the sand of the beach beyond. The room was fancy, but all Flash cared about was Kelli.

"Kelli?" he asked gently. She looked up at him with a small furrow in her brows he longed to soothe away. "Talk to me," he said softly.

"The room is nice."

That wasn't what he meant.

"What are you thinking? Are you all right? You're really quiet. I'm worried about you."

"I'm just...overwhelmed? That sounds stupid. I mean—"

"It's not stupid," Flash interrupted her. "An hour ago, we were sitting in the pitch darkness, telling fairy tales about possums turning into giants and a grasshopper named Fred. And then our life turned upside down. *Again.* In a good way this time, but it's jarring all the same."

She nodded. "It feels surreal. As if I was dropped into someone else's life. And my senses are going haywire. I could smell chicken cooking as soon as we got out of the van at the resort. And the salt from the ocean. The lights from the other cars and in the lobby almost hurt my eyes, they were so bright. It's hard to adjust."

"It is," Flash said, proud of her for articulating what she was feeling. "It gets better."

She nodded slowly. "It's better already. Now that we're not around so many people. Oh, no offense. I mean, I was happy to meet your friends and very glad they found us." She looked up at him. "I was rude, wasn't I? I should've talked to them more."

"No, you were fine. They understand. Trust me, they *definitely* understand. We've all been there. You want to check out your room?"

She tensed next to him and let go of his hand. That, out of everything he'd been through in the last day and a half, hurt Flash more than anything else. "What? What's wrong?" he asked.

She shrugged. "Nothing. Sure, we can look at my room. I'm sure you want to shower. So do I." But she was shrinking into herself again. And Flash wasn't going to let her pull away now. They'd been through too much together.

He reached out and grabbed her hand, then pulled her toward the dining table. He pulled out a chair and sat, yanking her onto his lap.

"Flash!" she protested, sounding more like the Kelli he'd gotten to know.

He put one arm over her thighs and the other was around her waist, holding her securely on top of him. To his immense relief, she didn't struggle. Didn't try to get up. If she had, he would've let her go. "What's wrong?" he asked again.

She sighed and closed her eyes, and Flash could feel her relax against him. He tightened his hold.

"I don't want to look at my room," she said quietly. "I want to stay here. With you. If that's okay."

Relief swept through Flash so fast it made him dizzy. "If that's okay?" he asked. "It's more than okay. I don't think I could've handled you being in another room very well."

"Because you think I'm weak?"

"No. Because *I* am."

That had her staring at him in disbelief.

"It's true. The thought of being away from you freaks me out. You've been my rock throughout this entire ordeal."

"Now you're being ridiculous," she said.

"No, I'm not. I was pissed that with all my training, all the warnings I'd had about leaving the resort, all the things I've done as a SEAL, I'd gone and gotten myself into a situation that could get me killed. You kept me focused on what needed to be done. If I'd been alone, I probably would've hurt myself trying to find a way out of that bus instead of staying calm, using my head to utilize what Heckle and Jeckle left for us, and waiting for my team. I've always just let MacGyver be the smart one. I've always been the muscle guy. You let me see myself in a new light—and I liked it. The thought of you leaving me now...frankly, it makes me nauseous."

"I think that's either hunger or our smell," she joked.

Flash wasn't sure he was ready to lighten the conversation, but he'd give Kelli time for what he was saying to sink in. That he wasn't blowing smoke up her ass. She really *was* his rock. And she'd done more for him in that bus than she realized.

Not wanting to think about what the next day would bring, the fact that they'd go their separate ways and he'd have to deal, Flash gave her a small smile. "Want to check out the bathroom?"

"Yes!" she said enthusiastically, showing some of the spunk he'd come to expect from her.

"I'll even let you go first," he said magnanimously.

She gave him a side-eye. "Is that because you're being nice, or because you want first choice of whatever your friend is sending via room service?"

Flash burst out laughing. "Busted," he said, although he hadn't even thought about that. But now that she'd said it, his stomach growled. Loudly.

He helped Kelli to her feet then took her hand once again. Glancing down at their fingers laced together, he saw how filthy they were. They both had dirt under their nails, and their skin was also covered in more grime, blood from her head wound, and rust flakes from the metal of the bus. But to him, she was beautiful no matter what. Simply because of who she was. How strong she'd been. How resilient.

"Flash?"

He stopped in his tracks. "Yeah?"

"Thank you."

He wasn't sure what exactly she was thanking him for.

"I'm well aware that you could've gotten away. You know, before we were put in that bus. You could've done your thing, your SEAL thing, and probably beaten Heckle and Jeckle to pulps. But you didn't because of me. You *let yourself* be put in that bus when you didn't have to. I..." She swallowed hard. "I don't think anyone has ever done anything so unselfish for me in my entire life."

"That's a shame. Because you're the kind of woman wars are fought over. Who make men act like fools because they're desperate to catch your eye. And I'll tell you something, if I had to do it all over again, I'd do everything exactly the same way, just to keep you safe."

"Flash," she whispered, clearly overwhelmed.

Taking a deep breath, Flash tried to ease up. He wanted this woman, but he didn't want to come on too strong.

Ha. Who was he kidding? It was too late for that. Way too late.

"Come on, let's check out the bathroom. Then I'll grab your suitcase from the connecting room so you can get your toiletries and stuff before you shower."

The bathroom was huge. Another step up from the basic rooms they'd had before. The shower was separate from the Jacuzzi tub and more than large enough for two people. But this was no time to think about anything other than their basic needs. Getting clean, eating, and sleeping.

Flash hurriedly grabbed her suitcase from the other room and returned. Kelli was standing in the middle of the bathroom, right where he'd left her, staring at herself in the mirror. She looked sad and freaked out again, so Flash came up behind her and wrapped his arms around her waist. He rested his chin on her shoulder and stared at their reflection.

They looked good together. Even with the blood on her skin and cover-up, the dirt on their faces and hands, the dark circles under both their eyes. They fit together perfectly. Complemented each other. His dark hair, her lighter strands. His six-two to her five-foot-two stature. His green eyes, her brown. His lean muscle mass, and her curvy figure. He loved how different yet compatible they were.

"We're a mess," she whispered, putting her hands over his forearms at her belly.

"Yup," Flash agreed. "But we're alive. Those assholes didn't win."

"Yeah."

He didn't want to let her go. Wanted to pull her into the shower and clean every inch of her body. Wash away the fear and uncertainty from their ordeal. But he knew it was too much, too soon. He'd give her the privacy she hadn't had much of recently, even if it killed him.

"I'll look at your head when you're done. Take your time. Seriously. We have no plans."

"Other than to eat. I swear, I could eat a horse."

Flash chuckled. He felt the same. "We might have to make due with some chicken and beef. Maybe pork."

"I'm all right with that. Flash? I'm sorry. I know it's silly that we have two bathrooms, and yet I don't want to go into the other room to shower."

"It's not silly. It's normal. Trust me."

"Okay. But I still feel bad that I'll be getting clean and you have to wait."

"Don't. I get first dibs on the room service, remember?" Flash joked.

He was rewarded with her smile. "Well, don't eat it all. Save some for me."

In response, Flash dropped his arms and shifted to her side. He kissed her temple, ran his hand lightly over the back of her head, then backed toward the door.

"I will," he reassured her, shutting the door as he left, her gentle smile burned into his brain as he lost sight of her.

It took a few moments for him to regain some control over his emotions. She was right there, on the other side of the door. Even so, he had to remind himself that she was fine. No one was going to break into the room through the wall and hurt her, or steal her away from him.

Forcing himself to step away from the door, Flash went into the bedroom and saw his own suitcase on the bed. He opened it and grabbed his toiletries and some clean clothes. In the kitchen, he brushed his teeth for what seemed like five minutes straight. That was one of his favorite things to do when he returned from missions. Cleaning his teeth properly. Tonight was no exception.

When he was done, he didn't dare sit on the couch in his dirty, smelly swim trunks and T-shirt. So he paced.

He couldn't stop himself from imagining what Kelli looked like in the shower. The memory of her in that black bathing suit, perched on his lap as they floated down the river in the same inner tube, struck him hard. The woman truly *was* a goddess, and she had no idea.

A knock on the door interrupted his thoughts, and Flash was glad for it. He needed to stop thinking about Kelli's body...and what it would look like *without* the suit.

When he opened the door, his vision filled with three carts covered with as many dishes as would fit on them. The attendants wheeled them in and put everything on the table and kitchen counter. The room filled with the most delicious-smelling food. It made Flash's belly clench painfully. He wanted to uncover every dish and stuff whatever was on each into his mouth, like an uncivilized heathen. But he restrained himself. Barely. He couldn't stand to eat without Kelli.

As if she could smell the food from inside the bathroom, the water shut off. Moments later, the door opened and her head appeared.

"Oh my God, that smells so good. I could smell it in the shower!"

Steam wafted around her as she peeked out the door, and Flash could see she was wrapped in one of the huge towels the resort was known for, swathed from chest to calves. Aside from her naked shoulders, she was more covered than she'd been in the last two days, and yet to him, she was even sexier. Her skin was clean and flushed from the heat of the water, and the smile on her face seemed brighter.

This was a woman who wasn't currently thinking about how

her body compared to anyone else's, how vulnerable she was in a room, naked under her towel with a man she'd met only a few days before. She was living in the moment. Focused on food and only the food.

"Get dressed and get out here, woman, and we can check out what MacGyver ordered for us."

Her head disappeared and the door shut behind her.

Flash grinned. He made a mental note that when his woman was hungry, nothing got in her way.

His woman.

Yeah, he liked that. A lot.

Kelli reappeared minutes later, skin still flushed, wearing a pair of loose cotton pants and a sweatshirt. She inhaled deeply and another happy smile broke out across her face.

"I'll never take food for granted again," she said. Then she turned to him. "Well? What are you waiting for?"

Flash reached for the nearest dish to uncover it, but Kelli stepped toward him, shaking her head. "No! I meant, it's your turn in the shower. It'll be slight torture waiting for you to get done, but it probably was for you too, me being in the shower when all this food came."

"You don't have to wait for me. Go ahead and start while I'm showering."

Kelli stubbornly shook her head. "No. There's no way I'm going to eat without you."

Damn. This woman. She slayed him. "I'll be fast."

"Take your time. The shower is awesome. The pressure is perfect."

That reminded him. "I need to check your head wound."

"After. Shower, Flash. It feels amazing. I would never deny anyone else feeling the way I do right now, especially you. The food will be here when you're done. I'm not going to die of starvation if I have to wait another twenty minutes or so to eat."

It wasn't going to take him twenty minutes to shower. That

was a given. Still, Flash wanted to hug her. Wanted to bend her over his arm as he'd done in that damn bus and kiss her the way he ached to. But now that she was squeaky clean, he didn't want to touch her with his disgusting self.

Knowing if he opened his mouth, he'd say something that was too intense, he simply smiled, then turned and headed for the bathroom.

CHAPTER TWELVE

Kelli stood where she was and stared at the bathroom door. She definitely wasn't feeling like herself. Being clean felt incredible, but in that bathroom...the second Flash was out of sight, she'd lost it. She'd ripped off her cover-up and bathing suit—neither of which she ever wanted to see again—got into the shower and sobbed.

For what she'd been through...in relief that she'd been saved...in thanks that she hadn't been alone through the ordeal...

And because she'd fallen head over heels for a man who, in the real world, would probably never have taken a second glance at her.

She'd gotten to know Flash better than anyone she'd ever dated, and some of those men she'd been with for months. He was her rock. He made her feel safe—and tomorrow she'd have to say goodbye to him.

It wasn't until she'd shampooed her hair twice—gingerly, since her head was still sore from where Jeckle had hit her— slathered on a ton of conditioner, and soaped herself up several times over that she began to feel a little better. Her tears had dried up and she'd felt oddly hollow inside.

And then she'd smelled the food.

Now, standing in the middle of the little sitting room, staring at the covered dishes, was akin to torture. But she refused to eat without Flash. They'd shared that callaloo and those peas, they'd passed that water bottle back and forth. She wouldn't stuff her face while he was still hungry. She couldn't do it.

Though, the smells emanating from the plates were making her mouth water.

It felt like she'd been standing there for hours, but when she checked her watch, Flash exited the bathroom exactly seven minutes after he'd entered.

Looking over at him, Kelli couldn't help but stare. He looked... holy crap, he looked good. Somehow being with him in the dark for so long had actually made her forget how handsome the man was. But seeing him fresh out of the shower, his hair wet and sticking up at odd angles, his neatly trimmed beard emphasizing his full lips and square jaw, those piercing green eyes...it made her want to rip off all her clothes and beg him to have his wicked way with her.

"Man, that felt good. The first shower after a mission always does," he said with a small smile. "You ready to see what we've got?"

Kelli swallowed hard and nodded.

She expected Flash to head toward the table, but instead he walked straight to her. Without a word, he wrapped his arms around her. Sighing in contentment, Kelli laid her head on his chest and held onto him just as tightly as he was holding her.

The moment was charged. And Flash smelled amazing. She needed to find out what soap he used and invest in gallons of it. She felt her nipples hardening under her sweatshirt and regretted not putting on a bra. She figured she was just going to eat then go to sleep, so there was no need to bother, but now she kind of felt as if she needed the extra layer of protection between her and Flash.

It was scary how much she wanted this man. How much she needed him. He made her feel as if she could conquer the world. It didn't matter that she didn't have any friends, or a career she loved. She'd survived being kidnapped and buried alive. Thanks to *him*.

It was the sudden urge to beg him never to leave her that had Kelli taking a deep breath and stepping away. She needed to get a grip. This wasn't a movie or a book. Real life didn't work like the romantic stories she watched and read about.

"Does your head hurt?"

Blinking, it took a moment for his words to sink in. "Oh, no. Not really."

"Can I take a quick look before we chow?"

In response, Kelli turned, presenting him with the back of her head. The second his hands were in her hair, she tensed. Not because what he was doing hurt, but because her damn nipples were hard again, and it was taking all her control not to shift where she was standing and rub her thighs together. She prayed he wouldn't be able to smell her arousal.

"It looks pretty good, all things considered. You could probably use a round of antibiotics just in case, but I agree with Kevlar that you don't need stitches."

"That's good," Kelli said, turning back around and desperately trying to control her lust for this man.

"Yeah. Come on, let's eat."

Flash took her hand in his, and it felt like coming home. Their clasped hands simply felt right.

He brought her over to the kitchen, where they both grabbed plates from the cabinet. He let go of her hand, but this time Kelli barely noticed...because he'd begun to uncover the dishes.

There was enough bread for a dozen people. Chicken strips, French fries, green beans, steak, various local vegetables, and those cheesy potatoes they both loved so much. It was as if the entire buffet had been brought up to their room.

At first, Kelli took tiny amounts of everything, but when she saw Flash loading up his plate, she mentally shrugged and began to do the same. They shared a smile when they both passed on the peas and callaloo. While she'd been grateful for the food in the bus, and it tasted amazingly good, thinking about consuming it now just brought up bad memories.

When their plates were overflowing, they opted for the couch instead of the dining table, pulling the coffee table close before picking up their silverware.

Flash grinned at her again before he speared a piece of chicken and brought it up to his mouth.

"Oh my God," he mumbled with his mouth full. "This is the best chicken I've had in my life."

The next twenty minutes went by with very little talking from either of them. They were too focused on filling their bellies. Flash went back to the little buffet two more times, while Kelli only managed one refill. Soon, she was slumped against the couch, feeling as if she was going to pop. Her belly was slightly bloated with all the food she'd consumed, and Flash was in much the same position.

"I owe MacGyver big time," Flash said with a satisfied smile. "That was awesome."

"Yeah," Kelli agreed.

When he got to his feet, she started to follow, but he shook his head. "No, stay there. Relax. I got this."

"I can help," Kelli protested.

"I know you can. But you don't need to. I'm just going to shove everything we didn't eat into the fridge for tomorrow morning. There are enough plates in the cupboard that I don't even have to wash these, I'll just rinse them and leave them in the sink. You can head into the bedroom and get ready for bed if you want."

At that, Kelli stilled. She looked up at Flash with big eyes.

"Unless you don't want to stay here. I'd understand. We're practically strangers and—"

"No!" Kelli interrupted. "I want to stay. I just...I wasn't sure if *you* wanted me here."

In response, Flash put down their empty plates and leaned over her, momentarily caging her in on the couch. "I want you here," he whispered. His gaze flicked to her lips, then back to her eyes, before he straightened.

Kelli felt paralyzed for a moment longer, then she forced herself to stand. Groaning with how full she was—wow, how unsexy did she feel?—she waddled into the bedroom. She did what she needed to do in the bathroom as quickly as possible, then crawled under the covers still wearing her stretchy pants and sweatshirt.

She heard the clinking and clanking of dishes in the other room, and not too much later, Flash appeared. He smiled at her before heading into the bathroom.

Kelli was tense. All of a sudden, this felt awkward. She should've gone into the other room. She was simply torturing herself by being here with Flash. It was one thing to sleep in his arms while they'd been captive in that bus, but now? Sleeping with him in a comfortable bed?

She was an idiot.

But as soon as Flash got under the covers, slid over to where she was lying on her back, and pulled her into his arms, contentment and a rightness she'd never felt in her life swept over Kelli.

"So much better than that hard metal floor," Flash sighed.

Kelli couldn't agree more. Although she'd had the better end of that deal, as Flash had let her use him as a pillow.

Neither spoke for a long time; they just held each other in the dark room...both lost in thought.

For Kelli, her life was irrevocably changed. This was her guy. The one those books and movies talked about. The person who was made for her. Soul mates. She knew that without a doubt. But it wasn't as if this was the end of the book. Life went on. She had no idea if things would work out between them, but for the first time ever, she was determined to go after what she wanted.

"I'm sorry I'm not the best conversationalist. I'm so damn tired," Flash said quietly.

"*Shhhh*. No need for talking. I'm exhausted too."

Flash fell asleep first. Kelli felt his deep breaths under her cheek as she lay practically on top of him. His arm was around her shoulders, his other hand grasping *her* arm, splayed over his chest. One of her legs had hitched up to rest upon his. They were as intertwined as they could be, and while she'd never slept with someone like this, Kelli had never been more comfortable.

With the feel of his heartbeat in her ear, Kelli followed Flash into a deep sleep not long after. She'd just been through the worst thing she'd ever experienced in her life, and yet, she was grateful it had provided the chance to get to know this man. He'd changed her forever, and even if they ended up as nothing but friends, she'd find a way to be all right with that...as long as he was in her life.

* * *

Brant Williams scowled as he stared straight ahead at the airplane seat in front of him. Nothing had turned out the way he'd planned. He'd been so careful, spent more money than he had to set everything up. It wasn't cheap to strip that bus and pay to have it buried in the middle of fucking nowhere. He'd been *so sure* the US government would pay to get that asshole back!

But he'd been wrong. And that stung.

He'd been waiting for the money to show up in his bank account when he'd gotten word that a group of Americans had arrived on the island. The information network was fast and effective on the island, and before long, word came down that the men were at Errol Brown's house...asking questions.

Brant knew without a doubt that he was in deep shit. He'd packed as much as he could in two suitcases and headed straight to the airport. Errol wasn't loyal to him and would definitely squeal. Would tell the Americans and probably the police all about the kidnapping and ransom plan—and how Brant was behind it.

He needed to get off the island. Disappear.

It didn't take him long to decide where to go. He thought about the IDs he'd buried in his luggage. The addresses he'd memorized.

California. He had some unfinished business in the States.

It was only a matter of time before the bitch and the asshole were discovered...with Errol's help. Because of course he'd blab. No one would find his hidey-hole in the jungle otherwise. It was too perfect. The *plan* had been perfect.

He'd just picked the wrong person to partner with.

He couldn't get to Errol though, who was apparently in police custody. Couldn't make him pay for snitching. But he might be able to get to the American...especially once the asshole was back on familiar territory. He'd never guess he was being followed. Never dream that anyone might still be after him. Even though he was some supposed badass Navy guy, important enough that his government didn't hesitate to send people to the island to find him, Brant had no doubt he could outsmart him—and anyone who stood in his way. Especially when the man's guard was down.

This wasn't about money anymore. It was about following through. Wade Gordon and Kelli Colbert weren't going to get away so easily, especially after fucking up all his plans.

Once they were home, they'd assume they were safe. That

they could just go on with their lives. Fucking Americans! Thought they were better than everyone else.

Well, he knew where they lived. Both of them. They hadn't seen the last of Brant Williams. He vowed to finish what he'd started. He'd get what he wanted in the end...the satisfaction of knowing he'd won.

CHAPTER THIRTEEN

For the first time in his life, Flash dreaded going home. Not because he'd wanted to stay in Jamaica, but because it would mean leaving Kelli. How he'd become so attached so quickly, he had no idea. But he had. And he didn't regret it.

When he'd woken up that morning, he'd had a moment of confusion. He didn't do one-night stands. Didn't sleep with women—*sleep* sleep, that was. And yet, he'd woken up with his arms around a soft body, flowery scent in his nose, and a hard-on that was almost painful.

But the confusion dissipated almost immediately as memories returned. He was at the resort. With Kelli. They were safe, clean, and he'd had the best night's sleep that he could remember in quite a while.

Moving slowly so as not to jostle the still-sleeping woman in his arms, Flash had stuffed a pillow under his head so he could see Kelli more clearly. Her hair had been strewn across his T-shirt-covered chest, her hand next to her face. One of her legs was thrown over his thigh, and as he'd shifted a little, she'd snuggled deeper into him, as if wanting to make sure he didn't move away from her.

Flash remembered thinking...*This. This is what my life is missing.*

That feeling of being wanted. Of being needed.

How long he watched her sleep, Flash didn't know. But he couldn't keep the smile off his face when she woke. She'd smacked her lips and frowned a little. Her brow furrowed. She was fucking adorable.

Eventually she'd taken a long, slow breath—then her entire body tensed. As if she'd just realized she was cuddling up to an actual living, breathing person and not a pillow.

Not wanting her to be embarrassed, Flash had wished her good morning, then slipped out from under her to use the bathroom. When he'd returned, Kelli was sitting up in bed, giving him a shy smile.

He'd reheated leftovers from the previous night for breakfast, and by the time they were packed and ready to go, it was almost noon. Kevlar had called while they were eating and informed Flash that Brant Williams was gone, along with what looked like most of his clothes. He'd obviously heard about their little visit to Errol and fled.

A phone call to Tex confirmed he'd gotten on a plane the night before and left the island altogether. A disappointing outcome, as Flash would've liked to have had the chance to confront the man face-to-face.

But then Kevlar told him where Brant's flight was headed—and Flash's easy, non-stressful morning had changed in a heartbeat.

LA. The man who'd kidnapped him and Kelli, buried them in the jungle, tried to collect ransom money from the US government for him, had gone to Los Angeles.

It was way too close to Riverton for his peace of mind, especially since Williams had both his and Kelli's IDs...with their addresses.

Tex was currently trying to track the man, happy that he was at least on what Tex considered home turf, where there were cameras on every corner and you couldn't fart without some sort of electronic footprint.

It still wasn't what Flash had wanted to hear, nor had he wanted to freak out Kelli when she was so relaxed and content earlier that morning. He'd decided to tell her after they'd arrived back in the States.

Which was any minute now. They were finally about to land in San Diego. They'd flown home on a commercial flight, as opposed to the military bird the team had arrived on. The trip was uneventful and Flash felt comfortable, surrounded by all his teammates.

Kelli was seated by the window, with Flash at her side. To his surprise and delight, not long after they took off, Kelli had reached over and put her hand on his thigh. It wasn't a sexual move, not that he could tell. He assumed she just wanted to keep a connection with him, the same way he felt a need to always be connected to her.

Flash had placed his hand over hers, and she'd napped a little, never breaking their hold.

But now they were home.

Back to reality.

And Flash had no idea how the hell he was going to say goodbye to the woman who'd turned his life inside out. She'd literally changed his entire outlook on his future. He wanted to take her home with him. Move her into his small apartment. The thought of letting her just walk away was making him grouchy, and he scowled at his teammates as they talked about the schedule for the upcoming week as if nothing had changed.

He sighed. For them, nothing *had* changed. The trip to Jamaica had been a slight detour in their schedule, nothing more. But for Flash, the few days were life-altering.

He'd taken the time to talk to his sister and parents that morning, reassuring them that he was fine. They'd heard about what happened, of course, since Chuck had arrived home from the trip the night before, earlier than expected, and told Nova that he was missing. They were all freaked out, but Flash had been able to talk them out of flying to Riverton to see him. He promised Nova he'd call her later and tell her everything that happened.

Kelli had also called her mom, who didn't seem quite as emotional as his own family had been about the entire situation. She was relieved her daughter was all right, and wanted to hear all about what happened, but by the time Kelli had hung up, they were talking about things like her mom's latest trip to the grocery store and what her plans were for the week.

All-in-all, he and Kelli had been lucky. *Damn* lucky. If he wasn't who he was, if he didn't have the resources that he had, namely a team of highly trained Navy SEALs who had his back, the outcome could've been very different.

As soon as they exited the plane, Flash took hold of Kelli's hand as they walked toward baggage claim. He was already getting used to being around people again, but he could feel Kelli inch closer as they walked.

"It's crazy how chaotic this feels to me now," she said, glancing up at him as they walked.

"I feel like this a lot after missions. Our work is intense. Often times in the middle of nowhere and in complete silence. And when I come home, the noise and hustle and bustle always take me by surprise," Flash said, wanting her to know what she was feeling was normal.

When she giggled, he looked down at her.

"What? Was that funny?" he asked, confused.

"No. Not really. I mean, it makes sense, and I'm sorry you have to go through this all the time, because honestly, it's not very fun. I was laughing because you saying 'hustle and bustle' reminded me of Heckle and Jeckle." She shrugged. "I don't know, it struck me as humorous."

Flash smiled at her. "So if I said shake and bake, it would be even funnier?"

To his delight, her smile widened and she giggled again. "Artsy-fartsy," she said between giggles.

"Jeepers-creepers," Flash countered.

"Frick and frack."

"Gloom and doom."

"Holy moly guacamole!" Kelli said, laughing so hard it was almost hard to understand her.

Flash shook his head. "I think you win with that one." His face hurt from smiling so hard. He couldn't remember the last time he'd been this genuinely amused.

"What's so funny?" Safe asked, glancing at them over his shoulder.

Flash's gaze met Kelli's, and they both burst out laughing. Eventually he controlled himself enough to tell his friend, "It's impossible to explain and you wouldn't find it funny anyway."

Safe rolled his eyes but let it drop.

Flash's humor slowly died with each step closer to baggage claim. Now, he felt kind of sick. This wasn't a normal reaction, but he couldn't help it. It was probably because of what they'd been through together, although he'd never felt this way about one of his teammates after an especially gnarly mission. He couldn't explain it, and that made him uneasy.

The second they walked through the gate that separated the secure area of the airport from the public part, Flash blinked in surprise.

Instead of walking past the people waiting to pick up passengers, ignoring them as he was used to doing when he flew commercial...he stopped abruptly when he saw some very familiar faces.

Remi, Wren, Josie, Maggie, and Addison were all there. And instead of running to their boyfriends or husbands, they headed directly toward him and Kelli.

In seconds, they were surrounded.

Flash had to let go of Kelli's hand as his friends' women all hugged him and fussed, saying how relieved they were that he was all right. Glancing back at Kelli, he saw that her eyes were wide and she looked confused...and slightly freaked.

He met Kevlar's gaze, and his team leader obviously read what Flash was trying to tell him nonverbally, because he stepped up and wrapped an arm around Remi, pulling her back a little. "How about we give them a little space, sweetheart."

The others all claimed their own women, giving Flash and Kelli some room to breathe. Flash regained Kelli's hand as the group moved their reunion out of the way of other travelers. Then Flash said, "Thank you all for coming. I didn't expect it."

"Why not? You're one of us. Part of our group," Wren said.

"When we heard you were missing, we panicked," Remi explained.

"Thank God the guys were sent to find you so quickly," Josie added.

"Did they find the asshole who kidnapped you?" Maggie asked.

"I can't believe he had the balls to call and demand a ransom from the Navy. What an idiot," Addison murmured.

"Where are your kids?" Flash asked her. "You didn't leave them home alone, did you?"

Addison rolled her eyes and smiled. "Of course not. Caroline came over."

Flash nodded. Caroline was the wife of Wolf Steel, an infamous former SEAL who was a kind of mentor to Flash and the rest of his team. They'd become close to the man's former team, and their families.

"Are you going to introduce us?" Remi demanded, smiling at Kelli.

"Right. Sorry. This is Kelli Colbert. Kelli, this is Remi, Josie,

Maggie, Wren, and Addison," Flash said, nodding to each woman as he introduced them.

"It's nice to meet you," Kelli said politely.

"It's probably not," Josie said wryly. "We debated if we should come. The last thing we wanted was to freak you out. But we all love Flash, and we wanted to make sure he knew how relieved we are that he's all right. And you too. We've all kind of been in your shoes...you know, in shitty situations where someone feels as if they can make you do things you don't want to...so we thought you could use the support."

"Yes, and with that being said," Remi added, "I hope you'll come back to Safe and Wren's place with us."

"Wait—what?" Flash asked.

"Um...we kind of have a welcome-home, glad-you-got-away party going on," Wren said, with a sheepish grin. "We didn't actually plan on it, but one thing led to another and before we knew it, all Caroline's friends and your SEAL buds were wanting to come, because they needed to see for themselves that you were all right, and now everyone is waiting back at the house."

Flash stared at Wren for a beat, then moved his gaze to Safe. "Did you know about this?"

"Uh-uh. Don't look at me like that. I had no part in this," Safe said with a shake of his head.

"Come on, Flash. Please? You'll come, right? We don't really need a reason to get together and hang out, but it would be weird if you weren't there, since Addison made a huge cake that says 'welcome home.' And Alabama got a bunch of balloons, and Jessyka is in charge of the kids, who're making signs to put up all over the house to welcome you back."

"And you have to come too, Kelli," Remi pleaded. "We're so glad you're okay. I mean, we don't know you, but if Flash likes you, we will too. We're a rambunctious lot, but we mean well. I promise."

Flash glanced at Kelli, who tilted her head up to look at him. He couldn't tell what she was thinking.

"Can you give us a minute?" he asked his friends.

"Sure."

"Of course."

"Take all the time you want."

"But not too much, we have food waiting at home!"

The others began to walk toward baggage claim, but Flash stayed where he was. He turned to face Kelli.

"Talk to me. Are you freaking out? I swear I didn't know they'd all be here, otherwise I would've warned you. Don't feel obligated to do anything. What are you thinking?"

She squeezed the hand he was still holding and said, "I'm thinking you're a very lucky man."

That wasn't what Flash expected to hear. "What?"

"You were gone, like, one extra day, and everyone came here to the airport to see you because they didn't want to wait a moment longer than they had to. Your six best friends dropped everything to come to Jamaica to find you, and not only that, they did it literally in *hours*. And everyone's so happy that you're all right, an impromptu party formed because all your *other* friends wanted *their* chance to tell you how happy they are that you're back."

She was right. Flash was very lucky. But just because he had good friends didn't mean his life was perfect. It was missing something huge.

A partner.

"You're right. I'm a lucky man. So...you'll come with me? Meet my friends? Get to know them?"

"Well...I kind of feel as if I already know the women. You told me a lot about them."

She was going to say yes. Flash could tell.

"Okay. Thank you, yes. I'd love to come with you."

Relief and satisfaction swept through Flash. "I'll take you

home when you've had enough. All you need to do is let me know. It'll be crazy," he felt obligated to warn. "If you think Remi and the others are enthusiastic, wait until you meet Caroline's crew. They'll have you agreeing to sleepovers, girls' night out at Aces Bar and Grill, and who knows what other crazy schemes before the night is done."

"If you're trying to talk me out of this, you aren't succeeding," Kelli said with a smile. "I've never had girlfriends to do that stuff with before. I mean, not as an adult."

"Come on. Let's go find our suitcases and get out of here. I don't know about you, but I'm hungry again. That usually happens after missions or times when I haven't been able to eat properly. I'm ravenous for a few days until my body figures out that it's going to be fed on a regular basis again."

And just like that, Flash was happy. They didn't have to say goodbye yet. He'd bought himself a few hours. And getting her enmeshed with the women was one of the best ways he could think of to ensure he'd see plenty of Kelli in the future. No one could resist Remi and her posse. He hoped.

* * *

Kelli looked around in awe. Never in a million years would she have guessed this was where she'd be right now. In a small house, packed to the gills—with more people in the backyard—laughing with people she'd just met, feeling as if she'd known them her whole life.

All of Flash's friends were open and welcoming, kind and compassionate. And they seemed genuinely happy she was there.

It was...weird but awesome. Kelli wasn't the kind of woman most people were drawn to. She was used to standing in the shadows, watching others at parties and get-togethers. If someone *did* talk to her, it was obvious they were usually doing so simply to be polite.

But she got none of those vibes from the people here. She couldn't remember everyone's names, as she'd been introduced to a lot of men and women. Fiona, Summer, Mozart, Benny, Julie, Matthew...and it seemed as if the women called the men one name, and the men used nicknames. It was all very confusing. But Kelli was still happier than she'd been in a very long time.

And Flash hadn't been the only one who was starving. The cake that Addison made melted in her mouth, and it was all Kelli could do not to spontaneously orgasm right there in the kitchen at the first bite. But all the other food was just as good. There was a lot of finger food, which made it easier to eat and talk.

Kids ran everywhere, shouting too loud, running into people, and dropping food on the floor, but none of the adults seemed overly concerned. They just warned them to be careful, demanded they apologize when they almost knocked Kelli over, and generally shaking their heads at their exuberance.

Looking at her phone, which she was extremely grateful she hadn't brought on the tubing trip, Kelli saw that she and Flash had been at the impromptu party for three hours. It was hard to believe, as it felt as if they'd just gotten there.

Just as she had the thought about Flash, he appeared as if she'd conjured him up. He wrapped an arm around her waist, and she leaned into him as he bent down and spoke softly into her ear. "You okay?"

She nodded.

"How many phone numbers have you gotten tonight?"

Kelli chuckled. "Um...all of them?"

"Good. Invites to hang out again?"

"Three or four."

"Has Julie tried to steal you away to work in her secondhand clothing store yet?"

Her smile widened as she looked up at him. "How'd you know?"

"Because she's not an idiot. You tired?"

Kelli shrugged. She was exhausted. It was silly, really. She hadn't done much today. Slept in, eaten, then gotten on a plane, and now she was just standing around. But then again, traveling always made her feel as if she was dragging. Now her energy level was seriously flagging.

"I'm knackered," Flash admitted.

She couldn't help but smile at that. "Knackered?" she asked. "You have British blood in you that I don't know about?"

"Nope. But I love that word. Was pleased I had a chance to use it."

This man. He made her laugh, made her feel safe, and also scared the hell out of her. Mostly because the thought of losing him made her want to puke. And somehow she felt as if the second she said goodbye, that would be it. He'd go back to his life, with all these amazing people, and forget about her. The short, frumpy woman he'd somehow managed to get kidnapped with while on that one trip to Jamaica.

"You ready to go?"

She was and she wasn't. But since Flash was tired, and he was her ride home, she didn't want to hold him up. She nodded.

"All right. We'll make the rounds and say bye to everyone then head out."

Of course, saying goodbye took another full hour. As they moved around the house, then into the backyard to talk to the people out there, Flash never left her side. Either kept his arm around her waist or held her hand.

As they were finally walking out the front door, Flash said, "Whew! I thought we'd never get out of there."

"You're going to see your teammates tomorrow, right?" Kelli asked.

"Yup. Why?"

She shrugged. "Just wondering."

"It's a thing," Flash said, as if he understood what she wanted to know without her having to say it out loud. "We never leave a get-together without saying goodbye or see you later to everyone. We've learned the hard way that life is too short."

That made sense. And it explained a lot about how close these men and women were.

Flash led her toward a gray Honda Pilot SUV parked on the side of the road.

"Wait, is this your car?" she asked, as he opened the passenger front door.

"Nope. I'm stealing it," Flash said in a deadpan tone.

"Whatever. But how'd it get here?"

"Wolf and Dude went to my house and picked it up for me, and brought it here."

"How'd they get your keys?"

"Probably from Kevlar."

Kelli turned in the doorway before climbing in. "How'd *he* get them?"

Flash leaned in and put one hand on the door, the other on the roof of the vehicle, effectively caging her in. Oh, she could've ducked under his arm and gotten away from him, but why would she? She was right where she wanted to be. Surrounded by Flash.

"We all have copies of each other's house and car keys. We never know when we might have to leave our car somewhere, and one of the others will need to pick it up for us. It's just what we do."

"Oh."

"Yeah, oh. Now climb in. It's dark out here, and while the neighborhood has cleaned up a lot, it's still not totally safe."

With that, Kelli moved, getting up into the seat. To her surprise, Flash pulled the seat belt and held it out to her. She'd never had anyone do that before. It was...nice. Once she was buckled in, Flash shut the door and walked around to the other side.

He started the SUV and they were on their way. They didn't speak much as he drove her to her apartment in La Jolla. She gave him directions and before she was ready, he was pulling into her parking lot.

A ball of dread sat in her throat, and it was all Kelli could do not to burst into tears. She was feeling extremely emotional. It was silly. She was safe, not buried underground, her belly was full, and her phone was crammed with numbers from who she hoped were a bunch of new friends. But the thought of walking away from Flash was actually painful.

He went around to the back and got her suitcase someone had obviously put into his SUV, pulling the handle out after he'd placed it on the ground. Then he walked toward her, stopping a couple of feet away and holding out his hand.

He didn't speak, didn't simply grab her, he waited for her to reach out to him.

Which Kelli did without hesitation.

It wasn't even a question about whether he was going to walk her to her door. This wasn't like a first date, where she would be leery of letting a man she'd just met know where she lived. This was Flash. They'd been through hell together. She had no qualms about him knowing which apartment was hers.

Her complex was several stories high, and she was on the fourth floor. She had a great view and could just see the ocean between two other buildings. It wasn't super fancy, all the apartments had outside doors accessed via long walkways on opposite sides of the building. She'd heard some people complain that the complex felt like a huge motel, but Kelli had always loved it. Enjoyed being able to get fresh air when the ocean breezes were kicking.

Neither spoke in the elevator. Kelli didn't know what to say, anyway. Thank you? Don't go? I had a good time? None of those options seemed terribly appropriate.

Flash walked her to her door and stood back as she used her keys to open the lock. She pulled her suitcase into the small foyer, then turned to face Flash.

To her surprise, he'd stepped into her personal space while she was dealing with her bag. She let out a small, surprised gasp—and then his lips were on hers.

The kiss went from zero to one hundred in milliseconds. Kelli gripped Flash tightly as he bent her backward. She loved when he did that. Loved the feeling of weightlessness as she hung in his arms. She had no fear that he'd drop her. None at all.

They were both breathing hard when he finally lifted his head and brought her upright. But he didn't move his arms from around her.

"This isn't the end of us," he said gruffly.

"Okay."

"I told you that I wanted to take you out when we got home, and I do. I will."

"Okay."

"But I'm thinking you need some time."

"Time?" Kelli asked, confused.

"What we went through...it was intense. I'm not trying to be a jerk when I say this, but you relied on me to get you through much of it."

He wasn't wrong. Kelli didn't take offense.

"So I want you to be sure that it's *me* you really want to spend time with. Now that we're back in the real world, your feelings might change. You could realize that you want nothing to do with a military man. I'm gone a lot. Sometimes we have to leave at a moment's notice. I won't be here every single night, won't always be around to do the things most boyfriends do."

"Are you trying to talk me *out* of dating you?" Kelli asked. She was confused.

"No. I'm just being real. I don't want you putting me up on some pedestal because of our ordeal, and then being disappointed when you find out that I'm just a man. Someone with real flaws who does things that'll annoy you."

"I know who you are, Wade Gordon," Kelli said softly. "I don't need to wait."

His fingers tightened on her waist before loosening. "I need you to be sure," Flash said. "Because the way I feel about you...it would kill me if you decided that I'm not who you want to be with, after all. If our time together in Jamaica colored your version of the real-life man."

Kelli wasn't thrilled with his request, but she understood it. "And you might come to realize that I'm not who you thought I was either," she said with a small nod.

It looked like he wanted to say something, but instead just pressed his lips together.

"One week?" she suggested.

"One week," he agreed.

"All right."

"Okay."

"Can we...talk though?"

"Talk?"

"Yeah. Text. Call. It feels...*wrong* to just cut off all contact," Kelli told him.

"I'd like that. There are times I won't be available because I'm in meetings or something, but if you need anything, I'll do my best to get back to you as soon as I can."

"My life isn't that exciting, Flash. I'm not going to have anything come up where I need you to get back to me that second."

"Even so, I'm always available to you, Kelli. No matter what."

He was making it even harder to agree to his stupid week-long break. She nodded.

"In a week, I'll pick you up and give you a tour of Riverton. Show you Julie's shop, my favorite little beach, maybe take you to the naval base. We can have lunch somewhere...and if you want, we can go back to my apartment and watch a movie or something afterward."

"I'd like that." And she would. Especially the go-back-to-his-apartment part. She'd already come to the conclusion that she wanted this man. All of him. Naked and over her. Or under her. It didn't matter. She'd never desired anyone as badly as she did Flash. Sleeping with him had been nice, but falling asleep after he'd been deep inside her body, after he'd hopefully made her come? That would be heaven.

They stood there staring at each other for a beat before Flash took a deep breath. Then he leaned down and kissed her again. It wasn't as passionate as other kisses they'd shared, but it was no less knee-buckling.

"One week," he said softly as he backed away from her.

Kelli couldn't speak. All she could do was nod.

Then he was gone. Heading back down the walkway.

Kelli shut and locked her door, then she put her back to it and slid down until she was sitting on the floor. Wrapping her arms around her updrawn knees, she lowered her forehead and took several deep breaths. She didn't want to cry. She'd done enough of that. Flash hadn't said goodbye forever. Just for a week. She could understand him wanting her to be sure that she really did want to see him again, and not in the context of a savior. But that didn't mean it didn't suck.

Because while Kelli definitely thought of Flash as her savior, he was so much more than that. He wasn't perfect. Neither was she. They were flawed humans who'd been through an intense experience together, and who'd forged a bond.

A bond Kelli was sure would become stronger as time went by, instead of weaker. But if Flash needed time, she'd give him that.

Taking a deep breath, she stood and grabbed her suitcase handle. She brought it straight to the closet in the hallway, where her washer and dryer were stacked. She unzipped it and loaded all her clothes into the washer...minus the bathing suit and cover-up she'd left in the trash at the resort.

She took out her toiletries and other random items and put them away in her bathroom. Then she dragged the suitcase into her large bedroom closet and shoved it into the back corner. Finally, she sat on her bed and stared into space for a long while.

Her ringing phone scared the crap out of her, partly because she'd been lost in thought, and partly because no one ever called her. Looking down, Kelli smiled when she saw Flash's name on the screen.

"Did you forget something?" she asked in lieu of greeting.

"Nope. Just wanted to hear your voice."

The grin on her face widened.

"You in bed yet?"

"No. Just put my clothes in the washer and finished unpacking. You home?"

"Almost."

The conversation continued as Flash arrived at his apartment, went inside, unpacked, then fixed himself something to eat. Kelli got herself something small to eat as well, then got changed for bed. They talked about nothing and everything. There were no awkward silences.

It wasn't until Flash said, "I should let you go," that Kelli realized how long they'd been talking.

"You have to get up early tomorrow...or rather, today?"

"Yeah. We have PT in a couple hours."

"PT? You don't get a day off after what happened?"

Flash chuckled. "Nope. I also have to meet with my commander. Give my report. And he needs to know Jeckle is in the States. Not sure what, if anything, will come of that, but the fact that the man tried to ransom US government property is probably a crime."

"Not sure I like you referring to yourself as government property," Kelli mumbled. Flash had told her earlier that the man who'd kidnapped them had fled Jamaica and flown to LA. She wasn't thrilled about that, but she was determined not to give the man any more head space than he'd already taken from her.

He chuckled. "It is what it is. I'll call you tomorrow?"

"Yes, please."

"What's on your plate?"

"Nothing as interesting as your day. I'll probably go see my mom. Then talk to my boss at the travel agency, see if I still have a job, since I was supposed to work today and when I didn't call in, I might have been terminated."

"Surely after they find out that you were kidnapped, they won't fire you? Or at least they'll *rehire* you."

"Maybe. I'm not sure I want to go back anyway. I think I might stop by the community college and talk to an advisor. It's about time I figured out what to do with my life. If what happened taught me anything, it's that I want to make a difference in my little corner of the world. I don't want to spend the rest of my life working jobs I don't enjoy."

"I think that's great. We can talk tomorrow night, and you can tell me all about what you found out. I'll be your sounding board."

Contentment spread throughout Kelli's veins. "Thanks."

"Sleep well. It's gonna feel weird to not have you sleeping on top of me tonight."

"Yeah."

"We'll talk tomorrow," Flash told her.

"Tomorrow."

"Bye."

"Bye."

Kelli hung up and realized she was smiling. She should've been asleep hours ago, but at least she could sleep in and didn't have to get up at five to go work out like Flash did.

Grabbing an extra pillow, she hugged it to her chest as she closed her eyes. It wasn't the same as using *Flash* as a pillow, but it would have to do...at least for another week.

Then all bets were off.

CHAPTER FOURTEEN

The following week was surreal for Kelli. She was plunked back down into her life, and while she felt as if she was a changed person, nothing else around her seemed to change. Her annoying next-door neighbor still played his music too loud, her mom, while happy she was all right, hadn't really asked much about what happened and was back to being consumed with her own life. Traffic still sucked, the weather was still beautiful, and bills still needed to be paid.

One thing that *had* changed...Kelli had indeed been fired for not calling in and missing work. It didn't matter that she'd literally been buried alive in a foreign country. Apparently, policies were policies. But she wasn't upset about it. She'd done what she told Flash she was going to do...she went to the community college not too far from her apartment and met with an academic advisor. She wasn't any closer to deciding what she wanted to do with her life, but it still felt as if she'd made a positive step forward.

She also seemed to have an entire girl posse of friends. That was *definitely* new. She'd received either texts or emails each day. Remi was the first to check on her, letting her know that if she wanted to talk about what happened, she was there. After all, she'd been through something similar, even if she was buried only a tiny fraction of the time Kelli had been underground. Wren and Josie had also texted. Out of the blue, Addison offered to bake her cookies or a cake. And Maggie, even though she was dealing with some morning sickness, had emailed and said she'd love to get together the next time she headed up to LA for a meeting. Apparently, that was where her biological father and brothers lived, and where she had to attend meetings every now and then for her job.

And it wasn't only Flash's teammates' women who'd contacted her. Caroline, Julie, Jessyka...she'd gotten occasional texts from all of the older former SEAL wives, as well.

Having so much support and friendship felt like a dream come true. Kelli wasn't sure *why* everyone was being so nice to her, but she wasn't going to do anything that might make them change their minds about being her friend.

But the best change was that, every night, she talked to Flash for about three hours...or more. One evening while they were FaceTiming, they'd talked so long she'd fallen asleep on him. When she woke up in the middle of the night, she looked at her screen and saw that Flash had propped up his phone on the table next to his bed and left his lights on, so she could watch *him* sleep.

Some people might think that was weird, but for Kelli, it was...intimate. She liked it. A lot. She'd ended the call and sent him a text apologizing for falling asleep, and making a comment about how empty his bed looked with only him in it.

It was a risky move, but given how much they talked, and how often Flash reminded her of the hours left in the week before he was taking her on a date, she felt pretty confident that what she'd said wasn't out of line.

Today, Flash had a meeting that he said would run a little late. They were in the middle of planning their next mission, which, honestly, kind of worried Kelli. But she refused to let what he did for a living discourage her. After all, him being a SEAL was the sole reason they'd survived their ordeal. Without his survival knowledge, their situation would've been a lot worse. And they certainly wouldn't have been rescued as quickly as they had without the resources and knowhow of his friends.

If she wanted any kind of relationship with Flash, she'd have to figure out how to live with him being gone on dangerous missions. She decided talking with the women who'd been through it already, and who obviously had wonderful relationships with their men, would be a good place to start. She had a lot of questions.

But she was also jumping the gun. Flash was right. They'd been through something extreme and traumatic together. More for her than him, he was used to that kind of situation, but still.

She had every intention of dating Flash. Doing normal guy-girl things. Dinners, movies, hanging out, getting to know him even more. She wasn't going to jump into a relationship simply because she was grateful he was with her when the worst had happened in Jamaica.

But...the man ticked all her boxes. He was kind, patient, hot as hell...

Kelli wrinkled her nose, a little disgusted with herself for that last thought. Honestly, looks didn't matter as much as other positive traits. It was possible he could go bald, or get fat, or his ears would grow three sizes as he aged.

Giggling, Kelli put the bags of groceries she'd bought today on the counter. She was being stupid. Thinking about what Flash may or may not look like as he aged was ridiculous. What mattered was the kind of man he was. Did he have a temper? She didn't think so, but time would tell. Was he possessive? Or *overly* so? Would he get annoyed that she had plenty of money in the bank and didn't need to be "taken care of"?

Deep down, regardless of the answers, everything in her was

screaming that Flash was the real deal. That he could be the man she spent the rest of her life with. It was too fast, they'd just met, but circumstances being what they were, they'd gotten to know the important things about each other very quickly.

Flash made her feel protected. He paid attention when she spoke and didn't look at his phone or everywhere around him, as if trying to find something more interesting to do. When she was with him, she felt as if she was the center of his world. And she hoped he felt the same way. She wanted any man she was with to have no doubts that she was right where she wanted to be.

Which she knew was why he was giving them both a week's time-out.

She smiled at that. Was it really a time-out when they talked for hours every night and constantly texted each other to ask how the other person was doing? She wasn't sure. All she knew was that she missed Flash. Even talking to him didn't feel as if it was enough. She wanted to see him. Touch him. The feel of her hand in his was the ultimate in comfort for her now.

Just as she'd finished cutting up vegetables and chicken and arranging them on a cookie sheet to bake, her phone vibrated.

Looking at the counter, she saw Flash had texted her.

Flash: Bad news, won't be able to call until late. New intel just arrived and we're staying later than planned to analyze it.

Disappointment hit Kelli, but she pushed it down. She had no idea what information he'd received, but she was proud of him for doing what he could to keep the world safe.

. . .

Kelli: It's okay. I don't have any plans tonight. Am going to think a bit more about what kind of career I want, maybe watch another episode of *Alone* so we can talk about it later.

Flash: Can't wait to see what you think about who taps out tonight. And it's been six days. I'm going to come up and take you out tomorrow night...if that's okay with you. Think about where you want to eat.

Kelli's nipples immediately hardened. Apparently, when Flash said something, he was serious. He'd said a week, and tomorrow was a week. She was more than ready to see him again. To see if the connection they had was real. She thought it was, but she'd find out for sure tomorrow. She couldn't wait.

Kelli: It's definitely okay with me.

Flash: Good. I'll text when I'm done here. If you're asleep, not a big deal. We can talk tomorrow.

It was a big deal to Kelli. She hadn't realized he might be *that* late. She liked her sleep, but lately she'd been staying up later because of their calls.

Kelli: Okay. I'll miss talking to you.

Flash: Not as much as I'll miss talking to you. Gotta go. Getting the stink eye from Kevlar.

Kelli: Later

Flash: Later

. . .

Kelli sighed. She wished it was tomorrow already. There were plenty of amazing restaurants she could take him to, she'd just have to wait and see what he was in the mood for and what he liked.

The rest of the evening went by fairly quickly. Her dinner was delicious, even if it was a bit lonely. She'd gotten used to eating while talking to Flash. The episode of *Alone* was exciting and she couldn't wait to discuss it with him. She was amazed at how resilient the contestants were. They made it seem as if camping outside in negative temperatures wasn't a big deal. Not to mention hunting and killing squirrels and other animals and attempting to fish when conditions, frankly, sucked.

She supposed some people would say what she'd done was just as amazing, but she'd been with Flash, who'd done all the work. She could probably survive living in sub-freezing temps if Flash was with her. She could sit in the shelter—that he made—and cook the animals he caught and skinned.

Kelli laughed at herself. No, she'd hate that. Wouldn't like feeling as if she wasn't pulling her weight.

Looking at her watch, she was surprised to see it was nine o'clock. Not terribly late, considering what time she'd been going to sleep this past week, but late for Flash to still be at work.

Kelli turned off the TV and headed to her bedroom. She put on the long-sleeve top and boy shorts she wore to bed before padding back into the hallway, to the only bathroom in her apartment. When she was finished, she climbed into bed, crawled under the covers, and put her phone on the nightstand. She grabbed her tablet and brought up the book she'd been reading.

She didn't think she'd be able to pay much attention, since she was waiting to hear from Flash, so she was pleasantly surprised when she got lost in the story.

Flash eventually sent a text over an hour later, saying he was exhausted and heading home to bed. But he promised to call early tomorrow so they could arrange a time for him to come over and take her to dinner.

Instead of going to sleep herself, Kelli continued to read. She wanted to find out who the bad guy was in her book.

And that was why she was still awake around midnight... when an out-of-place sound from the front of her apartment caught her attention.

Kelli froze, tilting her head, as if that would make it easier for her to hear.

The tell-tale squeak of the hinges on her apartment door had her adrenaline immediately spiking.

She'd locked the door, she knew she had, but had she thrown the dead bolt? Put the chain on? She didn't think so. Her hands had been full of the bags she was carrying. She had a feeling she'd forgotten.

No one except her mother had a spare key to her apartment, so whoever had just entered wasn't anyone she'd want to come face-to-face with in a dark apartment in the middle of the night.

She was moving before she thought about what she was doing. Kelli leaped out of bed, looking around frantically. Where should she go? If she left the bedroom, whoever had broken in would see her immediately. It wasn't that big of a space. The bathroom was in the hall, so that was also out. Not that anywhere in there would make a good hiding place. And she couldn't hide under her bed because it was a captain's bed...there were drawers filling in the space.

For a second, she panicked—then Kelli swore she heard Flash's voice in her head. Telling her to take a breath. To be smart.

Whipping around, Kelli quickly and quietly remade her bed, pulling the covers up so it looked like she hadn't been there at all. Of course, the sheets were still warm, but she couldn't do anything about that.

Grabbing her phone, she went to the only place that was an option.

Her closet.

It was fairly large, something she'd been thrilled about when she first rented the place. She had two racks of clothes against one wall—her shirts on the higher one, her pants on the lower. She could hide behind the pants, but there wasn't much room and whoever had broken in would surely spot her.

Her frantic gaze finally landed on the suitcase she'd unpacked a week ago. It was lying in the back corner where she'd left it, too lazy to so much as zip it closed, much less put it in the hall closet where it was usually stored.

Moving instinctively, and thanking her lucky stars that she was only five-two, she opened the top, stepped inside, and crouched down. She curled into a fetal position, lowered the lid, then fumbled with the zipper.

Whoever had broken in was moving down the hall. She could hear their footsteps coming closer and closer.

Finally, she was able to get hold of the tab and partially close the zipper around the suitcase.

She held her breath when she heard a male voice swear as he entered her bedroom.

Kelli had never been so scared. Not even when she'd had a gun pointed in her face. And she realized it was because at least then, Flash had been there. His presence hadn't made it any more or less likely that she'd be shot, but simply going through that experience with someone else made it not quite as terrifying.

Lying in the dark, curled into a ball, hearing whoever was in her apartment throwing things around, was *more* than terrifying. It almost paralyzed her with fear.

Feeling her hand throbbing, Kelli suddenly realized that she was gripping her phone so tightly, it was surely leaving marks on her palm.

Her phone! In her panic, she'd completely forgotten she'd grabbed her cell from the table next to her bed!

She was about to dial 9-1-1 when the intruder entered her closet. The light came on and Kelli realized she was seconds away from being discovered and probably raped and maybe killed.

The man—she could definitely tell it was a guy now, because he was constantly swearing and muttering under his breath—shuffled through her clothes. Then a large crash made Kelli flinch in her hiding place. She felt a weight settle on top of the suitcase. He'd pulled one of the entire racks of clothes off, and it had obviously landed right where she was hiding.

But that was good. Not the destruction he was wreaking on her belongings, but that she was buried under clothes. It meant he had no reason to believe she was there, in that suitcase. Right under his nose.

She still refused to risk moving even an inch while he was in the same room. The light from the phone screen might show through the open portion of suitcase. Or he'd see the clothes moving if she shifted even a fraction. No, she had to stay completely still and silent.

Of course, right then, her nose started to itch.

If she sneezed, she was as good as dead.

Closing her eyes tightly, Kelli did her best to suppress her body's involuntary reaction to her surroundings.

To her immense relief, the man left the closet. She could still hear him throwing things around in her bedroom. So the danger was still very real.

Taking a chance, Kelli looked at the phone she still held in a death grip and tapped the screen. The light made her wince, but she quickly turned it down, brought up her recent calls, and clicked on Flash's name.

It was stupid. She should call 9-1-1. But the first and only person she thought to call was Flash. He'd help her. He knew where she lived. He wouldn't hesitate to come. Of that, she had no doubt.

Awkwardly, she brought the phone up to her ear, because there was no way she could put it on speaker, not if she wanted to stay hidden. It rang twice before Flash answered.

"Kelli? What's wrong? Are you okay?"

Opening her mouth to tell him that, no, she definitely wasn't okay and she needed him, she froze when the intruder reentered the closet.

"Kelli?"

His voice sounded loud. Too loud. But once more, Kelli was afraid to move even one muscle. Why had the man come back? Did he know she was there? Had he figured out there was literally no other place for her to hide?

"If you don't answer me, I'm coming over. Understand?"

Yes, she understood, and she closed her eyes as a tear escaped. Kelli's breaths were coming faster and faster. She felt as if she wasn't getting enough air.

Flash must've heard her hyperventilating through the speaker, because his voice calmed and his tone lowered. "I've got you, Kelli. I'm coming. Slow your breathing down. You can do this."

She couldn't. She couldn't do this! Panic was taking hold. At one point, whoever was in her closet actually kicked the edge of the suitcase. She was certain he'd figure out that it was much too heavy and he'd find her.

But he simply swore some more, then left again.

"I'm in my car now. Hold on, Kelli. Hold on."

Kelli thought for sure whoever had broken in would leave now, but instead, she heard him continuing to stomp around her apartment, smashing more stuff.

It would take Flash almost half an hour to get to her place. Maybe less since it was the middle of the night and traffic was probably light. But so much could happen in thirty minutes. Or even twenty.

"Scared," she whispered in a voice so low, she was sure Flash wouldn't be able to hear her.

But somehow he did.

"I know. I can hear how fast you're breathing. What's going on? Did you have a nightmare?"

"No. Break-in."

"Fuck, someone broke into your apartment? I need to call Dude, he lives closer to where you are."

Panic almost overwhelmed Kelli. He couldn't hang up! If he did, she'd completely lose it. He was the only thing keeping her from springing out of her hiding place and running screaming through her apartment, trying to reach the door.

"I'm going to patch him into the call. I'm not hanging up. Hang on."

Relief made her dizzy. Or maybe that was lack of oxygen. She wasn't sure. All she knew was that he wasn't going to hang up.

"Dude? Flash. I need you. Someone's broken into Kelli's apartment. She's hiding."

"Address?"

Flash recited it to his friend.

"Where are you?" Dude asked.

"On my way but I've still got fifteen miles or so."

"Right. I can be there in ten minutes."

"I may or may not beat you there. Kelli?"

"Yeah?" she whispered, feeling so much stronger knowing someone—two someones—were on their way.

"Is he still there?"

She paused and strained to hear something, anything. Then, to her surprise, she didn't hear the intruder...but she smelled something.

Bacon.

The asshole was *cooking*? She had some of that microwaveable bacon in her fridge. She preferred the real stuff, but when she had a hankering for bacon, it was easy and less messy to cook a piece or two in the microwave.

"Kelli?" Flash's agitated voice brought her back to the conversation.

"Yes," she said.

"All right. Stay where you are. Stay quiet. We'll be there soon. You're doing good. So good, sweetheart."

She didn't feel as if she was doing good. Her nose still itched, her body felt as if it was cramping because of the position she was in, and breathing still wasn't easy, especially now that she'd gone and started crying.

"Do we know who it is?" Dude asked.

"No."

That had Kelli thinking. Who *was* in her apartment? What did they want? She was on the fourth floor. In the middle of the hall. Not exactly a prime position for someone to choose to break in. Had they watched her? Did they know she was a woman living alone? She hadn't noticed anything out of the ordinary, but that didn't mean much. She was no Navy SEAL, she wasn't trained to look for anyone who might be casing her apartment.

It could be the maintenance guy. He was kind of strange. Or the manager, he had a master key as well...but unlikely at this time of night.

The question of who could be in her apartment, who'd trashed it, who was in her kitchen even now, microwaving *bacon* of all things, was a complete mystery.

"I'm hanging up. I'll see you shortly," Dude said succinctly.

"Kelli?" Flash asked after a moment. "You still there?"

"Yes," she whispered.

"One of my favorite memories of Jamaica was Fred the grasshopper. Remember?"

She did. It had been her turn to come up with a fairy tale.

She'd made up the silly story about Fred, and Flash had laughed so hard.

"I think you should write it down. It would make a great children's book. Have you thought about doing that for a living? Telling stories?"

She knew what he was doing. Trying to distract her. Amazingly, it was working. Flash continued to talk to her in an even, calm tone as he made his way toward her. She couldn't hear anything from her bedroom or beyond now. And the smell of bacon had diminished. There was no telling if the person who'd broken in was still there or if he'd left.

Suddenly the image of Flash bursting through the front door, only to be met by a guy with a gun, had her shaking almost uncontrollably.

"I don't know if he has a gun," she whispered. "I didn't see him."

"It's okay, Kelli. I've got this. Don't worry."

Don't worry. Yeah, right. Kelli was one big ball of worry at the moment.

"I'm going to be there in three minutes. No matter what you hear, I want you to stay hidden. Don't come out until I give the all clear. I can't do what I've been trained to do if I'm worrying about you getting hurt. Okay? Will you stay put until you hear me call out Fred? I figure that's as good a code word as any."

His words ramped up her stress level, but Kelli managed to say, "Yes."

"Good girl. This will be over soon. I promise. You've been so brave. So smart to hide where he couldn't find you. I'm impressed. Okay, I'm pulling in. Dude just arrived too. I'm going to hang up, but I'm here. You'll see me soon."

Kelli swallowed hard. "Be careful," she whispered.

"I will. I have a hot date tonight that I'm not going to miss for anything. Soon, sweetheart."

The line went dead. Shockingly, Kelli found that she was

smiling at his date comment. How the hell had he done that? Made her *smile* in the middle of what was a truly terrifying situation? He was stressed, she could hear it in his voice. And yet he was still focused and calm. Much as he'd been in that bus in Jamaica.

Flash was always in control—and *that's* why Kelli could smile. Because he was good at what he did. And that was the reason she'd called him instead of the police. If whoever had broken in was still there, Flash would take care of him. Subdue him. Hold him until the police could arrive and arrest him. She just had to stay quiet and hidden until he said the code word.

Taking a deep breath, Kelli strained to hear anything from her hiding spot. The suspense was killing her, but she wouldn't move, not one inch, until Flash said it was all right. She trusted him with her life. Period.

CHAPTER FIFTEEN

Flash leaped out of his SUV and nodded at Dude. They took the stairs up to the fourth floor of Kelli's apartment two at a time. There was no one around. The place was deserted, but that didn't mean whoever had broken into Kelli's apartment wasn't still in there.

Acting as if they'd worked together all their lives—once a SEAL, always a SEAL—Dude went to one side of the door and Flash took the other. It was obvious the door had been tampered with. There were what looked like pry marks on the doorjamb and the door wasn't closed all the way.

Flash held his pistol at the ready, as did Duke, and his fellow SEAL's narrowed eyes and pressed lips indicated he was just as prepared to act, no matter what they might find inside.

Dude nodded at the door, then at Flash. He held up three fingers.

Flash returned his nod and stepped back a bit, giving the other man room to work.

Dude squared himself with the door, counted down on his fingers—three, two, one—then lifted his leg and kicked the door as hard as he could.

It flew open, slamming into the wall in the small foyer of Kelli's apartment.

Strangely, the smell of bacon was the first thing Flash noticed as he quickly swung into the apartment, weapon at the ready.

He and Dude moved forward, scanning the living area and kitchen. It was empty. Ignoring the absolute destruction, Flash moved down the hall. Checking the bathroom and finding it empty, they continued to the master bedroom.

The sheets and blankets had been pulled off the bed, the tables on either side kicked over and smashed. Knickknacks and books were strewn everywhere. Pictures that had clearly once been on the wall were now on the floor, stomped on, leaving broken glass behind. The bookcase had also been knocked over.

Whoever had done this was...angry. This wasn't a random break-in, Flash would bet his life on it.

Dude moved to check the closet, and when Flash reached him, he saw that it had suffered the same kind of destruction as the rest of the apartment.

The rods had been ripped down and clothes were strewn all over the sizable room. Flash shook his head at the needless destruction. It didn't seem to him that whoever had done this was looking for anything valuable. He'd just broken stuff and destroyed Kelli's belongings because he could. It made the situation more dangerous in Flash's eyes. If the intruder had no intention of stealing anything...what *was* his intention?

"Where is she?" Dude asked.

Flash had no idea where Kelli had hidden herself. Granted, he and Dude hadn't done an extensive search, but he hadn't seen any place where she might have squirreled herself away.

"Check the bathroom again?" he suggested.

When they did and still found no sign of Kelli, Flash's adrenaline spiked even higher. And it was already pretty damn high. Where was she? Had she left? Had whoever done this found her?

Had the intruder taken her down via the elevator while he and Dude were running up the stairs?

No...he was sure that hadn't happened. He hadn't hung up with her until he'd pulled into the parking lot. And he hadn't seen anyone lurking around, hadn't seen Kelli being forced into a vehicle or carried over someone's shoulder. She was here somewhere. She simply had to be.

Then he remembered what he'd told her. That he'd give her the all-clear code word. He'd totally forgotten in the heat of the moment.

"Fred!" he called out loudly.

"What the hell?" Dude asked, giving him a look.

"Fred!" Flash yelled again, walking into the bedroom.

Then he heard it. A rustling coming from the closet.

"We checked the closet, right?" he asked Dude, even as he was striding toward it.

What he saw made his legs go weak. The large mound of clothing in the corner was moving slightly. "Help me!" he exclaimed, dropping to his knees and frantically clearing the space of the clothes.

Dude was at his side in a heartbeat, pulling parts of a rack, pants and shirts, and even shoes off of the massive pile. Under it was a suitcase.

"Kelli?" Flash asked in disbelief, even as tiny fingers appeared in the opening between the top and bottom of the case. Next he saw an eyeball, and finally Kelli's body as the top of the suitcase flew open to reveal her hiding space.

"Holy shit!" Dude exclaimed.

Flash was already reaching for the woman who'd crawled under his skin and refused to leave. She threw herself up and out of the suitcase, and he ended up on his ass on the closet floor with a shaking, freaked-out woman in his arms.

"You came," she whispered into his neck.

"Of course I did," he soothed. His own heart was beating out of control. It was just settling in that he could've lost her. That whoever had broken in could've seriously hurt her. Assaulted her in a way that she might never have recovered from.

Or even killed her, if the destruction the intruder had caused was any indication of his rage.

He didn't know how long they'd sat on the floor of the closet, just holding each other, but eventually Dude walked back in—when he'd left, Flash had no idea—and said, "The police are on their way. And I called Kevlar. I know it's two-thirty in the morning, but your team would kick my ass, *and* yours, if they weren't informed as soon as possible about what happened here."

He wasn't wrong. If the tables were turned and he found out something had happened to any of his teammates or their women, and he hadn't been called, he'd be furious...and a little hurt. "Thank you," Flash said a little belatedly.

"At the risk of sounding like Tex, don't fucking thank me," Dude complained.

Flash found himself smiling at that. Tex was notorious for being cranky when someone tried to thank him for anything. It was part of his charm.

"Right. Can you please help me up then?" Flash asked. He had no intention of letting go of Kelli anytime soon.

Dude nodded, taking Flash by the upper arms. He hauled him upright while he was holding Kelli as if he was picking up nothing heavier than a piece of paper. "Good?" he asked gruffly.

"Good." He cradled Kelli in his arms and carried her through her bedroom. Dude walked in front of him and cleared a space on the couch. Flash sat with her on his lap. Throughout it all, Kelli didn't protest, didn't say much of anything, and it was worrying him.

"Kelli?" he promoted.

She finally lifted her head and met his gaze. "You came," she repeated.

"I'll always come if I'm able to," he said. Flash wanted to tell her that he'd always come for her without question, but the truth was, there were times he'd be physically unable to be by her side. But she needed to know that even if *he* couldn't be there, his friends would. Like Dude.

As if she could read his mind, Kelli looked over at Dude. "I appreciate you getting out of bed in the middle of the night and coming too."

Dude nodded. "As if I'd ever say no."

Then Kelli's gaze shifted, and Flash knew the exact moment the destruction of her things sank in.

"We'll get it all cleaned up," he told her quickly.

She took in her apartment, her head swiveling from side to side. "I heard him out here, the crashes and stuff. I didn't know exactly what he was doing."

"How did you know he wouldn't find you in that suitcase?" Dude asked, as the sound of sirens began to pierce the quiet night.

"I didn't," she said with a small shrug, looking up at him. "I was awake, reading, when I heard my door open. The hinges creak. I got out of bed and realized it was too late to get to the bathroom, or anywhere really. He'd see me as soon as I left the bedroom. I made my bed, hoping he'd think I wasn't home, then went into the closet. I was going to hide behind the clothes. Thank goodness I didn't, since he pulled down the rods. Then I saw my suitcase. I usually stow it in the closet in the hall, but I'd been too lazy this week to do that yet. I climbed in...almost couldn't believe I fit...then zipped it as much as I could before he reached the bedroom and held my breath, hoping he wouldn't think to look there."

"And it was a guy? You heard him?" Flash asked.

"It was a guy," she confirmed. "He swore a lot. And..." She paused, lifting her head to sniff the air. "I thought I smelled bacon. I guess he made it before he left?"

Flash was gobsmacked. He'd smelled it as well, but he just

assumed it was the lingering scent from a late-night snack Kelli had made or something. "*Why?* Why would he do that?"

She shrugged. "I have no idea."

"Sorry, I wasn't really asking you for an answer. Was just expressing my shock."

"You need to be sure to tell the detectives. Maybe he left some fingerprints on the fridge or packaging."

Kelli nodded, and Flash noted the look of shock settling on her face. She wasn't hurt, but mentally, she was dealing with a lot coming at her in a short period of time. The break-in, the destruction of her things, the thought that whoever had broken in was still out there.

"After we talk to the cops, I'm taking you home."

She looked up at him in confusion. "Home?"

"My home."

The relief that flashed across her face was reinforcement that he'd made the right decision.

"Okay," she said softly.

At that moment, two police officers appeared in the doorway, their weapons drawn and pointed at the three of them.

"Hands up!" one yelled.

Kelli immediately turned her head into Flash's neck once more, even as she obediently thrust both hands up where they could be seen.

Realizing his weapon was still on the floor of Kelli's closet—where he'd put it when he saw that pile of clothing move—Flash lifted his own hands into the air. It didn't take long for the cops to be reassured that they were no threat.

It took longer for Kelli to tell them the story of what happened. It took even longer to *retell* the story once the detectives arrived. Then when NCIS showed up, she had to recount the evening all over again.

By that time, Kevlar had arrived with the rest of his team and the sun was peeking over the horizon. Kelli had literally been up all night, and Flash could tell she was on her last leg. He needed to get her someplace safe where she could sleep.

Dude had been the one to tell Kevlar and the others what happened, so Kelli didn't have to tell it a fourth time. It wasn't until she was talking to her apartment manager that Kevlar approached Flash...and reminded him of something that hit him hard.

"Brant Williams is still in the wind. And he took both your IDs in Jamaica, which have your addresses. Could this have been him?"

Flash's first inclination was to say no. No way. But he stopped himself.

Why *couldn't* it be him? The man had to be pissed that his kidnapping plan was foiled. Not only that, but the bus he'd probably paid a good amount of money to modify and bury was no longer viable for future kidnapping plots. He'd had to leave the country to escape the long arm of the law and was now a wanted fugitive. So why wouldn't he come after Kelli in the States? Or Flash, for that matter?

"Fuck," he said belatedly. It wouldn't be safe to bring Kelli back to his apartment. Not if this was Williams...not when the man knew where he lived.

"Here. Stay at my place," Smiley said, holding out a set of keys to Flash. "He doesn't know where I live, and I can stay at your place. Sit in wait. If he does dare show his face, he'll regret it."

It was a very generous offer but Flash hesitated, reluctant to put Smiley in danger, even if he knew his friend could handle himself. Plus...he really wanted to get his hands on Williams.

"Take them," Kevlar prodded. "It's a good solution. Since the rest of us have our women to look after, it makes sense."

Because Kelli's safety was more important than his own pride —and his desire to take Brant Williams down himself—Flash took the keys. "Thank you," he told Smiley. "Be careful."

"It's not me who should be careful," Smiley said with a pissed-off glint in his eye. "And don't thank me yet," his friend said. "You haven't seen the place. In fact, it kind of looks a little like this." Smiley gestured to the mess around them with his head.

Flash groaned as his teammates chuckled.

He saw Kelli heading toward him and immediately turned his back on his friends to meet her halfway.

"I feel bad that the police are asking the manager so many questions," she said, when Flash took her hands in his.

"Don't. He has a key to your place, it's normal for them to question him."

"Still."

Flash didn't feel bad in the least. In fact, he was pretty sure Preacher and MacGyver were making plans to talk to the man themselves after the cops left.

"You ready to head out?" he asked.

Kelli looked around her apartment. There were still crime techs coming and going.

"Remi, Wren, and Addison are coming over in a bit to start going through your things...separating out what can be salvaged from what will have to be thrown away. Wolf and Mozart are going to replace your locks, probably with something that will take four keys and a fingerprint scan to open. Josie and Maggie will talk to Julie about replacing any clothing that was damaged, and they'll wash the rest so everything's fresh and clean."

"Oh. They don't have to do that," Kelli said.

"Of course they don't. They want to."

"I just..." Her eyes filled with tears.

Yeah, she was definitely at the end of her rope. "Come here," Flash said, pulling her into him and holding her tight.

"I don't know what to say. To do."

"You don't have to say or do anything. What you need is some sleep. Things will look brighter when you wake up."

He felt her take a deep breath. "Are we still going to your place?"

This was the part he didn't really want to tell her...but he wouldn't keep secrets from this woman. "Change of plans. We're going to stay at Smiley's apartment for a while."

She frowned up at him. "Why?"

"We don't know who broke in. But Williams hasn't been found yet."

"And he knows where we both live," Kelli finished for him.

Flash should've known he wouldn't have to explain. His woman was smart. "Exactly."

She sighed. "All right. But I hate feeling as if we're kicking Smiley out of his apartment."

"We aren't. He's more than happy to stay at my place. In fact, he *hopes* Williams is behind this and dares to come to my apartment."

"I don't want him getting hurt," Kelli said softly.

"No way in hell is anyone getting the drop on Smiley. He's been a mean son-of-a-bitch lately, ever since Bree Haynes disappeared like a puff of smoke again."

"That's the woman he found in Vegas, right?"

"Right. And she's the one who saved Ellory and Yana from the man who'd sold them for their organs."

Kelli frowned. "Is there anything we can do to help?"

Lord, Flash adored this woman. She was in the middle of her own shitshow, and yet she was still thinking about others. "No. Bree's clearly in some kind of trouble, but she also knows a thing or two about staying under the radar. We're all hoping she musters up the courage to talk to one of us at some point."

Kelli swayed in his arms, and Flash was officially done talking. He put an arm around her shoulders and physically turned her toward the door. They'd already gotten the okay to leave from the detectives, who had both their contact info and would get in touch when they had any information about the break-in or if they had more questions.

Flash waved at his teammates, and they all gave him chin-lifts in return. Kevlar had promised he'd talk to their commander and let him know what was going on, and why Flash wouldn't be at work that day. The others were going to be helping the women get Kelli's belongings straightened out. There would probably be lots of food being delivered to Smiley's apartment by that afternoon, if he had to guess.

Flash had never been as grateful for a group of friends as he was for his, right about now.

Dude approached when they reached Flash's SUV. Kelli turned to him and, as if she'd known the man for years, gave him a long, heartfelt hug. "Thank you for coming when Flash called."

"You need anything? *You* call. If Flash and his team are deployed, my friends and I are always available. No matter what. Understand?"

"Yes, sir," Kelli sassed lightly, smiling up at him. But what she saw in his face made her amusement fade.

"Never gets old," Dude said with a small chuckle, before turning her back toward Flash and giving her a gentle push into his arms. "Take care of her," he ordered, before spinning around and heading across the lot to his own car.

"He's...intense," Kelli muttered.

"You have no idea," Flash said. Everyone knew about Dude's sexual preferences. How he liked to be completely in charge in the bedroom. Sometimes his dominance leaked out in other aspects of his life...and it was obvious that, while Kelli didn't fully understand the vibes he was putting out, she was still affected by them.

"Come on. I need to get you to a bed."

Kelli smiled up at him. "I like the sound of that."

Flash shook his head. He hadn't meant that the way it

sounded, but now that he thought about it, the idea of holding her in his arms as they both slept was extremely appealing.

As he drove them toward Smiley's apartment, Flash's mind turned to the question of who had broken into Kelli's apartment. Why? What did they want? Would they come back?

Was it Williams?

He had too many questions and not enough answers. But whoever it was had failed...because Kelli had held her composure. And if he tried again, he'd find Kelli was no longer alone. Flash vowed to stay by her side until the perp was found.

And if it *was* Williams? The asshole who'd kidnapped them and buried them alive?

He was a dead man. *No one* messed with what was his.

And Kelli Colbert most definitely belonged to Flash.

* * *

Brant Williams scowled as he watched the hubbub die down outside the bitch's apartment. How the fuck had he missed her? Where was she hiding? He'd scoured the apartment and assumed he must've missed her leaving at some point. But he hadn't. She'd been there the whole time! He'd fucked up *another* chance for a big payday.

Yes, he was in the US mostly because he hated that the Navy guy and the bitch had escaped, and because he wanted to prove he was smarter than that asshole and all his friends. But it was expensive in the States. After just a few days, Brant realized the money was too important. He needed it. A lot of it. So he could move on with his life...in luxury, like he deserved. So tonight, he'd planned to take the woman and hold her for ransom, just as he'd intended back home.

Then the Navy guy had come to the rescue.

And in the last week, Brant had learned he wasn't just *any*

Navy guy...he was a fucking SEAL. No wonder he'd been found so damn quickly.

But Brant wasn't giving up. Not yet. He'd be patient. He knew where the SEAL lived. That was probably where he was taking the bitch right now.

Eventually, he'd figure out a way to show both the bitch *and* the SEAL that in the end, *he* was the smarter man. He'd get his money one way or another. And he didn't care who he had to kill for that to happen.

He needed a new plan—*again*—but he'd figure it out. And when he did...both the bitch and Wade fucking Gordon would die. The end goal was money, but almost as important...he wanted those two to pay for fucking up all his original plans.

CHAPTER SIXTEEN

"Where are we going again?"

Flash looked at the woman next to him and was in awe of her all over again. The hits for her just kept on coming, and yet she always bounded back, taking one day at a time. She was exactly the kind of woman he'd been looking for. Someone who didn't sweat the small stuff, sure...but Kelli wasn't even sweating the *big* stuff.

She had every right to be upset. To be lamenting the fact that she couldn't go back to her apartment because the person who'd broken in could still be watching and waiting for her. Didn't cry about life being unfair. Didn't complain about only having enough possessions that could fit into a single suitcase.

She was still friendly, upbeat, and trusting.

And Flash wanted her more with every passing day. It was getting harder and harder to sleep next to her and not take advantage of their situation. Namely, the fact that Smiley's apartment only had one bed...a queen-size at that. Yes, he could sleep on the couch, but Kelli had put her foot down and said that if he took the couch, she'd sleep on the floor. Which was ridiculous.

So every evening since her apartment had been broken into,

they'd crawled into bed together and slept in each other's arms. For five torturous nights now. Flash wasn't sure how much longer he could hold out and not slip his hand under those sexy boy shorts she wore to bed every night...show her just how much he admired and wanted her.

"Flash?"

Oh, she'd asked him a question.

"Aces Bar and Grill. It's owned by Jessyka Sawyer, who's married to Benny. You remember them, right?" When she nodded, he added, "I thought it would do us both some good to get out."

She murmured her agreement. Then changed the subject abruptly. "I think I've decided what I want to do. You know, as a career."

Flash looked over again, this time in surprise. She'd been poring over the literature she'd gotten from the advisor at the community college, and they'd even had a couple of conversations about the pros and cons of a few different jobs. "Yeah?" Flash asked, genuinely interested.

"Uh-huh. Electrician," Kelli said with confidence.

"Wow! Electrician. Okay, how'd you come up with that?"

"I just thought, what's something I could do that would be seriously useful? I mean, there are tons of jobs that are important, but are they truly useful in our own everyday lives? Like... linemen or surgical technologists. They're both vital in our society, but it's not as if I could use those skills when I came home at night. But if I knew the ins and outs of electrical stuff, I could totally help our friends if they needed something looked at, or I could install fancy lights in my apartment. If I ever own a house, I can put up a gazillion holiday lights and know how to manipulate the electrical system so it's not overloaded." She shrugged. "It was either that or plumber...and I think I'd gag if I had to unclog a poopy toilet."

Flash couldn't help but laugh at her verbiage. "I think that's great."

"You do? You aren't just saying that or humoring me?"

"Not at all. If that's what you're interested in, go for it."

"Thanks. I feel good about the decision. I'm going to go back to the community college as soon as I get the chance and see about signing up for classes."

He was proud of her all over again.

"Flash?"

"Yeah?"

"Is the food good at Aces? I'm not trying to be rude by asking, it's just that some bars have great drinks but crappy food. Like it's all frozen and they just throw it in a fryer."

"I know what you mean. And Aces has excellent food. Jessyka has done a great job in making sure her establishment is safe for women—and men, for that matter—and that it has a welcoming atmosphere, good food, and a wide assortment of drinks."

Flash pulled into the parking lot of the bar. He tried to see it from the eyes of someone who'd never been there before. It appeared somewhat run-down. It didn't have any flashing lights, it wasn't modern-looking, but it was like a lot of things in life...it was the inside that mattered.

After parking, Flash got out and met Kelli at the front of his SUV. He took her hand in his and smiled down at her. "It doesn't look that great from the outside, but trust me, it's a hidden jewel for sure."

"Of course I trust you," Kelli said, as if it was a given. She gave him a crooked smile. "Did you notice that the S in the Aces sign is out? I could fix that...I mean, after I learn how in my classes."

Flash chuckled. "That you could," he agreed. He opened the door and when they walked in, he heard several people call out his name in greeting.

Kelli giggled from next to him.

"What?" he asked, leading her toward the bar, where Jessyka was beaming at them.

"It's just...walking in with everyone saying your name reminded me of that old show, *Cheers*. Remember? Everyone would yell 'Norm!' when that one guy entered."

Flash knew exactly what she was talking about, and he supposed Aces was kind of like the bar Cheers.

"It's about time you brought her here!" Jessyka admonished when they got close. "Hi, Kelli! It's so good to see you again. How're you doing? After the break-in, I mean. Did the police find out who it was? Did they catch him?"

"Breathe, Jess," Flash told her with a grin.

"Sorry. I tend to talk fast because it's a given that someone will need me and if I don't get all my questions out quickly, I'll forget what I wanted to ask when I have to step away to deal with something else."

"It's good to see you too," Kelli said happily. "And I'm good. Flash doesn't think it's smart to go back to either of our apartments yet, and Smiley's been so generous in letting us use his place. And yes, the police ran the prints they found on the container of bacon the person handled when they broke in...and it's exactly who Flash and his friends thought. The guy from Jamaica."

"Holy crap! Really? And he went to your apartment? Why?"

"Money. Revenge," Flash guessed, already wanting to change the subject. He'd brought Kelli out to try to relieve some of the stress from everything going on, not rehash the details. "Benny has kid duty tonight?" he asked.

Jessyka beamed. "Yup. He said he was going to have a karaoke night. Trust me, I'm glad I'm missing that. I love my children, but they can't carry a tune to save their lives. What can I get you two?"

"I'll take whatever's on tap," Flash said.

"I think I'll have a rum and Coke," Kelli told her.

"Coming right up. You want to sit here at the bar or at a table?"

"Table," Flash said.

"Sure thing. I'll bring your drinks out when they're ready. Here, take a menu with you. I'll take your order when I swing by."

Flash took two menus from a stack on the bar and put his hand on the small of Kelli's back, leading her away from the hubbub of the bar, and also away from the pool tables on the opposite side of the room.

They sat, and Kelli said, "I like it. This place feels...homey."

"Jess and Benny have worked hard to make customers feel safe and comfortable."

"Well, they've succeeded. It's wonderful."

By the time Jessyka arrived at their table with drinks, they were ready to order.

"I think I'll have the Santa Fe burger with fries, please."

"Oh, good choice. We make the guacamole in-house and that chipotle mayo is so addicting. Flash? What are you having?" Jessyka asked.

"I think the hickory burger. I haven't had that in a while and I'm craving your barbeque sauce. I don't know what you put in it, but I swear it's of the not-quite-legal variety."

Jessyka chuckled. "Nothing illegal, promise. And I agree, it's so good."

When she'd left, Flash put his elbows on the table and leaned toward Kelli. She looked great tonight. The jeans she had on clung to her curvy legs, making him think way too much about how they'd feel wrapped around his waist. And the shirt she chose was dark blue with a V-neck, giving him small glimpses of her ample cleavage. It was enough to drive a man crazy. He loved it. She was classy and sexy at the same time.

Her gaze was fixed on him, making him feel as if he was the

center of her universe at that moment. He'd noticed that about Kelli; when someone was talking to her, she maintained eye contact, letting whoever she was chatting with know that she was one hundred percent engaged.

"How are you *really* doing with everything that happened last week, Kelli? And I don't want to hear platitudes. It wasn't that long ago we were in quite the precarious situation. And then you came home, had the shit scared out of you with our kidnapper breaking into your apartment, had to move out, go to a stranger's apartment with almost none of your stuff...and I leave you alone all day while I go to work. I'm worried about you. Worried that you're pushing your feelings down in order to try to make me feel better about everything that's happened."

Kelli reached out and took his hand in hers. "Here's the thing, Flash," she said quietly, looking him in the eyes. "Bad shit happens in life. It's inevitable. But I'm here. I'm alive. I survived. And I'll keep on surviving whatever life dishes out. I learned from a young age, when my dad was killed, that crying doesn't help. Being a bitter bitch doesn't work either. All it does is make me feel bad. I firmly believe that anyone who's experienced tragedy looks at life differently. Losing a job...dropping a full cup of coffee right after walking out of the store...getting stuck in traffic? It's nothing compared to the trauma I experienced with my dad."

She shrugged. "I learned how to process something really bad at a pretty young age, so now when I'm faced with things that aren't very fun, my brain also processes *those* things differently than a lot of people would. It's just how I'm wired. Yes, being kidnapped sucked, but I wasn't alone. It would've been a very different situation if I was. And yes, I was terrified when someone broke into my apartment and I had to hide, but you were on the other end of the phone, and you said you were coming. That made it more bearable.

"And of *course* I wish I didn't have to move out of my place, and that this Brant guy wasn't still out there, apparently looking for me...but silver lining? I've gotten to spend more time with you. And I'm here at an amazing restaurant, about to eat a humongous burger, having a great time being with a man I admire and like a whole lot.

"So I'm fine, Flash. More than fine."

It took all Flash's control not to stand up, haul Kelli to her feet, and drag her out of Aces back to his car. He wanted her. *Now*. But more than that, he needed her brand of positivity in his life. Her unique way of looking at the world was a direct result of trauma when she was younger, but he couldn't deny that it was extremely addicting. And attractive.

"What? Why are you looking at me like that?" Kelli asked, her cheeks turning a rosy pink from his scrutiny.

"I'm falling in love with you," he blurted.

Kelli's eyes widened.

"I'm not telling you that to freak you out. But just so you're forewarned. I'm addicted to you. I want to be around you all the time. I think about nothing other than getting back home to you when I leave for work each morning. And when I walk through the door and see your welcoming smile, and we talk about our days...it's as if a weight has been lifted from my shoulders every damn time.

"So...just as I warned that I was giving you a week to decide if going on a date with me was what you really wanted, I'm giving you advance notice that two years from now, I want to already have my ring on your finger, and yours on mine. I want you to be round with our baby, and I want us to have a house of our own. When I look at you, I see my future in your eyes, Kelli...and instead of freaking me out, it soothes me."

"Flash," she whispered.

He had no idea if that was an appalled whisper, or a yearning one.

"I'm sorry. I know. Too much, too soon. I just thought you

should know where I stand on whatever's happening between us. That this isn't a casual thing for me. I don't usually move in with women I've met while on vacation or on the job...no matter *what* might've happened between us."

Kelli licked her lips but didn't say anything. Just stared at him with those big brown eyes of hers.

The door opened, and they both looked up to see who'd entered. Kevlar and Remi smiled as they saw them, making a beeline for their table. Flash wanted to wave them off, tell them to sit somewhere else, because he and Kelli were having a very important discussion. The most important discussion of his life. But he supposed it might be good for Kelli to let what he'd said sink in.

He just hoped he hadn't scared her, fucking things up between them for good.

"Hey! Can we sit with you?" Remi asked.

"Of course," Kelli said.

As his team leader settled into the seat next to Kelli, Flash noticed that he looked a little...off. He couldn't put his finger on what was up, but his friend definitely wasn't his usual laid-back self. He wanted to question him, but not in front of the women.

Maybe he was worried about the mission they were researching. It would be an intense op. They were headed to Greenland, of all places. It wasn't exactly a hotspot for terrorism, but there'd been chatter about a group recently setting up a home base for getting operatives into the US. Their team would be heading to the country soon to take out the man in charge of the operation, before things could get too out of hand.

Cold-weather missions weren't Flash's thing—weren't *any* of their favorite kind of op—but taking out bad guys before they could injure or kill innocent civilians was what they did, no matter the temperature.

Jessyka stopped by their table and took Remi and Kevlar's drink and food orders, and she apparently put a rush on them, because by the time Flash and Kelli's burgers arrived, the salad and steak Remi and Kevlar had ordered were also delivered.

Kelli seemed happy to chat with Remi, and while Kevlar kept up his side of the conversation, Flash was still aware that he seemed tense.

The question of *why* was answered after they'd finished eating, when Remi was telling Kelli all about sleepovers at Caroline's house and how much fun they were.

Kevlar suddenly stood up.

Remi didn't seem too surprised by his abrupt movement, until he moved around to where she was sitting—and went down on one knee.

It felt as if everyone in the entire bar stopped talking at once.

"Remi. I told you once that I was going to marry you. Was going to put my ring on your finger, my baby in your belly, and that I'd glare at anyone who dared look sideways at my beautiful wife. You've been through several deployments. You've had more than enough time to know what you're getting with me. I'm not perfect. I can be a dick. But I love you more than I ever thought I could love another person. Will you marry me? Have my babies? Grow old with me?"

Remi was beaming. "And I told *you* that when you asked, I'd say yes. I think I knew you were the man for me back when we were floating in the ocean together and you shared your air with me. Yes...to the ring, the baby, and even though no one is going to look twice at me, I'll let you glower—not glare, you said *glower*, when you first warned me of your future intentions. Yes, Vincent! Yes to it all!"

Kevlar stood up and lifted his now-fiancée out of her chair, spinning her around in a circle. They were both grinning like fools as the entire bar cheered and clapped for them.

Flash looked over at Kelli, and saw she had an ear-to-ear smile on her face. It was obvious how happy she was for her new friend. Flash couldn't help but reach over and take her hand in his. She turned that happy grin to him, and it felt as if they were the only two people in the world. If he could bottle this moment, her happiness, and bring it out when life got tough, he would.

Kevlar put Remi back on her feet and slid a beautiful emerald-cut diamond ring on her finger. It wasn't ostentatious, but it definitely would tell anyone who might care to look that this woman was off the market.

"And we're having our party here, right?" Remi asked. "I talked to Josie, and she already asked me about a double ceremony with her and Blink. I love that idea! He means so much to me, and you too, I know. I may or may not have already brought up the idea of having the reception here at Aces to Jessyka. She said yes, that all she needs is a date. She'll close the bar to everyone but our people. Oh! And Josie wants to make sure Blink's twin and his helicopter friends can come too. And of course, Wolf and his team and all their families. Marley is already looking for the perfect dress to wear, even though I told her that I'm not sure I want the traditional bridesmaids. How could I choose who would stand up with me? It's impossible! I have too many people I love and I don't want anyone to feel slighted. It'll be a tight fit for everyone here at Aces, but this is the perfect place! It's casual, friendly, and the food and drinks are perfect—"

"Breathe, Remi. We can do whatever you want. All I care about is you being mine, and belonging to you officially in return."

"You're already mine, and I'm already yours," Remi said almost casually, as she put her hand on Kevlar's shoulder so she could admire her ring.

"Damn straight."

"Champagne on the house!" Jessyka announced loudly from behind the bar, holding up a bottle.

Cheers rang out all around them once more as everyone celebrated not only Remi and Kevlar's official engagement, but also free alcohol.

Flash kept hold of Kelli's hand as Remi and Kevlar sat back down, swapping seats this time so Remi could show off her ring to Kelli.

"Congrats, man," Flash said, slapping Kevlar on the shoulder.

"Thanks. Honestly?" his friend said quietly. "I'm glad that's over. Lord, I knew what her answer was going to be, and yet I was still nervous as hell."

"I could tell. Glad that's what was up, because I was getting a little paranoid over here," Flash joked.

"Wait until it's your turn," Kevlar warned. "You'll see what I mean. Even though you know you love your woman, and she loves you, there's just something nerve-racking about actually asking the question."

Flash wasn't sure about that. He looked at Kelli. When he asked her to marry him, he wasn't going to do it in public. It would be an intimate thing between the two of them. Not because he'd be afraid she'd say no, but because he wanted to spoil her, make her feel like the most cherished woman in the world. Visions of flowers, a dinner for two, maybe a beautiful view sprang to his mind, as he thought about where and how he'd ask her to marry him.

It wasn't until she laughed at something Remi said that he shook his head and concentrated on the here and now. He was getting ahead of himself for sure. But he knew down to his bones that this woman would wear his ring one day. Just as he'd wear hers.

The party atmosphere in the room lasted for quite a while. There was just something about a successful marriage proposal that made everyone happy.

So when Flash's phone rang, he was still enjoying the jovial mood. Looking at the screen, he saw it was Smiley calling.

"Hey. You'll never guess what our team leader did. He finally got the nerve to ask Remi to marry him," Flash said. "Looks as if another one is biting the dust," he joked.

"That's great. Listen, there's no good way to say this, so I'm just gonna say it. Someone tried to burn down your apartment complex tonight."

Flash's blood ran cold. *"What?"*

"Everyone's fine and it was caught before any real damage could be done. But from what the firefighters are saying, the origin was your balcony. Someone doused it with gas and made an incendiary device. A neighbor saw it smoking and called nine-one-one, then they were able to grab a hose from the apartment next to yours, and they got the fire under control before it did more than burn the shit out of the crap you had outside...like your grill and that patio chair."

"Shit! All right. You're okay?"

"Yeah. I was inside...and maybe it's TMI to admit this, but I was in the bathroom. Didn't hear a thing until the shouting outside from your neighbor."

Flash's stomach rolled. Smiley could've been hurt. Hell, an entire apartment complex full of people could've been hurt, or at the very least, lost everything. Thank God for his observant neighbor. He owed the man a beer. No, a lifetime supply of beer. "I'm going to drop Kelli off and then I'll be right there."

He was aware the conversation around the table had stopped and he was being stared at, but for the moment, all he could concentrate on was Smiley.

"No need. Things are fine here. I've given the detective on scene your phone number and gave him the rundown about Williams. I'm sure he'll be in touch soon, and you might have to go in and give a statement, but things here are under control."

"You need to come back to your place. I'll take Kelli to a hotel."

"Don't be stupid. Stay put. Both of you. I'm good here. I kind of like your kitchen. And I'm currently binge watching your

DVDs of *Criminal Minds*. I know it's on streaming, but there's something so old school about watching it on disc."

Frustration ate at Flash. "We need to find him. Stop this shit."

"I agree," Smiley said. "Which is why I told Tex to step things up. To get that chick from New Mexico involved. He's busy. Has his hands in a million different pies, as usual. We need someone on this exclusively. And…I think her name is Ryleigh, or something like that…she's just as good or even better than Tex, even though he doesn't like to admit it. She might be able to find this asshole, tell the cops where he is, maybe even provide the evidence they need to lock him up for good."

"All right. If you need anything—and I mean *anything*, Smiley —you call. Understand?"

"Of course. I'll see you at PT in the morning."

When his friend hung up, Flash looked up to see three sets of eyes locked on him.

"What happened?"

"Is Smiley all right?"

The first question came from Kevlar, the second, not surprisingly, from Kelli.

"There was an incident at my apartment complex. Everyone is fine."

"Williams," Kevlar said. It wasn't a question.

"Most likely," Flash confirmed.

Kelli frowned. "What should we do?"

"For now, nothing except stay vigilant. Keep our doors locked, our eyes open. You aren't going to like this, but I'm going to need you to stay inside Smiley's apartment while I'm at work. If you need something, you can order it to be delivered, or let me know and I'll pick it up on my way home."

"I can drive her somewhere if she needs to go out," Remi volunteered.

"I appreciate that, but this asshole might know about you

and the other women by now. I don't want him deciding to follow one of you to find out where we're staying. And I *definitely* don't want him using you to get to either Kelli or me."

"Should I leave?" Kelli asked quietly. "I can go to Florida. Or New York. Hell, Maine. It's pretty rural there."

"No!" Flash exclaimed. He took a deep breath. "No. Smiley is going to ask Tex to put his computer genius friend from New Mexico on this exclusively. She'll locate Williams, so the cops can put him away. We just have to be patient for a little while longer."

Kevlar frowned. "I don't like this."

Flash snorted. "Neither do I."

"I'm willing to be cautious, but what if this computer person *can't* find him? I don't want Brant to win by having you and I hiding and not living our lives. And what happens if he's not found before you guys get deployed? Am I supposed to hide in Smiley's apartment forever? That's not acceptable. I want to live my life! I want to start classes at the community college so I can become an electrician and fix Jessyka's sign." Kelli was breathing faster now, almost panicking by the time she finished speaking.

Flash shoved his chair back, reached over, and pulled Kelli out of her seat. He settled her onto his lap so she straddled him and they were eye-to-eye, holding her face in his hands. "Do you remember what I told you before Remi and Kevlar arrived?" he asked.

He saw her swallow hard, then nod.

"You think any of that can happen if we have to hide out? It can't. So I'm going to fix this. I'm going to find that coward and make sure he knows he picked the wrong people. The day he decided to put us in that bus was his downfall, he just doesn't know it yet."

"I don't want to lose you," Kelli whispered.

"Lose me? How?"

"If you kill him, you could go to jail."

"I'm not going to jail," Flash told her confidently. He wasn't going to promise that he wouldn't kill Williams—because if he got the chance, he was definitely taking the man out. If the guy simply went to jail, the opportunity for him to get out would hang over their heads forever. And Flash had no doubt that if Williams was let out of prison, he'd be gunning for them once again.

He didn't know how, or when, but Brant Williams was going down. He wasn't going to stand in the way of Flash and Kelli living the life he saw in his fantasies. No fucking way.

Kelli closed her eyes, took a deep breath, then looked at him once more and nodded.

Her trust, her belief in him, was a gift. And it was something Flash would cherish and protect with his life. He always wanted to see her looking at him as she was right now. With hope and their future in her eyes.

Turning his head without taking his hands off Kelli's face, he told Kevlar, "I'm going to need you to talk to the commander. Take me off the next mission. I'm not leaving as long as Williams is out there."

Kelli started to protest, but he ignored her.

"Done," Kevlar said with a nod.

"Shhh," Flash murmured as he pressed his lips to Kelli's forehead. "It'll be fine."

"I'll call Wolf too. Let him know what's up. Tell him to get word out about Williams. Every former and current SEAL in the area will be on watch for this guy. We'll catch him. I have no doubt," Kevlar said.

"Instead of Smiley's place, can you maybe come stay with us instead? I mean, there's strength in numbers, right?" Remi asked.

"Maybe," Flash hedged. She wasn't exactly wrong, but still, putting anyone else in this asshole's crosshairs felt wrong. Smiley was single. Staying with Remi would mean leaving two women alone while he was at work.

He ached to go to his apartment and check out the damage. Make sure Smiley hadn't downplayed any injuries that himself or his neighbors might have incurred. But his desire to stick by Kelli's side was stronger. He'd see Smiley soon enough.

"You ready to head home?" Flash asked Kelli.

She nodded.

"We should be going too," Kevlar said.

"I'm sorry we ruined your night," he told his friend, as he helped Kelli off his lap.

"You didn't ruin anything," Kevlar said, sounding exasperated. "Remi agreed to marry me, we're going to have a huge party here at Aces...what's to ruin?"

"Exactly," Remi agreed, giving Kelli a long hug. "Trust Flash. He'll figure this out."

Kelli nodded and gave her friend a small smile.

Flash waved at Jessyka, and she waved back from behind the bar. They'd paid the tab earlier so nothing stopped them from heading straight for the door.

Looking around, Flash saw nothing out of the ordinary as they exited. Visiting the bar again might also be out of the question until Williams was found. The last thing he wanted was the thwarted kidnapper deciding to take his frustrations out on the place where Flash and every other SEAL liked to hang out.

The drive back to Smiley's apartment took longer than usual, as Flash made a lot of extra turns, doing his best to try to evade Williams if he happened to be following. He wouldn't breathe a sigh of relief until they were inside the apartment, with the door double bolted behind them.

Williams could always try to burn Smiley's complex down, but he was fairly sure the man didn't know where they were...yet. Which was probably why he'd taken out his irritation on Flash's apartment. The man was a menace and had to be stopped.

But for tonight, Flash had different plans.

There was no telling what the future held. What plans

Williams had up his sleeve. And Flash had no intention of letting one more day pass without showing Kelli how serious he was about wanting her in his life...forever.

Of course, anything happening would be up to her. She might be too distraught after hearing about Williams' latest attempt to fuck with them. But tonight, when they got into bed, she'd know without a doubt that he was serious when he'd told her what he wanted.

And what he wanted was her. Under him. Over him. Any way he could get her. His mouth watered with thoughts of tasting her, of spreading her thighs and seeing her pussy soaking wet for him.

He was ninety percent sure she wanted him too. Her signs of arousal weren't as obvious as his, but she hadn't once shied away from his touches. And when his hand slipped under her shirt and rested on the small of her back the night before, she'd arched into him.

His timing wasn't great, and if she really was too worried about Williams, he wouldn't push. But with the way her gaze flicked between his legs and how often she blushed, he had a feeling they'd both get a break from their real life tonight. By losing themselves in each other. He couldn't wait.

CHAPTER SEVENTEEN

Kelli was torn. She was kind of freaking out that Brant had tried to burn Flash's apartment down. But she couldn't help noticing that Flash seemed different since leaving Aces. More focused. More touchy-feely. She liked that last part. A hell of a lot.

She'd been with men before. She wasn't a virgin. But none had made her feel the way Flash did. As if her skin was too tight, her body temp too high from the constant blushing. And right now, she was fidgety and she couldn't keep her eyes off him. As he drove, she saw the muscles in his arms flexing, which made her think about how they'd do the same thing as he propped himself above her.

When he glanced her way, she saw something in his gaze that hadn't been there before. A heated interest he was no longer trying to hide. And those looks shot straight through her. Making her embarrassingly wet between her legs.

She should be worried about Smiley. Should be trying to come up with a plan for what they'd do if Brant found them and confronted them. But instead, all she could think about was later tonight...when she climbed into bed with Flash.

Should she make the first move? Should she come right out and tell him she wanted him? What if he wasn't ready for more physical intimacy? What if all his declarations earlier were just a heat-of-the-moment kind of thing?

She mentally shook her head. No. That wasn't Flash's style. She hadn't known him long, but if he said something, he meant it.

And just like that, she was turned on again.

By the time they were walking up to Smiley's apartment hand-in-hand, Kelli still wasn't sure what would happen when they got inside. She knew what she *wanted* to happen, but she also felt bad that she couldn't stop thinking about sex when Flash was probably worried about his apartment almost burning down.

When the door to the apartment closed behind them, Kelli felt awkward all of a sudden. She was still full from the amazing burger she'd had at Aces, so killing time before bed by cooking something was out. They could watch television, but she wasn't really in the mood.

Then Flash, being Flash, took control. Didn't give her time to try to come up with something to say or do.

He abruptly turned and backed her up against a wall in the small living area.

Then he lowered his head and kissed her.

Kelli swore she saw stars—and just like that, her libido, which was already in overdrive, shot even higher. His kiss was like someone had lit a thousand candles inside her. One second she was barely managing to hold back her lust for this man, and the next she was burning from the inside out.

She gave as good as she got. Kelli wasn't a passive participant in the kiss. She grabbed Flash's hair and held him tightly as their tongues dueled. She hitched one leg around his hip and rubbed herself against him as best she could as they kissed.

Without a word, Flash pulled back, stared at her for a beat, then reached for the hem of his shirt.

Yes. Kelli was all in. Without thinking about her size, or awkward moments when she'd gotten naked in front of past lovers, she copied Flash's movements and took off her own shirt. Then it was a race to get undressed. Flash's hands were at the fastening of his pants and they were around his ankles in seconds.

Kelli giggled when he almost tripped over his feet because he hadn't taken his boots off before attempting to kick off his jeans. While he was sorting that, she managed to get her own pants and shoes off. She was reaching for the clasp of her bra when Flash straightened.

He was completely nude, and Kelli stared at his dick in awe.

She couldn't believe he'd been hiding that monster in his pants. She'd seen that he had an impressive bulge in his swim trunks, and she'd felt it under her ass while sitting on his lap in the tube on the river, but seeing him erect was...daunting.

"Let me," Flash said in a husky tone, as he reached around her for the clasp of her bra.

His dick brushed against her belly and left a smear of wetness that made her legs weak. She wanted this man. Right now. If she didn't get him inside her, she was going to die.

Okay, she was being dramatic, but she didn't even care.

The second her bra loosened, Kelli shrugged her shoulders forward and let the damn thing fall to the floor between them. Then she dropped to her knees before Flash could move and wrapped her fingers around his cock.

"Holy fuck," he groaned, pushing one hand into her hair and bracing himself on the wall behind her with the other.

Kelli didn't hesitate, she opened her mouth and took him inside.

His fingers tightened in her hair as she bobbed her head up and down. He felt amazing against her tongue, the musky taste of his precome filling her mouth. The knowledge that she, Kelli Colbert, was turning on this amazing specimen of a man filled her with confidence. She could feel her pussy weeping, readying itself for him.

"Easy, Kelli. We have all the time in the world," Flash murmured above her.

But she didn't want easy. She wanted hard and fast. Desperate. Exactly how she felt.

Her free hand went around Flash's body and gripped one of his ass cheeks, as she did her best to give him the most amazing blowjob he'd ever had. Her reward was the tortured groan that left his lips and another tangy spurt of precome. She moaned around him at the taste.

"Fuck, woman!" Flash said, right before he reached down and grabbed her by the upper arms, pulling her off the floor.

Kelli let out a squeak of complaint. She wasn't done. She wasn't a fan of swallowing, but for this man, she would do just about anything. But apparently that wasn't on his agenda for the night.

Feeling giddy about how easily he handled her, Kelli held on as he swung her up into his arms and carried her over to the kitchen table. Thankfully, Smiley's apartment was devoid of many personal touches, and the table was bare.

The wood was cold under her ass, even through her underwear.

Flash put a hand in the middle of her chest and gently pushed her backward. Kelli lay down and arched her back as he reached for her underwear.

She prepared to lift her bottom, thinking he was going to slide the cotton over her hips—but to her surprise, his arm muscles bunched as he ripped it off her instead.

That was so damn hot, Kelli was panting. "Yes," she muttered, spreading her legs apart. The table was the perfect height, and Flash's cock was lined up with her pussy. She waited for him to take her. She was ready. More than ready. She wanted this. Needed it. Needed *him*.

It felt as if she'd waited forever for this moment, when in reality she'd really just met this man not too long ago. But what they'd been through together had forged a bond that was stronger than any she'd ever felt before.

"So fucking beautiful," Flash said, as his gaze devoured her from her head to her toes. He leaned over a little and palmed her ample breasts. "I'm gonna spend a year worshiping these beauties. Gonna suck and lick and maybe get some clamps."

Kelli's pussy spasmed. She'd never been interested in anything like sex toys or pain with her sex, but as Flash pinched her nipples, the zings of arousal shooting down between her legs made her think she'd been missing out.

"But right now, all I can think of is getting inside you."

"Yes," Kelli breathed.

To her surprise, Flash suddenly turned and walked away from the table.

She frowned, confused. Was he...leaving?

She watched as he hurried across the room, turning away to pick up his pants and rifle through the pockets. Then he dropped them and stalked back toward her, his cock still hard, bobbing in front of him like a flag waving in the wind.

He reached for his dick, and it was then she realized he'd retrieved a condom and was now putting it on.

Honestly, Kelli was surprised. With all his talk about knocking her up, she kind of thought he might "accidentally" forget to bring up the subject of birth control. But he hadn't even asked if she was on anything. He simply did the right thing, making sure she was protected.

When he finished with the condom, he frowned when he realized she'd closed her legs. Forcefully shoving her knees apart, he grabbed her and pulled her ass to the edge of the table. Falling onto her back, Kelli smiled up at him.

But he wasn't looking at her face—his gaze was glued between her legs. "So wet," he murmured, running a thumb up her slit, ending up on her clit and rubbing it somewhat roughly.

Kelli loved this. She loved how rough he was being. But he wasn't hurting her. Not in the least.

He showed no mercy as he strummed her clit. She bucked, but Flash put a hand on her belly and held her down as he brought her to the edge of orgasm faster than she thought possible.

"Come for me," he ordered. "You're wet, but I need you soaking. Dripping. I can't be gentle this first time, and I don't want to hurt you. You're tiny, and I'm not."

Kelli choked back a laugh. Had anyone in her entire life told her she was tiny? No.

But she had no time to contradict him. To tell him she could take whatever he wanted to give her. Because she was orgasming, her entire body shaking as pleasure overwhelmed her.

And while she was still coming, Flash pushed her legs even farther apart, notched his cock between her legs, and entered her with one hard thrust.

***

Flash felt as if he was burning up from the inside out. He couldn't hold back from kissing Kelli the second the door shut behind them. He wasn't expecting more than a kiss there in the living area before he planned on taking her hand and leading her to the bedroom, where he would hopefully make long, sweet, slow love to her for the first time.

But she obviously had other ideas.

When she'd taken off her clothes and gone to her knees in front of him, he swore his vision had gone black for a moment. Before he even realized what was happening, his cock was in her mouth and he was living his greatest fantasy. Seeing her lips stretched around his dick, Kelli looking up at him with fuck-me eyes, made him lose all control.

He managed not to come in her mouth, barely, and it was all he could do to move her to the kitchen table. There was no way he would have made it to the bed. He'd needed inside her. Now. Right this second.

He'd faltered in his goal when he'd seen her pussy for the first time. She was perfect. She'd trimmed her pubic hair into a slender strip, and the sight made his mouth water. But his dick was more insistent. He needed to be inside her more than he needed to breathe.

Spotting his dripping cock made him suddenly realize he wasn't wearing a condom. As much as he wanted to fill her to the brim with his come and get her pregnant so she'd never leave him—which was an outdated notion to be sure...women didn't automatically stay with men when they got pregnant anymore—he wasn't about to do something so disrespectful as make love to her bare, not without first having a serious conversation about their past sexual histories, and future wants and desires when it came to babies.

So, Flash had stomped back to his pants—and his wallet with the condom he'd put in there just that morning. He'd hated the look of uncertainty on Kelli's face when he'd returned to the table. As if she thought he'd changed his mind, or maybe even assumed he was leaving her.

Not a chance in hell. He wasn't that strong.

She'd closed her legs, which offended Flash. He'd pushed them apart, almost embarrassing himself when he saw how slick her pussy was. It took every ounce of strength he had not to fuck her right then and there. But he didn't want to hurt her. Had to make her come before he entered her.

It didn't take long. Male satisfaction had welled up in Flash at how fast she'd come. She was primed and ready for him. While she was still shaking, still in the throes of her orgasm, he'd shoved himself as deep inside her as he could get.

Now, every muscle in his body tensed as he fought not to come then and there. She was tight. So damn *tight*. Her pussy rippled around him as her orgasm waned. Flash had never felt anything like it.

Swallowing hard, he held still, letting her get used to his size and enjoying the feeling of being inside the last woman he'd ever make love to for the rest of his life.

Kelli was it for him. Period. Done. He just had to convince her that he was the man for *her*. That he'd never let her down. That he'd bend over backward to be her rock, her cheerleader, someone she could count on.

"Flash?" she asked, staring up at him with glassy eyes.

"Yeah?" He was amazed he could still talk. All the blood in his body felt as if it was in his dick right now.

"Fuck me."

He was moving before the second word was out of her mouth. They both groaned at how good the friction of his cock pistoning in and out of her snug body felt.

Her tits bounced on her chest with every thrust, and Flash had never seen anything so gorgeous in all his life. He wasn't into BDSM, but as he'd told her, he itched to adorn her nipples with clamps...maybe jeweled ones. See if a bite of pain enhanced her pleasure.

His hands moved of their own accord, and he palmed her generous tits, even as his hips never stopped moving. He squeezed and massaged her breasts, then moved his fingers to her nipples. They were already tight and hard, and when he pinched them, she groaned and lifted her hips to meet his thrusts.

Yeah, she liked that. *Fuck*, she was perfect.

Flash pinched her nipples in time with his thrusts, and he felt her fingernails digging into his arms as she held him tight.

Eventually he had to let go of her tits to hold her hips, she was writhing and thrusting under him so hard. Her face was dewy with sweat, her entire upper chest flushed a bright pink, and he felt her heels digging into his ass as he moved, trying to take him deeper.

In short, she was glorious. He'd never be able to eat at this table—hell, *any* table—and not think of this moment. The first time he'd made love to the woman he loved. His soul mate.

His balls tingled, but Flash refused to come. He wanted this moment in time to last forever. To be right where he was for the rest of his life. He'd always enjoyed sex, but this was…life-altering.

He'd never felt so connected to another person. It was as if he were a part of Kelli, and she were a part of him. It was corny as hell, but there it was.

Then she blew his mind by moving one of her hands between their bodies and flicking her clit as he fucked her.

"Oh!" she exclaimed, and Flash could feel her inner muscles clench hard around him.

"That's it, Kel, give yourself what you need."

She didn't need his permission to touch herself, but it was a huge turn-on that she wasn't afraid to give herself an orgasm.

One second he was looking down and watching Kelli strum her clit, and the next he was coming. He wasn't able to hold back any longer. Flash felt as if he was being turned inside out. He'd never come so hard or so long before.

By the time the blackness receded from the corners of his eyes, Flash realized he was lying on top of Kelli, probably squishing her. The tabletop couldn't be that comfortable. Lifting up, he looked into her eyes…and what he saw there had his dick twitching deep inside her.

She looked happy. Content. Satiated.

"Hey," he whispered, suddenly tongue-tied.

"Hey," she returned.

"That shouldn't have happened," he blurted.

Flash realized he'd fucked up the second the words left his lips. He didn't need to see the happiness in her gaze turn to confusion, then hurt, to know that. He hurried to reassure her. "I mean, I meant to take you to bed. Give you a massage. Make slow, sweet love to you. Not this…out-of-control, fast fuck on a table."

Kelli licked her lips and brushed a lock of hair out of his eyes. "For the record? I liked this fast fuck on a table. It was a first for me, and I loved that you were so excited to have me that you couldn't wait."

"*Me*? You were the one who went down on me as if you couldn't last another second without having my cock in your mouth," Flash retorted.

To his immense relief, Kelli laughed. He felt it from the inside out. Her skin was still dewy and flushed from their lovemaking, her hair was fanned around her head, and she looked like a freaking goddess. *His* goddess.

Not willing to leave the warmth of her body, Flash put one hand on her ass, holding her against him, and the other went behind her shoulders, pulling her into a sitting position. "Hold on," he ordered.

Her arms went around his neck, and he picked her up and turned toward the bedroom.

She giggled, and once again, Flash could feel the sound along the length of his dick. It was an unusual feeling, and one he already couldn't get enough of. He carried her into the bedroom and threw back the covers before falling forward, placing Kelli on her back on the bed.

"Are you okay?" he asked. "I wasn't too rough?"

"I'm perfect," she reassured him. "And no, you weren't too rough, not at all. I loved it."

Knowing he had to pull out and take care of the condom that was full to the rim, otherwise wearing it would be for naught,

Flash propped himself over Kelli and said sternly, "Don't move. Stay right here. Just like this. I'll be right back. Gotta get rid of this condom and grab a new one."

"How many do you have in your wallet?" she asked a little cheekily.

"I only had one, smartass. But the box I bought is in the bathroom."

"You know, I'm on the pill," Kelli said almost nonchalantly.

Flash stared down at her as the words sank in. "What are you saying?" he asked quietly.

"Just that...it's been a long time since I've been with anyone. Depending on your sexual history, if you know that you're... okay...We don't have to use them. Condoms."

A red haze of lust covered Flash's vision. He could take Kelli bare? Fill her with his come? Watch it leak out between her pussy lips?

It was all he could do to swallow and speak. "I haven't been with anyone in over a year. And we get tested by the Navy regularly. I'm good."

"Right, so, if you want proof, I can show you the pills in my overnight bag in the bathroom, then we could—"

Flash didn't let her finish her sentence. He pulled out of her warm body, removed the condom, tied it off before tossing it over the side of the bed, then pumped his cock twice before thrusting right back inside Kelli's wet pussy with a deep groan.

"I guess you believe me," she said dryly, with a tiny smile.

"You've created a monster," Flash warned, even as he thrust his hips. "I'm gonna spend as much time as I can right here. You have no idea how good you feel. God, and it's even better without anything between us. I apologize now for how sore you're gonna be tomorrow. But I can't stop. Please don't make me."

She writhed under him. "Why would I want you to stop doing something that feels so good?"

"This is gonna work out," Flash said with determination.

"What is?"

"Us. I'm gonna be the best boyfriend you've ever had. You'll see. I'm not going to give you any reason to want to leave. I'll never cheat, never hurt you, physically or otherwise. I'll be protective and possessive, but not in an abusive, assholey way. I'll give you space when you need it, and be right by your side when you don't. I'll bend over backward to do anything you need so you can become the best electrician Riverton's ever had. You'll be so in demand, you can charge hundreds of dollars an hour to change people's frickin' light bulbs, and they'll gladly pay just so they can say *the* Kelli Colbert did it for them. And maybe one day...it won't be Kelli Colbert, but Kelli Gordon changing their light bulbs."

"Flash," she whispered, as she stared up at him with big eyes.

"Too soon. Yeah, I know. Sorry. But I did warn you what I wanted," he told her.

"How about we take things one day at a time and not plan our wedding quite yet."

"Deal," he said, inordinately pleased that she wasn't demanding he get off of her, freaking out that he'd basically planned the rest of their lives together. "You tell me if anything I do doesn't feel good. Or if you get tired."

"I will. I do have one question."

"Yeah?"

"You gonna leave that used condom on the floor all night?" She was smiling so widely when she asked, Flash knew she was teasing him.

"Yup."

"I'm gonna tell Smiley," she threatened.

"If I can't make you forget about it by morning, I haven't done my job," he told her.

Then her smile faded, and she wrapped a hand around the back of his neck. "I feel as if this is a dream. Like I'll wake up and we'll be back in that bus. Hungry and scared. I don't want this to end."

"It's real, and it won't end. You'll wake up with me curled around you every day from here on out."

"Promise?"

"Promise," he vowed. Then he got to work making his woman forget about everything except for him.

CHAPTER EIGHTEEN

Kelli sighed in frustration. She was ready to start classes at the community college. The more she thought about becoming an electrician, the more excited she got. But because Brant Williams was still out there somewhere, lying in wait for the chance to make whatever move he had up his sleeve, she'd been stuck in Smiley's apartment, waiting.

Things with Flash were good, at least. Better than good. She'd never been so satisfied, both sexually and in general. He was a wonderful man. He had his flaws, but showing her how much he cared for her wasn't one of them.

He was currently at work, and Kelli was bored. She wanted to go for a walk. Go see Remi or one of the other girls. Maybe head to Aces and have another delicious hamburger. But for now, she was basically a prisoner in the apartment.

And it sucked.

Still, she wasn't going to do something stupid like defy all common sense and head out on her own. That would just be asking Brant to grab her, and this time do something worse than just bury her underground inside a bus.

She had to be patient. Had to believe that this Ryleigh

person would find Brant. Once that happened, her life could go back to normal. But what *was* normal, now? Would she move back into her apartment up in La Jolla? She'd be pretty far from Flash if she did that, and she'd gotten very used to living with him. It was scary just how easy it was to move in together. How right it felt.

She'd talked to her mom about the situation, who'd simply told her, "When you know, you know," and that was that. She also wanted to meet Flash, but with everything going on, her mom agreed Kelli should just lay low, and she'd meet him when the time was right.

Flash called or texted pretty much every hour, wanting to make sure she was okay, that everything at the apartment was calm. Kelli appreciated it, and only partly because the memory of Brant breaking into her place was still fresh. Texting or talking with Flash also made her smile, made her feel not quite so lonely.

Yes, she texted with Remi, Josie, Maggie, Addison, and Wren too, but it wasn't the same as when Flash contacted her. She got butterflies in her belly and she felt all warm inside when he took time out of his day to check on her. She was aware that he'd been taken off the deployment rotation, at least until Brant was caught, but he was still working hard to make sure his friends and teammates would be safe when they left for whatever mission was currently in the planning stages.

Kelli had just finished texting Flash yet again, and was settling on the couch to read one of the thrillers Smiley had on his bookshelves, when there was a knock at the door.

Immediately, her mouth went dry.

Who could that be? Not any of the girls; they would've let her know they were coming over. And she'd just talked to Flash, so she knew it wasn't him.

Getting up cautiously, she tiptoed over to the door. She made sure to stay completely silent as she gazed through the peephole.

She saw a woman standing there, looking extremely nervous. She was biting one of her fingernails and kept glancing down the hallway, as if expecting the boogie man to appear at any moment.

She looked to be in her mid-thirties and couldn't be much taller than Kelli. She had reddish-brown hair that came down to around the middle of her back, and hazel or light brown eyes, it was hard to tell in the low light of the hall. The jeans she wore were baggy, and the sneakers on her feet were worn. She was wearing a plain black T-shirt, with no markings on it at all.

But what stood out to Kelli most were the faded bruises on her face. They were yellow, meaning they were almost healed, but the woman hadn't used any concealer to cover them. Actually, it didn't look like she was wearing makeup at all.

Despite the danger the woman might pose, Kelli was intrigued.

When she reached up and knocked on the door again, it startled her so badly, Kelli almost fell backward onto her ass.

Should she answer it or not? Indecision tore at her. Flash had told her not to open the door to anyone, no matter what, but this woman looked...she looked freaked out. Would someone hell bent on doing Kelli harm look so nervous? She didn't think so.

Taking a deep breath, she made a split-second decision—and prayed she wouldn't regret it. She unlocked the two bolts and took the chain off, then opened the door.

The two women stared at each other for a long moment. The woman at the door looked confused.

"Hi. Can I help you?" Kelli asked, sounding more confident than she felt inside.

"Um...I'm sorry. I think I have the wrong apartment. I thought this was Jude Stark's apartment."

Kelli had heard the other girls mention that Smiley's real name was Jude. At the time, they'd been discussing how cool it was. That it was basically a superhero's undercover name. They weren't wrong.

"It is."

"Oh. Um, is he here?"

"No, he's at work." Kelli wasn't going to tell this woman anything important until she found out who she was and why she was looking for Smiley. There was a chance she was working with Brant, a slim one, but a chance nonetheless.

For some reason, the woman looked...heartbroken? It made no sense. Kelli was pretty sure Smiley wasn't seeing anyone, so she didn't understand what was going on here.

Abruptly, the woman turned to leave.

Understanding hit then. The woman thought Kelli was dating Smiley. She *was* in his apartment, after all.

"I'm dating Flash. Smiley's friend," she blurted, before the woman got too far away. "Some things went down, and my boyfriend and I are staying here. Smiley let us swap apartments. He's at Flash's place." Her words were rushed, and for some reason, Kelli really wanted the unknown woman to believe her. "I like Smiley but he's kind of...intense for me. Not in a bad way, I just like my men to be a little friendlier. No—that makes him sound mean, but I didn't mean it that way."

"It's okay, I understand," the woman said.

"Do you want to come in?" Kelli asked. Flash was going to give her hell for inviting a stranger into the apartment, but everything was screaming at her that something was...maybe not *wrong*, but definitely off with the woman. There were those fading bruises, yes, but also, there was no gentle way around it... she stunk. As if she hadn't had a shower in a long while. And her clothes were dirty.

Something within Kelli was screaming not to let her walk away.

"Um, no, that's okay."

"Please? Look, my name is Kelli. I'm bored out of my mind. I can't leave the apartment because there's a guy out there who'd love nothing more to get his hands on me for nefarious purposes. So I'm kind of hiding out until Flash and the others can find him. And I don't want to put Remi or any of the other women at risk, so they really can't come over and visit. I'm sick of watching TV and there are only so many of Smiley's thriller books I can read. So you'd be doing me a huge favor if you came in and visited for a while."

Kelli was laying it on a bit thick, but the more she thought about it, the more she thought this woman *needed* to come in. She obviously came here to talk to Smiley for some reason, and she hoped she could get her to relax enough to maybe tell her why.

The woman looked up and down the hall. Then slowly nodded.

Feeling as if she'd accomplished something miraculous, Kelli smiled and took a step back from the door, giving the woman some room. Making sure the door was locked and dead-bolted behind her mysterious guest, Kelli gestured toward the kitchen.

"Are you hungry? I was about to make some lunch. Don't get too excited, it's nothing super-fancy, just some ham and cheese sandwiches."

"I don't want to put you out," the woman said.

"Oh, you aren't. Seriously." Kelli led the way, and it didn't escape her notice how interested the woman seemed to be in checking out Smiley's apartment. It was if as she was drinking in every little detail.

"I'm sorry, I didn't catch your name," Kelli said, knowing full well the woman had never said it.

"Oh...I'm Bree."

It was all Kelli could do not to gasp and gawk at the woman. *This* was Bree? The woman Smiley had been hunting all over Riverton? And the bruises had to be from when she'd helped save Ellory and Yana from the guy who'd sold them to someone overseas for their organs.

Her heart started beating fast. The woman was nothing like what Kelli had pictured in her head. For one, she felt sorry for her. Now that she was inside the well-lit apartment and not in the dingy hallway, Kelli could see that she looked *really* bad. Dark circles under her eyes, those faded bruises, the clothes were even dirtier than she'd thought...and there was that smell emanating from her.

As Kelli made the sandwiches, she babbled about nothing in particular. She simply wanted to fill the silence, as if that would prevent Bree from deciding to leave. She also wanted to text Flash and let him know who was there, right now, but she had a feeling that would make Bree bolt.

As they ate their sandwiches at the table, Bree asked, "So, Smiley is at Flash's place and you guys are here?"

Kelli nodded. "Yeah. To make a very long story short...well, actually, I guess it's not *that* long. I was in Jamaica for my cousin's bachelorette party. We went tubing, Flash's tube broke, we kind of got left behind on the river together, were the last ones off. On the way back to the resort, we got kidnapped, put in this bus that had been buried underground. Flash's friends found us, and we came home. But the kidnapper had our IDs, and he came to the States. A week after we got back, he broke into my place. I hid so he couldn't find me, but since it isn't safe for me to stay there anymore, and since the bad guy has Flash's address too, Smiley said we could stay here."

"Is he in danger?"

Bree's worry for Smiley was obvious; she wasn't even trying to hide it.

"Honestly? I don't think so. I had the same question, but the guys are SEALs...I think they'd probably *love* for the kidnapper to come after one of them."

"Yeah," Bree said, but her brows were still furrowed and she still looked worried.

Kelli didn't know Smiley all that well, but she figured having someone worry about him the way this woman was couldn't be a bad thing. He was kind of standoffish and grumpy. Maybe having a friend like Bree would be good for him.

"I'm sorry you guys have to hide. That's no fun."

Kelli studied the woman. She sounded as if she knew what she was talking about. Then she remembered what Flash had told her about the woman's situation...and she realized she knew *exactly* how Kelli felt.

She felt an instant connection with Bree.

When Bree had introduced herself as the woman Smiley was so desperately searching for, Kelli's first inclination had been to text Flash and let him know, so he could tell Smiley and he could get his butt over to the apartment. But the more they talked, the more she suspected if she did that, Bree would probably leave and never return. Yes, she'd knocked on the door expecting to talk to Smiley, but she still seemed extremely skittish, and Kelli didn't want to do anything that might make her run off again. It was obvious Bree needed a friend, and Kelli suddenly wanted to *be* that friend.

As if she could read her mind, Bree's gaze met Kelli's, and she asked, "Are you going to tell Smiley I was here?"

"Do you want me to?" she returned.

"I don't know," Bree whispered. It was obvious she was conflicted. "I came thinking I was finally ready to talk to him, but now that I'm actually here? And Smiley isn't home? It kind of feels like maybe this was a sign...like it's not the best time."

"I'm sure he could help you," Kelli said. "I mean, I was kidnapped and buried underground and before I could blink, he and his team were rescuing us."

"My situation isn't quite the same," Bree said.

"Look, Flash told me a little about you. Nothing personal,"

she said, quickly seeing Bree tense. "Just that Smiley met you in Vegas when they were there to find Josie. He was distraught when you disappeared."

"I had to," Bree said.

"Yeah, but you should know that when you saved Ellory and Yana...now *all* the guys want to find you."

"They can join the club," Bree muttered.

"Don't take this the wrong way," Kelli said. "But you look like crap."

To her surprise, Bree burst out laughing. "I bet I do."

"I want to be your friend, Bree. I won't tell Smiley you were here, but...what if you visited me during the day while Flash is at work?" Then she spoke faster, as if that could keep the woman from saying no. "You can shower, we can do your laundry, you can eat something hot. And you'd be keeping me company while the guys do their thing to find my kidnapper."

"Why? Why would you help me?" Bree asked.

Kelli shrugged. "Because. One, I like you. I know we just met, but there's something about you that tells me you're trustworthy and a good person. And two, I'm lonely."

Bree stared at her for so long, Kelli was sure she was going to refuse, say she needed to go. Then she sighed. "I need help," she whispered. "I'm exhausted. Sleeping in my car sucks. I'm sick of fast food. And I think the man who's after me has figured out where I am. I don't know how, but I'm pretty sure he's here in Riverton."

"That's why you came here, isn't it? To talk to Smiley."

"It's stupid. I only met the man once, and it was on the worst day of my life. But I couldn't stop thinking about him. His name, the fact that he's a SEAL, that he seemed so...pissed off about my situation."

"Smiley would bend over backward to help you. The rest of his friends too," Kelli said earnestly.

"I don't want to involve them," Bree said.

Kelli laughed. "I'm not being rude—okay, laughing probably *is* rude—but one thing I've learned about Flash and his friends is that they love to be involved. In everything. They're regular ol' busybodies. But they have the connections and the ability to solve just about any problem. Stay, Bree. Let them help you."

"I know that's why I came, but now I...I can't. Not yet."

"All right," Kelli said calmly. "Then how about you shower and we'll do your laundry. You can make the decision about what to do next after that."

"Are you going to tell Smiley or your boyfriend that I was here?"

Kelli struggled with that question. She wanted to. But she wanted Bree's trust more. "No. Not until you tell me I can."

"Why?"

"Because I'm guessing you've had enough decisions about your life taken away from you."

"Thank you," Bree whispered, looking down at the table and the empty plate in front of her. "You have no idea what that means to me."

Flash was going to be hurt when he found out that Kelli had kept something from him. She hated that. But she truly believed Bree would find the courage to talk to Smiley before too long. She was more concerned with the woman's physical health and safety at the moment. Once she was clean, and had some healthier food in her belly, hopefully she'd find the courage again that had led her to Smiley's door in the first place.

"I *did* think you were his girlfriend, you know," Bree said.

"Smiley's? Yeah, I figured that out," Kelli said. "Come on. I'll show you where the bathroom is, and you can do your thing while I do the dishes."

Bree frowned. "You truly aren't going to call your boyfriend while I'm out of earshot?"

"I'm not. I promise."

Kelli hated that Bree still looked skeptical, but that made her all the more determined to not let her new friend down.

Not wanting her to leave, because she was afraid she wouldn't come back, Kelli enticed her with the promise of plenty of girly soap in the shower. And while Bree was taller than Kelli by a few inches, and much, much thinner, she suggested she wear a pair of her leggings and a T-shirt and sweatshirt, while her own clothes were in the washer.

While Bree was showering, Kelli stared at her phone guiltily and chewed on a thumbnail. She hated not being able to tell Flash about Bree…and she had a feeling Smiley wasn't the kind of man who would forgive and forget such a huge breach of trust.

But she wanted Bree's trust more than Smiley's. The man had countless people to rely on; Bree had no one. The woman needed a friend, and Kelli was determined to be that for her.

The woman who exited the bathroom looked like a completely different person than the one who'd entered. It was as if washing off the dirt and grime had somehow exposed a more confident version of Bree. Kelli convinced her to sit on the couch, and the time slipped by while they waited for her clothes to finish washing and drying.

To her delight, Kelli found Bree to be smart, funny, and down-to-earth. She was also very observant and empathetic. Somehow she found herself telling Bree all about her dad's death, how devastating it had been. How the money she and her mom had received didn't do a damn thing to heal her heart. She told her about wanting to become an electrician, and her frustration that she couldn't start classes until the man who was lurking had been caught.

It didn't escape her notice that Bree didn't seem confused when Kelli mentioned the other SEALs' women. As if she knew them somehow. Kelli didn't ask about that, nor did she question Bree about her past, simply because she didn't want her to bolt.

When her clothes were done, and after Bree had changed back into them, Kelli was genuinely sad that the time with her new friend was over. She followed her to the door and asked, "Will you come back?"

Bree hesitated, and Kelli's stomach fell. She was going to walk out the door and never return. That would hurt, and not only because Smiley and the others wouldn't understand why Kelli hadn't called immediately to tell them the woman they'd been searching for had shown up. She liked Bree. Her visit had made the day go by quickly.

"I think so, yes."

Relief made Kelli feel almost dizzy. "Good," she said with a huge smile.

"Be careful," Bree warned. "I know you said you aren't leaving the apartment, but that doesn't mean the guy doesn't know you're here. He could follow someone else, figure out where you are."

Kelli pressed her lips together. Bree wasn't saying anything she hadn't already thought of herself, but it was still scary to hear.

"Sorry, I'm used to being paranoid. I'm sure you'll be fine."

"No, I hear you. But Flash has to go to work, and it's not as if I can hang out there with him while he and the others discuss super-top-secret SEAL stuff."

"I guess not. How about if I help keep an eye out on the place for you? I mean, I'm already always looking over my shoulder. What does this Brant guy look like?"

"Average height, short dark hair, dark skin, the last time I saw him he was clean-shaven, but I guess that could've changed by now. He's slender...oh, and he walks with a slight limp. I don't know why."

"That's actually really helpful. I don't suppose you know what kind of car he's driving?"

Kelli shook her head. "No, sorry."

"It's all right. I'll keep watch, and if I see anyone who looks similar to what you described, I'll let you know."

"Thanks. Do you want to tell me what the guy who's looking for *you* looks like, so I can return the favor?"

"No."

That was it. Just one word. Kelli tried not to be insulted by being shut down so completely. "Right. I probably wouldn't be much help anyway, since I'm in this apartment all day. Be careful, Bree. I don't have a ton of friends, and it would suck if you left and I never saw you again."

"It would suck for me too," Bree said. "I don't know when I'll be back, but if I can do so safely, I will."

That didn't sound very promising to Kelli, but she nodded anyway. "Be safe out there," she said softly.

Bree nodded, then opened the door. Kelli watched her walk down the hall until she was out of sight. Then she closed and locked the door once more. The last few hours had been surreal, but she was very glad she'd met the illusive Bree Haynes.

CHAPTER NINETEEN

Something was up with Kelli, and Flash was frustrated because he couldn't figure out what was bothering her, and she wasn't talking.

He'd done everything he could to try to get it out of her. He'd apologized over and over that she was stuck in Smiley's apartment all day, but she shrugged it off. Said it wasn't his fault and that she was fine. He'd offered to take her to see her mom, but she declined, saying that they talked on the phone all the time, she didn't need to see her until they knew for certain it was safe.

He was doubly frustrated because Williams was still in the wind. It had been over two weeks since the fire at his apartment, and Ryleigh, the woman in New Mexico who was trying to find him, hadn't had any luck. He liked the woman, she was blunt and to the point, a lot like Tex. She'd found the bank account that had been set up to receive ransom money—and disabled it—but that was a dead end as far as finding Williams.

She'd even gone so far as to get his current credit card canceled, and she transferred the money in his Jamaican bank account to Flash's, just because she could, also rendering his debit card useless. She'd hacked into security cameras at all the places he'd last used his credit card before canceling it, and she'd also sent pictures of the man to all their friends. But she still hadn't been able to find him.

Canceling his cards had almost certainly pissed him off and hampered his ability to hide in shitty motels or rent vehicles... but it also cut off any ability to track him. Still, Ryleigh assured them that she would find him. That she was getting close.

Flash had to believe her.

Other than whatever was weighing on her mind that she wouldn't talk to him about, things with Kelli on a personal front were going extremely well. She was his perfect match in every way. Flash just hated that she couldn't be free to do what she wanted. To move on with her life by starting her electrician classes. He'd been a little skeptical about her decision, but the more time that went by, the more excited she got. And seeing her so hyped about her future made Flash happy.

Their sex life was more amazing every day. Kelli's passion matched his own perfectly. Most nights he went to bed telling himself that he was going to make love to her slowly, but within minutes, she'd blow all his good intentions out the window. She was a wildcat, and he loved it. She loved giving head, which was any man's dream come true. She wasn't as comfortable with him reciprocating, but she was learning the joys of being eaten out.

She also loved to experiment when it came to positions...and they hadn't kept their sexual activities to the bedroom, which Flash would never admit to Smiley.

Speaking of which, Flash was more than ready to get back to his own place. It wasn't that he didn't appreciate his teammate giving Kelli a safe place to stay while he was at work, it was more that he wanted to be in *his* space. He wanted to see her shoes in *his* living room. Her underwear in *his* laundry hamper. Her body in *his* shower. *His* kitchen. *His* bed.

Those thoughts were ridiculous, but he didn't shy away from

them. He wanted to be able to start his life with his woman on their own terms, not on Brant fucking Williams'. The man needed to be found. Pronto.

Maybe when that happened, Kelli would feel comfortable enough to talk to him about whatever had been bothering her for over a week now.

They were currently in bed, and he was running his fingers over her bare shoulder as she lay on top of him. He needed to get up soon, but for now, he was enjoying the quiet moment with the woman who meant everything to him.

"Are the guys going to be deployed soon?" she asked, seemingly out of the blue.

Flash frowned. "No. Why?"

She shrugged against him. "I don't know, I guess because you're all working really hard on whatever it is you're working on, I just figured that meant the mission would start soon."

"Sometimes we research for months before we head out. Other times we're sent out on the spur of the moment. It all depends on what the mission is. For instance, taking out an HVT...high-value target...could take weeks of planning to make sure we mitigate as many dangers as possible. But if there's a hostage situation, we might get no advance notice."

"That makes sense," Kelli said against his chest.

"You okay? What brought this on?" Flash asked, wondering if this was what had been bothering her.

"Nothing. I'm good. If they catch Brant, you'll get put back on the rotation to be deployed, right?"

He nodded. "*When* they catch him, yes. Are you worried about that? About me leaving?"

"No."

"No?" Flash asked in surprise.

Kelli picked up her head and rested it on the back of her hand, lying on his chest. "Why would I? I already know that you rock. I've seen you in action first-hand. And your fellow SEALs too."

Her confidence and absolute trust in him blew Flash away. "I know things between us have been fast, brought on by some not-so-great circumstances, but you can talk to me about anything, Kelli. Nothing is off limits between us. Understand?"

She put her head back down on his chest and nodded.

Her reluctance to meet his gaze made him even more sure that she was keeping something from him. And her next words cemented it.

She sighed, then said softly, "I trust you, Flash. More than any other man I've ever been with. I *can* talk to you about anything, which feels amazing. I need you to know that I'd never keep secrets from you. I'm an open book to you. But...sometimes there are things that affect *others* that aren't my place to talk about."

Flash frowned. "Does this have to do with Williams and what happened? Has he contacted you in some way?"

"No."

Her reply was so immediate and heartfelt, Flash believed her.

"Are you in danger?"

"Me? No."

That didn't make Flash feel any better. "But someone else is?"

"Maybe."

"Look at me," Flash ordered. He waited until Kelli had picked her head up again and met his gaze. "If someone is in danger, you need to tell *someone*. If not me, then one of my teammates. Or Wolf or someone on his team."

"I can't," she whispered. "I promised."

Flash didn't like that answer. Not at all. He didn't realize he was scowling until tears formed in Kelli's eyes.

"I don't want you to hate me. Please, that would destroy me."

"I could never hate you. I love you."

The words seemed to echo in the room.

"What?" Kelli asked.

He hadn't meant to blurt that out, but Flash didn't regret it. "I love you," he repeated. "You're my everything. It's too fast again, but I don't give a shit. It's how I feel, and how I'll *always* feel. And I'm willing to wait as long as it takes for you to love me back.

"No matter what's going on, I'm not going to hate you, Kelli. I understand loyalty. Hell, there are lots of things I'll never be able to tell you, because of my job. I just need you to promise that if someone's life is truly in danger, you'll talk to me or someone else you trust. The last thing you'll want is any guilt hanging over your head for not speaking up, only for the worst to happen."

"I know. And I will. It's just...it's a delicate situation."

Flash was baffled how this woman, who hung out in the apartment all day, could have found herself in the middle of a so-called "delicate situation." But he didn't question her. He'd have to trust that she'd come to him when she was ready. "Do *not* put yourself in danger," he warned.

"I won't. This isn't about me," she quickly reassured him.

But Flash wasn't particularly reassured. He made a mental note to check in with her more often during the day. Make sure she was all right, that whatever was going on truly wasn't putting her in harm's way.

Making a split-second decision, Flash leaned over and grabbed the small box he'd put on the table next to the bed. He'd had something made for her and was waiting for the best time to give it to her. Now seemed like that time. He rolled back over and held it out to her.

Kelli looked surprised. Then confused. Then a little worried.

"It's not a ring," he said quickly. "I love you, but proposing two seconds after I tell you that I love you for the first time is a bit much, even for me."

She grinned, then took the box and opened it without a word.

When she saw what was inside, her eyes widened and she let out a small gasp. "Flash," she whispered. "Is this..."

"It's the spoon. From the bus. The girls found it while they were helping you clean your apartment and since it didn't match the rest of your silverware, they asked me what they should do with it. I took it and was going to have it mounted in a shadow box or something, but decided on this instead."

"This" was a bracelet. He'd brought it to a jeweler Caroline recommended and the man had twisted and manipulated it, making it a beautiful piece of art. It was still obvious that it was a spoon, but now it was polished and cleaned up, even if it still had its little dents and dings. Kind of like both him and Kelli.

"I...it's perfect," she breathed. "Thank you."

Kelli looked up at him and Flash could see the tears in her eyes.

"Those are good tears, right?" he asked, suddenly nervous he'd overstepped and messed up.

"Of course they are. I'll treasure this forever. It reminds me of the hell we went through, but also that we came out on top. That we worked together to make the most of that horrible situation."

Flash reached for the bracelet. "May I?" he asked.

Kelli nodded, and Flash gently wrapped the spoon bracelet around her wrist. It was a cuff bracelet, the kind that didn't have a fastener, but could be tightened by squeezing it around a woman's wrist. It fit perfectly.

"I've never gotten a more thoughtful gift. Thank you, Flash."

"You're welcome." Rolling over, Flash pinned Kelli under him. "I have fifteen minutes before I need to get up," he informed her.

Her cheeks were still damp from her tears, but she smiled up at him. "We could sleep," she suggested with a glint in her eye.

"We could," he agreed. "Or we could do that Lazy Man position. You know, which I think is only fair, since I'm the one who has to get up and go to PT."

"You only like that one because it puts my boobs right in your face," Kelli protested.

Flash chuckled. "Can you blame me? You have a set of tits that wars are fought over."

Kelli rolled her eyes. Flash smiled and started to move to a seated position, with the headboard at his back, but Kelli stopped him. "Flash?"

"Yeah?"

"I love you too."

Flash immediately leaned down, his cock throbbing against her thigh, the urge to slam inside her and show her how much her words meant to him pushing at him hard. He kissed her... long, slow, and with every ounce of love in his body that he had for this woman.

It wasn't long before she was pushing at his shoulders, urging him to sit up. Neither of them had put on anything after they'd made love the evening before, so it was an easy matter for her to straddle him. She was right, this position put her tits right in his face, and Flash didn't hesitate to take one of her nipples into his mouth.

She groaned and arched her back. His cock was trapped between their bodies, but he knew it wouldn't be long before he sank home, where he belonged.

As usual, Kelli began to squirm, impatient with lust. She lifted up, and Flash moved with her, not wanting to lose the nipple he was biting and sucking on. She wrapped her hand around his cock and notched him between her legs.

They both gasped when she dropped down, taking him deep inside her body.

"Ride me, Kelli. Take what you want," Flash urged.

He didn't need to ask twice. Then he was no longer able to suck on her tits; they bounced too much as she rode him hard.

This woman. She slayed him. He loved her so damn much.

It didn't take long for either of them to reach orgasm. He loved how tussled Kelli looked after she came. There would never be any question if she'd had an orgasm or not, he could tell by the flush on her skin, the sweat on her brow, and the look of absolute satisfaction on her face.

The last thing he wanted to do was pull out of her warm pussy, but a glance at the clock told him he was already going to be late for PT. He took Kelli's face in his hands and kissed her. Then he said, "Stay safe today. We're getting off early. How about we go out tonight?"

"Really?" she said, the excitement easy to hear in her voice.

"Really. Smiley needs to come over and grab some more things—I think he's just lazy and doesn't want to do laundry, so he wants to get some clean clothes from here. After he leaves, we can go anywhere you want."

"There's an amazing Thai place in La Jolla."

"If that's what you want, that's where we'll go."

"I can show you my favorite beach up there too. Maybe we can watch the sunset."

"It's a date," Flash told her, leaning forward and kissing her once more. "Now, I have to get up or Kevlar's gonna make me do extra sand sprints."

Kelli grinned. "Wouldn't want that," she told him. Then squeezed her Kegel muscles, making Flash groan as his cock flexed in appreciation.

"That was just mean," he complained, easily lifting her off him as if she weighed next to nothing.

"I love when you do that," she said on a sigh, as she lay on her back next to him and stretched.

"Do what?" Flash asked, distracted by the way her tits moved on her chest.

"Lift me as if I were light as a feather."

"You are," Flash told her. Then he leaned down and kissed her forehead, knowing if he did anything more, he'd never get out of bed. "You need to get up and lock the door behind me, put the chain on," he told her. "Don't go back to sleep."

"I know, and I won't," she said.

Flash got out of bed while he still had the willpower, and within minutes, he was kissing Kelli at the front door. "I'll text you when Smiley and I leave work."

"Okay. What time...approximately, do you think?"

"Maybe three-ish."

"Sounds good. Drive safe."

"I will. I love you, Kelli. You've made my life so much better, and while I'd never admit that I was glad we were kidnapped, I *am* glad that your cousin decided to have her bachelorette party at the same resort as Chuck."

"Me too."

Flash kissed her one last time before heading out. He heard the bolts click into place and waited to hear the clink of the safety chain being slid on. Once he was satisfied that Kelli was as safe as she could be, he strode down the hall and did his best to turn his attention from his cock to the work that needed to be done later that day.

* * *

Kelli really, *really* hoped Bree showed up today. She hated keeping the woman's visits from Flash, but she'd been back twice in the last week and a half, and each time, Bree seemed to relax a little more. And she looked healthier too. The regular showers and being able to wash her clothes went a long way toward giving her some confidence. And it didn't hurt that Kelli plied her with as much food as she could while she was there, giving her fresh veggies and other healthy foods to take with her, as well.

She especially wanted Bree to show up today, since Flash had said Smiley would be there. If she happened to be there at the same time, maybe she'd work up the courage to talk to him. To finally ask for the help she needed. She'd seemed utterly despondent that first time she'd knocked on the door, and now that she wasn't quite as desperate as far as her personal needs went, maybe she'd be able to dig deep and ask for assistance with whomever was after her.

Smiley would be so relieved to have found her, and Kelli knew that he'd agree to help in a heartbeat. According to Flash, that had been his goal all along. To make sure she was safe and wasn't in the clutches of whoever she'd been sold to.

Looking at her watch, Kelli paced nervously. It was getting close to the time when Flash and Smiley should be here, and still no sign of Bree. She'd finally admitted that she'd been following the team; she knew where everyone lived and what they drove. If she saw Smiley's older-model Ford Ranger in the parking lot, she most likely wouldn't stop. That would mean Kelli would have to keep the secret of her visits from Flash even longer.

His words that morning nearly undid her. Her promise that she could talk to him about anything. She almost confessed everything. But then she'd been distracted by Flash telling her that he loved her.

It seemed so unreal. That she, Kelli Colbert, nerd extraordinaire, nobody special, had managed to make Flash love her. And the thing was, she had no idea how she'd done it. Or how to *keep* him loving her. It was why she hadn't said the words first, even though she'd felt them down to her soul. Flash was...he was a miracle. And not only because he'd been her everything when they were kidnapped.

He was a good man. Considerate. Protective. And as a bonus, he was amazing in bed. Kelli became a person she didn't know when she was with him. Like this morning, riding him like she was a cowgirl at a rodeo or something. But since he wasn't complaining, and she'd never felt so satisfied, she couldn't care if she was suddenly...overly exuberant in bed.

Stopping by the window to look out into the parking lot, Kelli didn't see Bree or her Subaru Outback. She'd spied on the woman after her second visit and saw her getting into the dark green car. She usually arrived early in the afternoon, wanting to make sure she was gone before Flash came home. It was already later than she'd normally visit...but she had no way to know the men would be getting off work early today, so there was still a chance that she'd stop by, and she and Smiley could actually come face-to-face.

Around the time Kelli got the text from Flash saying that he was on his way home, she reluctantly decided Bree wouldn't be visiting. She was bummed about that, since she truly thought the woman was ready to talk to Smiley, but she'd been running for so long, hiding, that Kelli knew it had to be scary for Bree to consider doing anything outside of her current routine.

She *did* manage to convince the woman to take Smiley's cell number after their last visit, and her own. She was worried enough about her, living in her car and on the run, that she'd wanted her to have an emergency way to contact someone. Just in case.

Kelli, at least, would be glad to see Smiley. After more than two weeks in the apartment, she was feeling cooped up. Stir-crazy. The day was beautiful. The sun was out and she longed to go outside, at least for a little bit. Get some fresh air. Surely under both Flash *and* Smiley's watchful eyes, she could do just that.

She wasn't resentful, not in the least. If she was on her own, still at her apartment, she'd be terrified. Wondering when Brant would return...and what he'd do to Kelli when he found her. Here in Smiley's apartment, even when she was alone, she felt safe. Brant still didn't seem to know where she or Flash were. And the Ryleigh person who was doing everything in her power to find him claimed she was close to figuring out where he'd been hiding.

Without his credit card or access to his bank account, he'd have to make a move soon. Which scared Kelli, but she was aware that meant she and Flash would hopefully be able to move on with their lives.

What would happen next for them was still to be determined. Would she go back to her apartment? She hoped they'd still date, figured they would...it wasn't likely Flash would tell her that he loved her one day and decide they were over the next.

Kelli removed the chain on the door after Flash's text, then waited impatiently in the kitchen for the men to arrive. When she heard the key in the lock, she walked around the counter.

Flash entered first, and Kelli beamed at him. He walked straight toward her and hugged her hard, taking her off her feet. It was how he always greeted her. As if it had been weeks since he'd seen her, rather than simply hours.

"You good?" he asked.

Kelli laughed. "Why wouldn't I be?"

"Just checking."

"Hey, Kelli," Smiley said in his gruff way. "I like what you've done with the place," he joked.

Kelli chuckled. "You mean cleaned it?" she asked. When she and Flash had moved in, the place looked like a tornado had hit it. Smiley was obviously not a very orderly person. But now there wasn't one thing out of place. It was spick-and-span. She'd cleaned the apartment from top to bottom...it was one way to keep busy during her long, boring days alone.

Looking around, Kelli figured Smiley was probably wincing inside at the shape of his apartment, how different it looked from when he'd seen it last. No dirty dishes in the sink, no mail piled up on the counter, and two blankets folded neatly and hanging off the back of the couch. She'd even straightened his bookcase and alphabetized the books by the last name of each author.

"Yeah, that," Smiley said. Then he stepped forward and gave her a hug as well.

Kelli was surprised. Smiley wasn't a touchy-feely kind of guy, and him being so...well...*nice*, made her feel guilty all over again. He'd been desperately trying to find Bree, and she was keeping the fact that she'd been here, in his apartment, using his shower, his washer and dryer, a secret from the man.

She felt like shit. She was a horrible friend.

Suddenly, guilt threatened to overwhelm her.

Luckily, Smiley didn't seem to notice. He stepped back and said, "I'll just go and pack some stuff."

The second he disappeared down the hallway, Flash wrapped his arms around her waist from behind and rested his chin on her shoulder. "What's wrong?" he asked quietly.

"Nothing, why?" Kelli asked.

"Because you seem...tense all of a sudden."

She sighed and turned around to face him. "I'm okay. I'm just feeling a little stir-crazy today. It's a beautiful day and I'm stuck inside."

Flash frowned. "When's the last time you were outside?"

Kelli gave him a look.

"Right. I'm sorry."

"For what?"

"For not truly understanding how difficult this is for you sooner."

"It's fine. I'm safe, and that's all that matters."

"That's *not* all that matters," Flash disagreed. "Your mental health is important too. And more than just feeling safe. I never want you to feel as if you're trapped."

"You said Ryleigh is getting closer to finding Brant, right?" Kelli asked.

"Yes."

"So, it won't be too much longer then. Hopefully."

"Hopefully. I still want to go to that Thai place you mentioned this morning, but maybe we'll go to the beach first instead of after. Let you get some sun on your cheeks. Some outdoor therapy."

"I'd love that," Kelli said with a smile. Just the thought of being able to sit in the sand, feel the breeze on her face, made her happy.

Ten minutes later, Smiley came out of his bedroom with three large duffle bags.

Kelli giggled. "Did you pack everything you own?" she asked.

"Not sure how much longer I'll be gone, figured I might as well get it all now."

Flash walked up to him and took one of the bags. "I'll help you carry these down."

"Me too," Kelli said, reaching for one of the two remaining bags Smiley had over his shoulders.

He stepped away from her, frowning. "No."

"Come on, I'm not *that* much of a weakling."

"No," he repeated.

Now Kelli frowned at *him*. "Why not?"

"Because."

She rolled her eyes. "That's not an answer. Flash, tell Smiley he's being ridiculous and to let me carry one of his bags."

"You know you sound like an eight-year-old tattling to her mom about something her brother isn't allowing her to do," Smiley told her.

Kelli frowned harder and put her hands on her hips. "So?"

Smiley didn't seem to be affected by her irritation in the least. He just walked toward the door.

"Wait a sec," Flash told his friend. He turned to Kelli. "You ready to go?"

"To the beach and dinner? Yes!" she said excitedly. "Let me

grab a sweatshirt. And my purse. Oh, and I need to change shoes!"

She heard Smiley chuckle and say under his breath, "I'm taking that as a *no*, she isn't actually ready to go."

"Shut it, Smiley!" Kelli called out, as she hurried toward the bedroom.

She was back in less than a minute, more than ready to get out of the apartment.

They all left, Flash making sure the door was secured behind them. As they walked down the hall, Kelli complained, "I could be carrying one of those bags for you."

"You could, but you aren't," Smiley said.

Kelli was actually amused now by his stubbornness. She didn't really care whether she carried one of the bags or not, it was just fun to needle the uptight SEAL.

The second they left the building, she winced at the bright light but gloried in being outside, touched by the sun's rays without a window as a buffer.

"It's such a gorgeous day!" she gushed. Stopping for a moment to close her eyes and lift her chin to the sky, she reveled in the warmth on her face.

She was still standing there, soaking in the moment, when suddenly she was almost jerked off her feet.

Kelli's eyes popped open as she stumbled backward, her hands instinctively moving up to her neck, where a strong arm was almost cutting off her air.

Her gaze flew to Smiley and Flash, standing by Smiley's pickup truck, one of the three bags at their feet and the other two already inside the bed of the truck. She had the wild thought that she'd never seen Flash—or Smiley, for that matter —look so...murderous.

The men were furious. If she didn't already know that she was in big trouble, their expressions would've given it away.

"Don't get any closer!" the man behind her growled, even as

he forced Kelli to walk backward. It was difficult to breathe, and all she could do was stumble along in the man's grasp.

"Let her go, Williams!" Flash ordered.

Brant. He'd finally found them.

Instead of being on alert, the first time she'd stepped outside in days, Kelli had to stop in the middle of the parking lot and close her eyes.

She was an idiot.

"No can do," he said. Kelli could smell his body odor, and it made her want to gag. Wherever he'd been hiding, he hadn't been taking care of himself, that was for sure.

"You're making a mistake," Smiley said. He and Flash were matching her and Brant step for step now, and Kelli swore she could see both men readying themselves to pounce.

"I wouldn't if I were you," Brant said, producing a knife out of nowhere and angling it toward her chest—right over her heart. "I'll kill her. Right here and now. I swear I will! How long do you think she'll live with a hole in her heart? Not long. She'll bleed out in seconds and it'll be *your fault*."

"What do you fucking want?" Flash said in a low, pissed-off tone.

"I want my money!" Brant screamed, sounding hysterical.

"What money? The money you tried to get out of the government? You're an idiot if you ever thought the Navy would pay a cent of that ransom."

"Well, they might not have paid, but *you* will if you want to see your precious girlfriend again. Now stop walking or I'll do it! I'll kill her!"

"Then you definitely won't get your money," Smiley said in a stone-cold tone.

To her surprise and horror, the knife in Brant's hand lowered —and she gasped in pain as just the tip penetrated her shirt and skin.

Flash reached out an arm, halting Smiley's forward motion.

"I'm serious! I have nothing to lose. Stop right there!" Brant yelled.

The knife still stuck in her chest hurt. *A lot*. Between that and the lack of oxygen, Kelli was having a hard time thinking straight.

"As long as you do what I say, she'll be fine. I want a million dollars delivered to a new bank account I set up this morning. And if you do *anything* to get it shut down, I'll send her back to you in pieces. An ear one day, a few fingers the next. The last thing you'll get is her heart. And don't fuck with me! I'll do it!"

A million dollars? Flash didn't have that kind of money. Even if he got help from all his friends, Kelli wasn't sure they'd be able to come up with that much cash. Brant had obviously gotten greedy, upping his demand significantly from the fifty thousand he'd originally hoped to get for this kidnapping.

Because Kelli was focused on getting air into her lungs—but not breathing *too* deeply, so the knife wouldn't be penetrating her skin any farther—she didn't realize they'd reached a vehicle. It wasn't until the arm around her neck loosened and Brant pushed her into an open door that she even thought about trying to escape.

But that idea was instantly foiled when Brant, still holding the knife, struck out and slashed her thigh.

Pain blossomed hard and fast. Kelli slapped her hand over the gash in her leg even as she cried out.

"Kelli!"

Flash's voice sounded as if it was very far away. Brant pushed her over until he was behind the wheel of the decrepit, older-model four-door car, then he peeled out of the parking lot before his door was even shut.

Looking out her window, Kelli saw Flash and Smiley running after the car. Then they abruptly stopped and ran back toward Flash's SUV.

Brant laughed. The sound so evil, it made the hair on the back of Kelli's neck stand up.

"Those idiots aren't going to catch up. I've outsmarted them! All I had to do was wait and be patient and today was my day. I knew you were somewhere, hiding out. I tried following your boyfriend, but he eluded me day after day. I couldn't find where you two were staying. But today, he and his friend were careless, and I followed them straight to you. I'm gonna get my money! One way or another!"

Kelli's throat felt bruised from the pressure he'd used with his arm, hauling her around. And her thigh was on fire. At least her chest no longer hurt as badly...but Kelli was terrified. Where was Brant taking her? She'd dropped her purse in the confusion, so she didn't have her phone to call for help or give any clues as to where they were heading.

Brant drove like a man possessed. He took corners way too fast, side-swiped a couple cars, went the wrong way on one-way streets, and generally broke every rule of the road. It wasn't long before Kelli realized he was right. Flash and Smiley weren't going to catch up to him.

He was getting away.

Surreptitiously glancing at the man behind the wheel, Kelli tried to come up with a plan. Some clever way to escape before he did more than just make her bleed. Because he was going to kill her—she had no doubt. Even if he got his money, he wasn't going to let her live this time. He was too pissed off that his kidnapping plan in Jamaica had failed. That she and Flash had escaped. That it took so long to find them.

Then something out of the corner of her eye caught her attention.

Tucking her chin and pretending to fuss over the cut on her leg, Kelli turned her head just enough to glance into the back seat—and was surprised to see a pair of hazel eyes staring back at her.

Bree Haynes was in the backseat! Sitting on the floor behind the driver's seat, covered by the clothes and other junk cluttering up the entire back of the car. It looked as if every possession Brant owned was back there...but how *Bree* came to be there was more than Kelli could comprehend.

Bree shook her head and put a finger up to her lips, warning Kelli to stay quiet, then held up a phone.

The relief that almost overwhelmed Kelli made her dizzy. Or maybe that was blood loss. She didn't know. She had no idea how the heck Bree was in this car, but the fact that she had a phone —and was hopefully using it to communicate with Smiley—was enough for Kelli to get her hopes up.

Brant hadn't won yet. Kelli might be bruised and battered, but she wasn't dead. And as long as she was still breathing, she had hope that Flash would find her.

Jerking her head so she was facing forward again, Kelli took a deep breath. Then another. She wouldn't do anything that would give Bree away. The woman was literally her best hope at getting out of this alive. For both of them getting away alive. Because if Brant found he had a stowaway, there was no telling what he'd do.

CHAPTER TWENTY

Smiley held onto the oh-shit handle of Flash's SUV as he took a corner on two wheels.

"Come on, come on," Flash muttered, as both men frantically searched for the piece-of-shit brown, four-door car that Williams had used to steal Kelli right out from under their noses.

The memory of Kelli's shriek of pain when the asshole cut her leg wouldn't be something Smiley forgot anytime soon. Nor the anguished noise that flew from Flash's lips. Seeing the woman he loved—yes, Smiley was aware that his friend was well and truly hooked on Kelli—being hurt, but not being able to do a damn thing about it, was terrifically painful for his teammate.

Seeing a car on the side of the road with its side all scraped to hell—and its front end bashed in from hitting a light pole—Smiley yelled, "Go right!"

Flash took another corner way too fast as they did their best to track the path Williams had gone by the destruction left in his wake.

Just when they thought they might've lost him, Smiley's phone vibrated in his pocket. Feeling like an idiot for not calling in backup immediately, he yanked it out and stared down at the text from an unknown number.

Unknown: This is Bree i'm in car w Kelli & asshole just passed 37th st

It took Smiley's brain a beat to understand what he was reading. He was confused as fuck. Bree? *His* Bree? How did she have his number? And how the *fuck* was she in the car with Williams and Kelli? Was she working with him?

What the absolute fuck?

Unknown: was visiting K when u guys came outside I saw what happened & got into car while he was distracted by u guys and hurting K we just turned on Aspen st

"Keep straight here!" Smiley told Flash.

"But I think he went west," he protested.

"Straight!" Smiley barked. Thankfully, his friend listened and continued straight instead of turning. "Bree's texting me. She's in the car with them. She's telling me where they're going."

"What the fuck?!" Flash asked.

That's what Smiley wanted to know, but at the moment, he needed intel on Williams more. He had no idea what Bree's intentions were, but if she could lead them to Kelli, he wasn't going to question her...not yet. Later? Yes. She had a lot to answer for. But Kelli needed to be his focus right now.

Smiley: Got it

. . .

He couldn't resist one question.

Smiley: r u ok?
Unknown: for now. passing 40th

Smiley continued to pass along the information Bree was giving him. A ball of panic sat in his throat, as there were now two women in danger instead of one. And because, for the second time, Bree was putting herself at risk in order to help one of his friends. When he got his hands on that woman, he'd make certain she understood that was unacceptable. That she needed to stop putting herself in danger.

Unknown: slowing down. going down cedar. pulling into drive. Brown hse, one sty, 47. We r at 47 cedar st!!!
Smiley: We're coming. Stay put. Do NOT leave. I mean it.
Unknown: I wont. Tired. Need help.

Smiley was almost as alarmed at the fact that Bree was admitting she needed help as he was that she'd stowed away in Williams' car in the first place. From everything he'd learned about this woman throughout his long and unsuccessful search for her, she was very stubborn and far too independent. Now, he didn't like how...defeated she sounded. Which was crazy, since it was just some words on a screen. But he couldn't shake the thought that she was definitely at the end of her rope.

He and Flash would take care of the Williams situation, then he and Bree Haynes were going to have a very long talk.

***

Kelli's eyes widened as they pulled into a driveway in front of a dilapidated house that looked like no one had lived there for a very long time. Brant didn't give her time to even try to open her door and run, not that she could've outrun him with her leg throbbing as badly as it was. He grabbed her by the arm and manhandled her across the front seat and pulled her out the driver's side door.

Without a word, he half dragged her to the front door. He kicked it hard, and it flew open. Dust swam in the sunlight coming through the door as he pulled her inside then kicked the door shut behind them.

"Brant, I—"

"Shut the fuck up," he growled menacingly.

Deciding it was in her best interest, Kelli shut up.

Her mind spun, attempting to figure out how the hell to get out of this situation. But she had no idea what to do. Brant slashing her leg made it impossible to walk very well, much less run. She could feel the blood oozing down her leg under her pants, making the material stick to her as she walked. Not to mention the wound in her chest. The knife hadn't gone in very deep, but it was still painful.

Brant hauled her to a room in the back of the house that was littered with trash and decaying food. There was a moldy mattress in the corner, and Kelli could see several used needles in the filthy mess around her. Brant shoved her—thankfully not at the disgusting mattress—and she fell onto her hands and knees in the middle of the filth. She immediately turned on her butt to face Brant. If he was going to come at her with that knife, she'd fight him as best she could.

But he seemed to forget she was there as soon as he let her go. He immediately began to pace, mumbling to himself as he walked.

Kelli kept her gaze on the man who'd obviously gone a little crazy, inching backward until she was against one of the walls. The only window was on the back wall, and it had so much dirt and grime on it, she wasn't sure it would even open. If Brant left her in the room alone, she could break it out, but that would alert him in seconds that she was trying to escape.

For now, she had to be content with the fact that Brant hadn't tied her up. He obviously thought, correctly, that she wouldn't be going anywhere, not with that wound on her leg.

Kelli's thoughts turned to Bree. How had she gotten in the car? Had she managed to tell Smiley where they were? Was she going to do something stupid and get herself killed? That would suck, especially considering Kelli's plan to get her and Smiley to meet face-to-face had failed.

She had no idea how long she'd sat against the wall, watching Brant pace and talk to himself. A matter of minutes. But when he finally stopped and faced her, Kelli tensed.

This wasn't good. Not good at all.

"It's time," Brant said, pulling the knife from a sheath along his hip. He ran his thumb over the tip and smirked. "I don't need you alive to get my ransom. I just need your boyfriend and his friends to *think* you're alive. Frankly, you've been a pain in my ass since Jamaica—and I'm done dealing with you."

Kelli shrank away from him and mentally berated herself for not doing anything to even attempt escaping sooner. Fending off a man armed with a *very* sharp knife—and she should know, she'd felt it first-hand, slicing through her flesh—would be far less fun.

But no matter what, she wasn't going down easy. She'd do what she could to get his DNA under her fingernails, to scratch him so it was obvious he'd been in a fight. Anything that would tell the police and forensic people that Brant was guilty as hell. She might not be there to see him put away, but she prayed with all her might that he'd pay for what he was about to do.

Regret hit Kelli hard as Brant stepped toward her. She loved Flash, more than she'd ever loved anyone in her entire life. He gave her confidence, made her believe she could be anyone she wanted, do anything. He made her laugh, sigh in pleasure, and she simply enjoyed being around him. And she regretted that she hadn't had more time with him. That she'd never get a chance at the future for them that Flash envisioned.

Taking a deep breath, Kelli focused on Brant's right hand. The one holding the knife. This was it. She'd either win or die trying.

Attempting to channel Flash's badass SEAL vibe, she waited for Brant to get close enough to make a move. She'd try to kick the knife out of his hand, make the first strike. Then the fight would be on.

* * *

Flash focused on not hitting any other cars as he sped through Riverton toward Cedar Street. He had no idea how the hell Bree Haynes was in Williams' car, but he wasn't going to look a gift horse in the mouth. All he could think about was getting to Kelli.

Watching Williams cut her had felt like his own flesh was being sliced. The expression on Kelli's face would stick with him for the rest of his days. He'd been injured in missions, and had seen many others get hurt too. But nothing had affected him as deeply as seeing *Kelli's* pain.

Fury churned under the surface. Williams was a dead man. Of that, he had no doubt. He'd dared put his hands on *his* woman. Had drawn blood. He'd answer for that.

"There!" Smiley practically yelled.

They were both amped up. Neither had called Kevlar or any of the other guys, and they'd probably all be pissed about that, but they'd understand...eventually. There hadn't been any time to stop and call them, or even text. Flash was concentrating on driving and Smiley was communicating with Bree, then looking up 47 Cedar Street on his map app.

Taking a deep breath, attempting to slow the adrenaline coursing through his veins, Flash turned down Cedar. His gaze immediately locked onto the piece-of-shit car Williams had been driving. It was sitting in the driveway of a brown one-story house, just as Bree had described.

It looked like a trap house, a place drug dealers used to sell their goods, or a place where junkies went to shoot up and party. The foundation was iffy and the roof literally had small holes here and there. Flash wouldn't be surprised if this was where Williams had been hiding out after his money disappeared.

Stopping three houses down, Flash and Smiley jumped out of the SUV and quickly made their way toward number 47.

Just as they were approaching the side of the house, a woman stepped out from around the back. Flash was startled for a moment, but Smiley didn't hesitate. He changed his trajectory and went straight toward her.

It hit Flash that this had to be the elusive Bree. The woman Smiley had been obsessed with for so long. When his friend got close enough, he reached out and grabbed her upper arm—and looked like he never wanted to let go.

"There's a window in the back that's broken. I think you can get in that way," Bree told them quietly.

She looked disheveled but in control of her emotions. Which was surprising, considering what she'd just done. Her hair was greasy and her clothes wrinkled. But she held her head up, her shoulders back, as she gestured them toward the back of the house. Smiley still hadn't let go of her, but she didn't seem to mind or really even notice.

The threesome crept around the house, and the back seemed to be in worse shape than the front. There used to be a fence but it had long since collapsed. The weeds were thigh-high, and the smell of rotting garbage was almost overwhelming.

But Flash only had eyes for the window. Bree was right, it wasn't too high off the ground and the glass was completely broken out. He and Smiley would be able to get inside easily. Especially since they weren't hindered by the packs and gear they usually carried while on missions.

Taking a few seconds to listen, Flash didn't hear anything from inside the house, which scared the shit out of him. Had Williams already hurt or killed Kelli? Was he even in there?

There was only one way to find out. If Kelli was hurt, she'd need medical attention. Hell, she was *already* hurt; he needed to get in there *now*.

Without waiting to consult Smiley, Flash grabbed the windowsill and pulled himself up. He was inside the house in seconds, crouched by the window, trying to work through what to do next. He had no weapons, nothing but his hands. Which were as deadly as a gun in *other* people's hands but he'd still need to get close, and if Williams panicked, he could hurt Kelli before Flash could get to him.

The knife he'd held at her heart was enough to make Flash pause before. He couldn't afford for Williams to get away a second time. He had to take the man out once and for all.

"Are you going to run again?" Flash heard Smiley ask Bree.

"No."

"I don't believe you."

"I know you don't. But I'm not lying."

A heartbeat later, Smiley was at Flash's side in the house.

Gratitude toward—and sympathy for—his friend and teammate filled Flash. It couldn't have been easy to leave the woman he'd been searching for so hard. The chance to get answers was literally in his grasp, and they were both aware that leaving her on her own outside was an open invitation for her to bolt yet again. She'd done what she set out to do, led Flash and Smiley to where Kelli was being held. She had nothing holding her there.

Nothing except the fact that she was still being hunted by a brutal sex trafficker.

"I'll go right, you go left," Smiley said in a barely there whisper.

Flash nodded—and just as they both moved, they heard a voice from a room to the right.

The plan shifted in a heartbeat. Both men turned to the right.

They paused outside the next door and Smiley held up a hand. He counted down on his fingers.

Three...

Two...

Before he got to one, a terrified and desperate scream came from inside the room.

Both Flash and Smiley moved at the same time.

Flash took in the scene at a glance. Kelli was against a wall, kicking at Williams, who was doing his best to stab and slash at her with the knife.

A red haze fell over Flash's vision.

He lunged for Williams, who was so focused on killing Kelli that he hadn't even realized they were no longer alone. Flash hit him from the side and they both went down. Hard.

Flash was immediately up and punching Williams over and over. He slammed his fists into his head, his throat, even his chest, hoping to hit hard enough to stop his heart.

"Flash, get Kelli!" Smiley yelled.

It took a minute for his words to penetrate, but as soon as they did, Flash turned.

Kelli was lying on the floor, not moving.

Scrambling on his hands and knees to get to her, Flash barely registered Smiley taking over where he'd left off on top of Williams.

"Kelli?" he croaked, as he hovered over her.

Nothing he'd ever experienced had ever brought him more relief than when her beautiful eyes opened, and she stared up at him.

"Flash?" she whispered.

"It's me! I'm here. You're safe. Where do you hurt?"

"You're bleeding," she said.

Flash blinked. He looked at his knuckles, which were indeed covered in blood. "I'm more worried about you. Talk to me, sweetheart. Shit, I need to call the police and an ambulance."

As soon as the words were out of his mouth, the sound of sirens wailed in the distance.

"It sounds like Bree already did," Kelli said with a little smile.

This woman. She amazed him. Blew everything he knew about strength and what it took to be brave right out of the water. He'd always admired his friends' women for being so strong, but until this moment, it hadn't sunk in just *how* amazing every last one of those women were. Especially his own.

"Seriously, talk to me, Kelli. Did he cut you again? When we came in, he was slashing at you."

"I think I kicked his knife hand. Then you tackled him."

Flash closed his eyes in relief. But only briefly. He had to get Kelli out of there. This was no place for her...this disgusting, filthy, probably disease-ridden room. "Your thigh?" he asked.

"Hurts."

"Right. Of course it does. I'm going to take you out of here. If anything hurts when I move you, let me know immediately. All right?"

"Okay. Is he..." Her voice trailed off.

Looking over his shoulder, Flash wasn't surprised to see Smiley standing next to a bleeding and unmoving Williams. The knife he'd had was lying a little ways away from the body and his neck was at a very unnatural angle.

"Had to defend myself," Smiley said with a shrug. "He kind of broke his neck in our altercation. Oh, and I'm gonna need you to hit me, brother. Pronto. Before the cops arrive."

Kind of broke his neck. Right. It took a lot of strength to break someone's neck, but Smiley had obviously no problem doing just that.

And Flash understood why his friend and teammate was asking for him to hit him. There was no way Tex or any of their other friends would allow Smiley, or Flash himself, to spend even one minute behind bars for killing this piece of trash. But a self-defense claim would go down a lot smoother if Smiley at least looked like he'd been in a fight. At the moment, he didn't have a scratch on him.

"What?" Kelli asked, as Flash stood. He didn't hesitate; he punched Smiley in the face. Once. Then twice.

"One more," Smiley grunted.

"Stop! Flash, what are you doing?"

Flash hit his friend once more, and the men shared a small, satisfied smile as blood began to drip from Smiley's nose. "That'll do," Smiley said with a nod. Then he turned and headed for the door, obviously eager to see if Bree was still around or if she'd fled, like every other time Smiley had gotten close enough to talk to her.

"What the hell?" Kelli asked, as Flash leaned over to pick her up.

"Self-defense," he said softly. "We had to defend ourselves, and unfortunately ended up killing Williams."

"Oh...Right," she said, as she wrapped her arms around his neck and he carried her through the filth toward the door.

The second they exited the house into the late-afternoon sunlight, Flash felt as if he could breathe a little easier. Probably because he literally could. The fresh air, not clogged with the remnants of rotting food and dust, was like a balm to his soul.

To his right, Flash saw Smiley standing next to Bree, his hand once more around her upper arm. He couldn't believe she hadn't fled, and he was thrilled for his teammate. Maybe now he could get to the bottom of what was still happening with the woman. His obsession and curiosity could finally be assuaged.

He'd be interested in hearing her story, himself...after making sure Kelli was all right.

Police cars were now swarming the run-down neighborhood, but Flash kept his eyes on the ambulance that was behind them, already moving toward the vehicle as the police screeched to a halt. When an officer jumped out of his car and tried to stop him, he barked, "Can't you see she's bleeding and needs medical attention?"

To his relief, the officer let him continue toward the ambulance. But he was right on their heels, clearly not willing to let either of them out of his sight until he knew what the hell was going on.

Flash gently lay Kelli down on the gurney in the back of the ambulance and forced himself to stand aside so the paramedics and EMTs could do their job. It was possibly one of the most difficult things he'd ever done, letting go of her, but Kelli holding his gaze and smiling helped him stay calm.

That had been close. Too close. Flash never wanted to be in that situation ever again. He could deal with his own life being in danger. Could deal with being surrounded by terrorists and being fired upon. But knowing one wrong move could mean the death of the woman who'd become his everything literally made him weak in the knees.

The only solace to this situation was that Williams was no longer a threat.

No...not the *only* solace. They could go back to their lives. Kelli could take her classes to become an electrician, he could move back into his own apartment, hopefully along with Kelli. They could get married, start a family, and live happily ever after.

And Flash couldn't wait.

CHAPTER TWENTY-ONE

Kelli gasped and threw a hand over her head to brace herself against the headboard as Flash thrust in and out of her, hard.

"Yes!" she exclaimed.

She'd needed this. After everything that happened, she'd needed to feel alive. And there was no better way than to have the man she loved lose control as he fucked her.

Yesterday had been scary. Terrifying. She'd come way too close to dying. If Flash and Smiley hadn't shown up...No, if *Bree* hadn't been in the parking lot at the exact right time, the outcome would've been much different.

But Bree *had* been there, and Flash and Smiley *had* shown up.

Her leg throbbed, but even in the throes of passion, Flash was careful not to grab the bandaged appendage. He'd been reluctant to make love to her at all, but Kelli was insistent. It was probably way too soon, but she didn't care.

She'd gone to the hospital, where she'd received stitches, and where Flash had paced and generally made everyone uneasy with the amped-up alpha vibes emanating from him. A detective from the Riverton Police Department had arrived and taken her statement while she was waiting for the doctor to stitch up her leg.

Since the man was already familiar with Brant Williams and their case, and he knew he was wanted for the kidnapping back in Jamaica, Flash and Smiley weren't in imminent danger of being arrested. Especially not after seeing Kelli, and hearing her harrowing story of how she was kidnapped...again.

Kelli didn't know where Smiley and Bree had gone, though she assumed they were at his apartment. He and Flash had immediately switched back to their own homes, the rest of their teammates generously pitching in to pack up and move everyone's belongings to the appropriate apartments. By the time she'd finished at the hospital the previous evening, they'd been able to go straight to Flash's place, where they both crashed hard.

However, Kelli had woken up just hours later thanks to a horrible nightmare, and she'd decided what she needed to get back on track, to wipe away the bad dream, was her boyfriend deep inside her. Injuries be damned.

And now here she was, getting fucked hard and fast, just the way she wanted it.

"Get there," Flash ordered, as he moved one hand between her legs and began to strum her clit, just as roughly as he was thrusting inside her.

Kelli had already been close, but his touch sent her soaring. She barely heard his triumphant yell as he let himself come deep inside her.

They were both sweaty, and Kelli could feel her heart beating hard in her chest. She smiled. Yup, this was what she needed. To feel alive...to celebrate the fact that they'd won.

"Damn, woman," Flash complained, as he gently eased out of her and arranged her carefully on the bed so he wouldn't jostle her leg. Then he snuggled up against her, on his side, one arm over her belly, his leg hitched up on her uninjured thigh, his head on her shoulder.

This position was a reversal of how they usually slept. Usually it was Kelli who was draped over *him*, but she actually loved being the receiver of the snuggles, rather than the giver.

"Did I hurt your leg?"

"No."

"Are you sure?"

"Yes."

"You were kind of...aggressive...are you sure you're okay?"

He wasn't wrong. Kelli *had* been aggressive. Insistent that he fuck her, overriding all his objections about her injuries. "When I was on that floor, looking up at him holding that knife, I knew that was it. I was going to die. Even when we were in that bus underground, I hadn't felt that way. I don't know how, but the possibility of us being able to escape was always there in the back of my mind. But yesterday? Even knowing Bree had been in the backseat, and that she had her phone, I didn't think anyone could get there in time. Not when all it would've taken was one quick stab. And the only regret I had was that I wouldn't get to see you again."

She felt Flash's surprised inhalation. But she kept going.

"I wasn't going to just lie there and let him stab me to death. I was going to fight, but I knew the chances were slim that I'd be able to hold him off for long. Life is short, Flash. I've spent too much time just going through the motions of living. I'm done with that. I'm sure people will look at our relationship and smile to our faces, but behind our backs, say that we won't make it. That we moved too fast. That I've got some sort of savior complex thing going...or whatever it's called. That I'm only with you because you rescued me...twice. But that's not it. Not at all.

"I love you, Wade Gordon. I want to spend the rest of my life with you. I want to get my degree in electrical technology and be able to go over to Remi's house and fix her lights when they conk out. I want to fix that light that's out at Aces Bar and Grill. I want to cry when you go on a mission, and rejoice when you return. I want to hang out with Wren and the other girls and get drunk and talk about how great our sex lives are. I want to be an honorary aunt to Maggie and Addison's babies. I want to have my own. I want to have wild monkey sex with my husband when we're in our fifties, sixties, and even later. I want it all, Flash. I'm greedy. And I realized all this as I watched Brant come toward me with that knife, with a maniacal look in his eyes.

"So, yeah. I was aggressive. Because I knew you weren't going to touch me, since you were afraid to hurt me. But you'd *never* hurt me. Ever. I know that down to my very marrow. I hope you don't mind that I jumped you...because I have a feeling I'm gonna be doing that a lot."

"Marry me."

Kelli stared at Flash. He'd picked his head up when she'd begun talking, so he could look into her eyes—and she was momentarily speechless.

"I want all that too. I want to be the loudest person in the auditorium when you get your degree. I want to take pictures of you in your overalls and tool belt as you're on top of a ladder, fixing shit. I want to come home to you after every mission, and after every day of work. I want to hang out with my SEAL buddies as we watch over our women, getting sloshed during a girls' night out, then bring you home and fuck you drunk. I want to be a father, have babies that look exactly like you, teach them to be strong and confident, just like their mom.

"And you already know I love you too. I almost lost my mind when I walked into that room and saw Williams trying to stab you. Fuck anyone who thinks we won't make it, because I intend to spend every day of my life making you happy. Proving I'm the man you think I am. Because the truth is, I'm kind of a dick. At least to people who annoy me. Marry me, Kelli. I'll gladly have wild monkey sex with you when I'm eighty, although I might need some medical assistance to get it up by then."

Kelli couldn't help it. She laughed. This was a momentous occasion in her life, and she was giggling. Which made it all the more perfect. She didn't need the grand gestures. Him going down on one knee. She just needed Flash.

"Yes."

"Yes?" he asked, as if he couldn't believe what he'd heard.

"Of course, yes. I love you," she said simply.

In response, Flash's head dipped, and Kelli knew he was trying to regain his composure. When he lifted his head again, she saw that his eyes were sparkling. Flash might think he was a dick, but not to her. Never to her.

"We're going to be wedding'd out in the next few months, huh?" she asked. "With Remi and Josie marrying Kevlar and Blink, our own ceremony, my cousin's and your sister's...it's going to be crazy."

"We're eloping," Flash said without hesitation.

"What? Really?"

"That is, if you agree. I want my ring on your finger, and yours on mine, as soon as possible. I don't have the patience to plan a big thing, and besides, the people who'll be at Kevlar and Blink's party at Aces are the same people we'd invite to our own reception. I'd rather put that money toward a down payment on a house."

"Yes!" Kelli said happily. "But we might need to invite my mom to whatever ceremony we have. I think she'd be heartbroken to miss it."

"How about Vegas? It's a little cliché, but we can invite your family and mine, and have a party there on the Strip afterward."

"Um...no offense, but after what happened to Bree in Vegas... no. Maybe we can just go to the courthouse here?" Kelli asked.

"Done. So we're doing this?"

"This?"

"Getting married, buying a house, making babies, having wild monkey sex when we're in our nineties."

Kelli giggled again. The age of them having this crazy sex kept creeping up. "We are," she confirmed.

Flash smiled, then got serious. "Thank you for not giving up," he whispered.

"Never," Kelli vowed. "Will your team be mad if they aren't invited to our wedding? They certainly weren't happy that they missed everything with Brant."

"They weren't happy because they knew you were in danger and scared. Because Smiley and I didn't have them as backup. They won't be upset if we go to the courthouse and get married. Promise."

"Okay. Um...do you think maybe we can take a short honeymoon to that resort in New Mexico?"

"The Refuge?"

"Yeah."

"They're pretty booked up, but I can at least call them," Flash said without hesitation.

That was reason number eight hundred and twenty-six why Kelli loved this man. "It's just that I'd love to meet the woman who tried so hard to find Brant. But with him staying in that abandoned house, I'm thinking there's no way she could've found him."

"I think that's a perfect idea. I've heard such great things about The Refuge. You know about Melba, right?"

"Who's Melba?" she asked.

"Their resident cow."

"No way!" Kelli exclaimed, her brows flying up.

"Yup. And they have a bunch of other animals too. And from what I understand, the owners and their wives have had their fair share of drama, but they're now all settled and building a mini village on the property, where they're all raising their kids together."

"That sounds awesome."

"Maybe we should find a large piece of land where we can do the same. Convince everyone to build there, so we can all live together."

"Can you imagine living with grumpy Smiley next door?" Kelli teased. Then she sobered. "He's not going to hurt Bree, is he?"

"No! Why would you ask that?" Flash asked.

"It's just...he didn't exactly look happy to see her."

"You have to understand, Smiley's been trying to find her for quite a while now. It was driving him crazy that she disappeared into thin air. He was worried about her. I think something about her touched him in a way that no one else has."

"She was scared," Kelli said. Then she sighed. "I have a confession. Bree was visiting me at Smiley's apartment for a week or so. She came to the door one day, looking for him. I think she was ready to ask him for help. And she thought I was his girlfriend because I was in his apartment. I invited her in, because she was in desperate need of a shower. I fed her, we did her laundry...and she came back a couple of times. That's why she was in the parking lot yesterday. She was coming to see me again. But it was later than she usually showed up."

"Is that what was bothering you? The secret you couldn't tell me?" Flash asked.

Kelli nodded, scared he was going to be really mad.

To her surprise, he just leaned up and kissed her forehead before settling back down at her side.

"I promised I wouldn't say anything to you or Smiley. She was gathering up the courage to talk to him face-to-face. I gave her my cell number, and Smiley's, just in case. And she used it when she hid in Brant's backseat. Are you mad?"

"No. I think you did the right thing. She was obviously very used to hiding, to staying under the radar. Making friends with her was a good thing."

Kelli relaxed. "For the record, I didn't like keeping her from you. But I promised."

"I know."

"What happens now? With her and Smiley?" Kelli asked.

"No clue. I'm guessing he's going to want to hear her entire story. Find out who her ex is, and who the asshole sold her to. Then he'll want to track that fucker down and do what he can to end his reign of terror and break up any sex-trafficking thing he's got going on."

"Um...is it going to be that easy?"

"Not at all. There are usually layers upon layers when it comes to exploiting women. And honestly, most women who get into situations like that are groomed for months. It's not just a matter of kidnapping strangers off the streets. So whatever is going on with Bree's situation is unique. And unique isn't necessarily good. I remember a story from a while ago about a woman who'd been kidnapped while she and her husband were in Vegas, and she was taken out of the country and held for a decade."

"Oh my gosh! But she was found?"

"Yeah, by her husband, who never gave up hope that she was alive. He formed his own group of former military men who tracked down trafficking victims, all in the hopes he could find his own wife one day. And he did. They live in Colorado now."

"That's amazing."

"Yeah. My point is...what *is* my point?" Flash mused.

"Bree."

"Right. Bree's situation is going to be tough because someone's still after her. He seems desperate to find her, actually, and follow through with whatever plans he had for her. Which... seems strange. So whatever is going on there, it's not good."

"And Smiley will be right there in the middle of it," Kelli surmised.

"Yup."

"Well, shit," she said with a sigh.

Flash smiled.

"Why are you grinning? This isn't funny."

"No, it's not. But I'm not upset that you're worried about my friend. That you care."

"I care," she agreed.

"How about we get some more sleep? It's still a few hours until dawn. We can save the world when the sun comes up."

Kelli rolled her eyes. "Flash?"

"Yeah, sweetheart?"

"I love you."

"Lord, I'll never get tired of hearing those words from your lips. I love you too."

Kelli sighed with contentment, ignoring the throbbing of her leg and the slight discomfort on her chest where Brant had pierced the skin over her heart. Both slight hurts reminded her that she was alive. And apparently engaged.

"Oh!" she exclaimed softly. "Am I going to get a ring?" she blurted.

Flash chuckled against her, and she felt his warm breath caress her chest. "Of course. I've already got what I want for you in mind."

"I don't want anything too big. That's not my style."

"I know. And it won't be."

"Okay. Flash?"

"One more thing, and then you need to sleep, Kelli," he said, trying to sound stern but failing.

She grinned as she said, "You're the man I've dreamed of all my life. My superhero. My Flash Gordon."

"That was corny as hell," he protested. "And I love it. Sleep," he ordered.

Kelli closed her eyes and fell asleep with a huge smile on her face.

* * *

Bree sat quietly on the couch as Jude mumbled to himself, pacing back and forth in front of her. He'd brought her straight to his apartment after the cops were finally done talking to everyone about what happened with Brant Williams, earlier that afternoon. He hadn't said much during the ride, and when they'd arrived at his place, he was surprisingly gentle with her. Getting her a glass of water, asking if she wanted anything to eat.

As a result, she wasn't scared. More relieved that her running —from *this* man, at least—was finally over.

He obviously wasn't completely happy though. The scowl on his face probably should've freaked her out. Had her running for the door, for the state line, for the other side of the *country*...but for some reason, it was actually comforting.

Because Jude wasn't pissed at her, per se—okay, he was a *little* angry with her for hiding from him for so long. But he was more upset over the fact that she had so few answers to his questions.

He wanted to know the name of the man she'd been sold to back in Vegas.

She didn't know it.

He wanted to know the name of her ex.

She'd told him, but then explained that he'd been found dead in an alley in Vegas, not too long after she and Josie had been rescued.

He continued to ask questions, and the more she didn't have answers to, the more he scowled and the more he paced.

What Bree *did* know was that, here with Jude, she could finally get a good night's sleep. She'd been looking over her shoulder for so long, feeling as if she was being watched, like she was seconds away from being snatched and disappearing forever.

But now that she'd revealed herself to Jude, she knew without a doubt the man wasn't going to let her out of his sight. He was too shocked she'd been able to stay under the radar for so long, that he hadn't been able to find her. Knowing he would be extra vigilant—if for no other reason than so she couldn't escape him—was a comfort.

She truly didn't know the name of the man who'd bought her, but she knew enough to know if he got his hands on her, she would wish she was dead. Whatever his plans for her might be, they weren't good.

"What *do* you know?" Jude asked, sounding exasperated as he finally stopped pacing and sat on the couch next to her, his brow furrowed and his hair mussed from him running his hand through it in agitation.

"That you'll keep me safe," Bree said without hesitation.

That seemed to fluster him. He stared at her for a long moment. "Damn straight I will," he growled, sitting up straighter. "But you might not like how I go about it."

"Go about what?"

"Keeping you safe. Just remember that *you* came to *me*. You showed up at my door. I might not have been here at the time, but that doesn't negate the fact that you came looking for help. And I *want* to help you, Bree. I haven't been able to stop thinking about you since you disappeared in Vegas. Haven't stopped worrying about you. Where you were. If you were safe."

His words made Bree feel almost light-headed. She'd felt alone for so long, and here was the man *she* couldn't stop thinking about, saying all the right things.

"I'm not an easy man, though," he said after a moment.

Bree snorted.

"I'm going to ask you to do things that will probably make you uncomfortable. That you might not want to do. But whatever I ask of you will be for your own good. To keep you safe. I need you to understand that."

Bree nodded. She was tired of doing everything on her own. Of feeling alone. Vulnerable. Helpless. She needed help. That's why she was here in the first place. "I need your help," she said out loud. "It's why I came to California. For some reason, I trust you, Jude Stark. When I trust very few other people in my life. I'll do what you say. And if you can figure out the nightmare that is my life, I'll be forever in your debt."

"I don't want your gratitude," Jude said, growling again.

Bree opened her mouth to ask what he *did* want, but he talked over her.

"I'll get you a shirt and a pair of boxers to wear to bed. We'll get your car, wherever you've stashed it, and the rest of your stuff. You can use my washer and dryer to clean your clothes. We'll also go to a store tomorrow and get you some new stuff, whatever you need."

Bree's head spun. He was obviously very serious. She wasn't sure if she should be freaking out or falling to her knees at his feet. Both reactions would probably piss Jude off, so she settled for simply nodding.

"You're tired," he said, in a softer tone.

"Yeah," Bree agreed.

"Shower, then bed," he declared, standing abruptly. "I'll be right back." Then he left the room.

Bree was actually pretty familiar with the layout of his place, since she'd spent some time there with Kelli over the last week, and figured he was headed for his bedroom.

Jude returned, holding some clothes in his hand. "You're sleeping in my bed," he stated. "I'll take the floor. I'm not risking you sneaking off in the middle of the night after you have some time to think, telling yourself that you made a mistake by coming to me for help."

Bree could've reassured him that she wasn't going to sneak off again, but it was obvious he needed some time to learn to trust her. She understood.

"I don't want you to sleep on the floor," she told him.

"I've slept in worse places. It'll be fine," he told her without batting an eye.

Again, Bree should've probably felt wary. It wasn't every day a man basically ordered her to sleep in his bed. But she hadn't been lying earlier when she'd told Jude that she trusted him. Besides, she was at the end of her rope. She literally had nowhere else to go. No one else to turn to.

Standing, she walked toward him to take the clothes, grateful to have something clean to put on...after she'd showered, of course.

But when she tried to grab them, Jude held on until she looked up and met his gaze.

"Thank you for saving Kelli," he said gruffly. "It would've destroyed Flash if she'd died."

That was all the reassurance Bree needed to solidify the fact that she'd done the right thing by coming to Riverton, and to Jude Stark. His friends were obviously important to him. And even though she could tell he was irritated with her, he'd still done what he felt was right and thanked her.

"You're welcome," she said softly. "For the record? What I did was stupid," she admitted. "Getting into the car was pretty reckless. And dangerous. I could've been seen. He could've killed me. I should've written down his license plate number and gone to you immediately. I'm sorry I didn't."

"Me too. I don't like that you put yourself in that situation. But...you did reach out to me. And you were able to tell me exactly where Kelli was being taken. It's very likely we wouldn't have found her in time if you hadn't done what you did. You did good, Bree. Really good."

His words lessened her guilt somewhat. But she vowed to try not to do something so stupid again in the future. To not put her own life at risk as she'd done earlier that day.

Being around this man was a balm to her battered and bruised soul. For too long, she'd been a nobody. A homeless person living out of her car. Ignored. Looked down on. A piece of property that someone had paid for. A commodity. But to Jude? She was more. She was Bree Haynes again. And it felt good.

So she simply nodded.

"Go on. Shower. I'll change the sheets and make the bed so it's ready for you when you're done." With that, he turned and headed for the bedroom, presumably to strip the sheets off the bed.

Without another thought, Bree did as she was told. She hadn't lied. She was tired. Bone-deep exhausted from trying to stay one step ahead of the man who'd bought her. From trying to stay under the observant SEALs' radars. From being terrified that one wrong move would end up with her in a situation she couldn't even fathom.

Bree needed Jude Stark. And she vowed to herself to do whatever he told her to do. It wasn't in her nature, but she'd do it. Because it was obvious the path she was on wasn't working. The truth was, she needed a knight in shining armor. And while Jude's armor was dented and not so shiny, she wouldn't want anyone else by her side while she tried to figure out who'd bought her from her ex, and why they still wanted to get their hands on her so badly.

* * *

Mateo Castillo stared up at the apartment building that his property had entered earlier that evening. He'd been looking for her for months now, and had almost run out of patience when he'd found her.

Turns out, her being here in Riverton was actually a good thing. It presented an opportunity that he'd waited two long decades for.

When he was in his mid-thirties, he was living in Mexico, part of a sex-trafficking ring. A low-level partner at the time, it had taken years for him to work his way back up the organization after one of their most expensive acquisitions had been stolen right out from under their noses.

He hadn't been at the camp when it happened; that was the only reason why he'd been allowed to live. The other dozen or so men who'd gotten drunk and passed out—allowing a US

Navy SEAL to sneak into camp and steal the woman out from under their noses, plus another female asset—had all been eliminated.

The senator's daughter, plus the mousy woman they hadn't been able to find a buyer for after three months of looking, had both been taken back to the States. But Mateo was a believer in fate...and here he was. In Riverton.

Where those same women were now living.

They'd moved on, married Navy SEALs. Were living what they thought were happy lives. But they'd soon learn that the past never truly went away. It could always come back to haunt you. And Mateo was there to take back what was his.

Julie Lytle and Fiona Rain Storm were *his*. As was Bree Haynes. It was just a matter of finding a way to snatch them all back...then he'd get his money's worth out of all three.

In the last decade, Mateo had partnered with a man in Peru named del Rio. He'd supplied the man with women from all over the world for his business, until del Rio's organization collapsed after he'd been killed by some assholes from Indiana. But Mateo had gladly stepped in. He was now based in Ecuador, and the current unrest in the country made it easier for him to get his property moved in and out under the radar.

He sold women to the richest men in the world, and even knowing the sexual appetites of these men were depraved and downright sadistic didn't deter him. In fact, their proclivities only made the men willing to pay any cost to have a new plaything delivered right to their doors.

Full circle.

Things were coming full circle. Mateo would take back what was stolen from him and make a shit ton of money in the process. Thumbing his nose at the very men who'd stolen from him all those years ago was a huge bonus.

If they came after him, he'd be ready this time. There would be no drunken parties in the jungle. No, the SEALs would die if they tried to take back what was his. And they would. They'd come for the women. Of that, Mateo had no doubt.

Smiling, he started the engine of his black Mercedes. He knew where Bree Haynes was now. She wouldn't be able to hide from him anymore. He could take her tonight, break into the asshole's apartment and take back what belonged to him, what he'd bought fair and square. But now that he knew this man was connected to the other two women?

He'd wait. Be patient.

His time would come.

He couldn't wait to see the looks on the other women's faces when they realized their worst nightmares were coming true... *again*.

And when Bree Haynes understood that running had only put off the inevitable?

Bliss.

The terror they'd feel made Mateo's dick hard. He might not have the reputation del Rio did, but when word got out that Julie and Fiona had been taken a second time, people wouldn't be able to deny his authority any longer. He'd be the most powerful man in South America. Respected. Revered. Feared.

Finally.

The black Mercedes drove off without a sound, without anyone looking twice at the vehicle. Never knowing evil was on the move, and with it, a black cloud of terror was about to descend on Riverton.

* * *

You've been waiting for Bree and Smiley's story for what seems like forever and it's finally here! And yes, I went there. I went back to almost the very beginning of my writing career and brought back a bad guy from *Protecting Fiona*...everyone is going to lose their minds when they find out the connection between the man after Bree and Fiona and Julie's ordeal. Everyone will have to band together to end this new threat once and for all. Get the last book in the SEAL of Protection: Alliance series now. *Protecting Bree!*

And...are you curious as to the story Kelli told about the grasshopper named Fred who left home to see the world, only to discover that what he'd been searching for was back home the entire time? Do you want to read it? I've put it on my website as a FREE little short-short story that you can read if you so desire. You can find it here:
https://www.stokeraces.com/fred-the-grasshopper2.html
ENJOY!

Scan the QR code below for signed books, swag, T-shirts and more!

Also by Susan Stoker

SEAL of Protection: Alliance Series
Protecting Remi
Protecting Wren
Protecting Josie
Protecting Maggie
Protecting Addison
Protecting Kelli
Protecting Bree (Jan 6)

Rescue Angels Series
Keeping Laryn
Keeping Amanda (Nov 4, 2025)
Keeping Zita (Feb 10, 2026)
Keeping Penny (May 5, 2026)
Keeping Kara (July 7, 2026)
Keeping Jennifer (Nov 10, 2026)

Alpha Cove Series
The Soldier
The Sailor (Mar 3, 2026)
The Pilot (Aug 4, 2026)
The Guardsman (Mar 9, 2027)

SEAL Team Hawaii Series
Finding Elodie
Finding Lexie
Finding Kenna
Finding Monica
Finding Carly
Finding Ashlyn
Finding Jodelle

ALSO BY SUSAN STOKER

Eagle Point Search & Rescue
Searching for Lilly
Searching for Elsie
Searching for Bristol
Searching for Caryn
Searching for Finley
Searching for Heather
Searching for Khloe

*

Box Set 1, Books 1-4
Box Set 2, Books 5-7

The Refuge Series
Deserving Alaska
Deserving Henley
Deserving Reese
Deserving Cora
Deserving Lara
Deserving Maisy
Deserving Ryleigh

Game of Chance Series
The Protector
The Royal
The Hero
The Lumberjack

SEAL of Protection: Legacy Series
Securing Caite
Securing Brenae (novella)
Securing Sidney
Securing Piper
Securing Zoey
Securing Avery

ALSO BY SUSAN STOKER

Securing Kalee
Securing Jane

Delta Force Heroes Series

Rescuing Rayne
Rescuing Aimee (novella)
Rescuing Emily
Rescuing Harley
Marrying Emily (novella)
Rescuing Kassie
Rescuing Bryn
Rescuing Casey
Rescuing Sadie (novella)
Rescuing Wendy
Rescuing Mary
Rescuing Macie (novella)
Rescuing Annie

*

Box Set 1, Books 1-4
Box Set 2, Books 5-8
Box Set 3, Books 9-11

SEAL of Protection Series

Protecting Caroline
Protecting Alabama
Protecting Fiona
Marrying Caroline (novella)
Protecting Summer
Protecting Cheyenne
Protecting Jessyka
Protecting Julie (novella)
Protecting Melody
Protecting the Future
Protecting Kiera (novella)

ALSO BY SUSAN STOKER

Protecting Alabama's Kids (novella)
Protecting Dakota
Protecting Tex

*

Box Set 1, Books 1-4
Box Set 2, Books 5-8
Box Set 3, Books 9-11
Box Set 4, Books 12-14

Delta Team Two Series
Shielding Gillian
Shielding Kinley
Shielding Aspen
Shielding Jayme (novella)
Shielding Riley
Shielding Devyn
Shielding Ember
Shielding Sierra

Badge of Honor: Texas Heroes Series
Justice for Mackenzie
Justice for Mickie
Justice for Corrie
Justice for Laine (novella)
Shelter for Elizabeth
Justice for Boone
Shelter for Adeline
Shelter for Sophie
Justice for Erin
Justice for Milena
Shelter for Blythe
Justice for Hope
Shelter for Quinn
Shelter for Koren

ALSO BY SUSAN STOKER

Shelter for Penelope

*

Box Set 1, Books 1-4
Box Set 2, Books 5-8
Box Set 3, Books 9-12
Box Set 4, Books 13-15

Ace Security Series

Claiming Grace
Claiming Alexis
Claiming Bailey
Claiming Felicity
Claiming Sarah

Mountain Mercenaries Series

Defending Allye
Defending Chloe
Defending Morgan
Defending Harlow
Defending Everly
Defending Zara
Defending Raven

Silverstone Series

Trusting Skylar
Trusting Taylor
Trusting Molly
Trusting Cassidy

Stand Alone

Falling for the Delta
The Guardian Mist
Nature's Rift
A Princess for Cale

ALSO BY SUSAN STOKER

A Moment in Time- A Collection of Short Stories
Another Moment in Time- A Collection of Short Stories
A Third Moment in Time- A Collection of Short Stories
Lambert's Lady

Special Operations Fan Fiction
http://www.AcesPress.com

Beyond Reality Series
Outback Hearts
Flaming Hearts
Frozen Hearts

Writing as Annie George:
Stepbrother Virgin (erotic novella)

ABOUT THE AUTHOR

New York Times, USA Today, #1 Amazon Bestseller, and #1 *Wall Street Journal* Bestselling Author, Susan Stoker has spent the last twenty-three years living in Missouri, California, Colorado, Indiana, Texas, and Tennessee and is currently living in the wilds of Maine. She's married to a retired Army man (and current firefighter/EMT) who now gets to follow *her* around the country.

She debuted her first series in 2014 and quickly followed that up with the SEAL of Protection Series, which solidified her love of writing and creating stories readers can get lost in.

If you enjoyed this book, or any book, please consider leaving a review. It's appreciated by authors more than you'll know.

www.stokeraces.com
www.AcesPress.com
susan@stokeraces.com

facebook.com/authorsusanstoker
x.com/Susan_Stoker
instagram.com/authorsusanstoker
goodreads.com/SusanStoker
bookbub.com/authors/susan-stoker
amazon.com/author/susanstoker

www.ingramcontent.com/pod-product-compliance
Lightning Source LLC
Chambersburg PA
CBHW010949020925
31959CB00048B/1802